CW00832991

Sleight of Hand

To Chief Inspector Ralph Arnott the bizarre death of Francis Swayne, QC, was the beginning of the end. Infuriated by what he saw as the unwarranted intervention of Special Branch in a routine investigation, he resigned early from the force.

But his young sergeant Judy Pullen knew the tough Yorkshireman too well to believe he could ever abandon interest in a case which had developed intriguing features. Encouraged by her, Arnott began investigating on his own and was soon drawn willy-nilly into the world of academic fraud which had blighted the careers and lives of several of those associated with Swayne, in particular his younger sister Sabina, now seemingly cocooned in a wealthy if difficult marriage.

The action shifts between London and Yorkshire, between the world of scientific research and glittering London lifestyles. Both seem alien to Arnott, but he finds himself drawn to the young woman whose promising career never got off the ground and to her brilliant but discredited professor, as he perceives in their distress at a life's work interrupted a curious parallel to his own. He also perceives that nothing about Swayne's death is as it seems . . .

VIVIEN ARMSTRONG

Sleight of Hand

THE CRIME CLUB
An Imprint of HarperCollins *Publishers*

First published in Great Britain in 1991
by The Crime Club, an imprint of
HarperCollins Publishers, 77–85 Fulham Palace Road,
Hammersmith, London W6 8JB

Vivien Armstrong asserts the moral right to be identified
as the author of this work.

© Vivien Armstrong 1991

British Library Cataloguing in Publication Data

Armstrong, Vivien
    Sleight of hand
    I. Title
    823.914[F]

    ISBN 0 00 232342 7

Photoset in Linotron Baskerville by
Rowland Phototypesetting Ltd
Bury St Edmunds, Suffolk
Printed and bound in Great Britain by
HarperCollins Book Manufacturing, Glasgow

CHAPTER 1

At nine o'clock Francis Swayne's cleaner placed her palm firmly against the front door and turned the keys in their soundless locks. The paintwork was already warm, almost tacky, under her fingers and the unbroken blue arcing overhead a fair approximation of her own Caribbean skies.

Humming cheerfully, Pamina waved to the milkman entering the cobbled mews. Squeezing herself plus two bulging bags of shopping into the house, she shut the door firmly against the sparkling sunshine as if to an uninvited guest. Plunged again into darkness, the mean hallway conceded small leeway in the shape of a curtained alcove to one side, the stairs rising sharply just inside the front door, leaving little space for the welcome mat.

As Pamina de Cassis bent to pick up the mail her shoulder-bag shot down her arm, toppling one of the plastic carriers, scattering contents in all directions. Breathing heavily, she felt about on the floor, patiently replacing the tins and packets, stacking the shopping against the wall and balancing her keys and handbag on top.

Switching on the hall light, she gathered up the letters: several bills, a picture-postcard from Rome, a handbill advertising a fête and three minicab cards. She stacked them on the radiator shelf before moving purposefully to the cupboard under the stairs to start her regular Monday morning assault.

It was a good job. Cleaning was cleaning but some folks she could mention . . . Well, some were not so special and the richer the worse. She shook her head and, filling a bucket with cans of polish and cloths, grasped the broom and made her way upstairs. It was more than twenty years since she had left St Lucia to come to this damp, cold land and Pamina still dreamed of black volcanic sands and secret forests. Her pace had never synchronized with these crowded city streets.

Upstairs, three doors opened off the landing: one entering the bathroom, another a study, and the third door opposite leading to the sitting-room overlooking the mews and the pub which faced the row of little houses. The bathroom door was ajar. Hands full, Pamina leaned against it. Jammed. Not exactly stuck but curiously obstructed. Frowning, she thrust a plump black forearm through the gap, feeling empty air. A whisper of unease fanned her cheek: her 'gentleman' was so tidy, so predictable. She shrugged, pushed firmly and stepped in, kicking aside a bath towel littering the floor.

The dim curtained room enveloped her in a cloying sweetish smell of aftershave and damp towels. Premonition, black as fear, slithered under her fingertips. Was someone there? The room had too many dark corners even on the brightest morning. With the window closely curtained, the only daylight filtering through emerged from a skylight above a lavatory discreetly hidden behind a wall backing a triangular bath. The opulent decor augmented by an arching palm and Moorish tiles suggested this was no mere washplace but an oasis for luxurious relaxation.

Pamina stood her ground, straining to penetrate the gloom and utter silence. Her eyes adjusted to the semi-darkness and she could pick out the shadowy shape of someone seeming to hover almost out of sight beyond the partition wall. A thief! A houseguest? A bathrobe hung up to dry?

Groping for the light switch, she hesitated, on the brink of apology, unsure in the unnerving quiet. She crept forward, peering round, gripping the broom. In the shaft of sunlight from the skylight a woman wreathed in some soft black stuff appeared slowly to turn towards her, unnaturally tall, bowed head almost touching the steel bracket supporting the sloping ceiling. Mesmerized as by a primæval memory, Pamina remained transfixed, sweat glistening above parted lips.

Suspended from a noose from the crossbeam, a woman swayed as if on a spotlit stage. She floated in the limelight, a wraith whose long narrow feet almost touched the floor, red satin rosettes and fishnet stocking glimpsed within the dark cloud of a chiffon negligee. Cascades of reddish hair entirely obscured the hanged woman's face, her head cocked awkwardly like the stem of a broken flower. Pamina froze.

In the square of sky shimmering above the body, a plane screamed its flight path towards Heathrow, the unearthly sound suddenly releasing Pamina's paralysis. Her shriek rose to meet the aircraft with the shrill reverberation of a human slipstream as she wrenched at the door. The knob slid from her sweating palm. She reeled back, the door slamming in her face.

She gasped for breath, the stench of the little room seeming to claim her very soul. Clutching her throat, dizzy with fear, she spun round, stumbled over the strewn towel and found herself lurching uncontrollably backwards, catching the suspended body a glancing blow. It twisted violently, dancing on its cord like a macabre puppet. Almost fainting, her senses swimming and dissolving, the woman became wildly disorientated as if in a nightmare. Trapped. She dropped to her knees, fingers clawing at the wall tiles as she struggled to rise. And then, as if a malevolent spirit played its trump card, the hennaed curls of the corpse fell, dropping softly as a bat on to Pamina's head, hooking in the frizzy braids.

Flinging up her hands in supplication, Pamina de Cassis howled in torment, flailing wildly as the sagging bald head of the creature hanging from the beam rotated as if to look down on her. Pamina, hypnotized by its rouged lips puckered grotesquely round a black stiffened tongue, met the popping bloodshot eyes of her employer, Francis Swayne, QC.

Crashing through the door, pursued by demons, Pamina hurled herself downstairs and into the astonished embrace of Kevin Bolton delivering a pint of Channel Islands Best.

*

Detective-Inspector Ralph Arnott abhorred suicide. And kinky suicide was the worst. Not for any spiritual reason. But taking one's own life struck him as the ultimate cop-out. Not an unfeeling man, but Arnott's well of sympathy lay untouched by what in his view remained cowardly violence.

He wished it possible to ditch the new detective, Pullen. But the Commissioner was adamant. Detective-Sergeant Judith Pullen was by no means to be shunted to rape, shoplifting and the normal 'soft options'. He sighed, closed the file and, shouting a few terse instructions to Minter, laboriously rose from his desk. He'd lost the flavour for this job: retirement glimmered like a string of Chinese lanterns in his mind.

Pullen was waiting in the car park looking cool in a linen jacket and blue dress. Arnott nodded briefly before sagging into the driving seat. Buggered if he'd open the door. These women wanted it all ways: equality plus the perks. After a small hesitation Judy Pullen got in, a waft of cologne sharpening the stale tobacco smell permeating the up-holstery, and snapped the seat-belt across her chest.

'Photography on its way, sir.' She smiled to herself, glancing at Arnott's profile set like a craggy outcrop of rock against the traffic. 'And the lab's sending Dr Foster. And a fingerprint buff.'

'Uncle Tom Cobleigh an' all, eh?'

'Swayne was a QC, sir. Can't be too careful. I made a few calls before we left but nothing fishy. Before this, of course.' He ignored this, accelerated and bored through the tunnel of Kensington High Street in the rush hour, the cacophony of the police siren ahead parting the traffic like the Red Sea.

Arnott grunted, swinging the wheel in a wide arc across a patient line of traffic. Five minutes later the car edged through a stone gateway and bumped over the cobbles of Sherbourne Mews.

Judith Pullen deftly extracted herself from the seat-belt,

grabbed her capacious leather bag and was already half out of the car when Arnott tapped her arm.

'Hold on, Sergeant.'

She slumped back, eyes wary, sensing the trickiness of Arnott too early in the day.

'Before you prance in there,' he said, 'just remember you're not on the telly. This is no scoop for Miss Sherlock Holmes and there's no need to make a splash. There's little enough in the papers in August and nobody will thank you for making a drama out of a sordid number like this. The blowflies from the press'll be round soon enough. So keep your 'ead down.'

Releasing her, he ponderously locked the car under the carefully blank countenance of the duty constable standing outside Swayne's front door. Two plain-clothes men lounging in the deep shadow of the passage jumped to attention as he entered. Biting her lip in suppressed irritation and amusement, Judy impatiently stood aside while Arnott gazed round the crescent of brightly painted little houses.

Sherbourne Mews formed a quiet backwater between Gloucester Road and Kensington High Street, twin exits impressively arched in sandstone at right angles to each other. Six converted coach-houses flanked a triangle of cobbles opposite the Ring of Bells, its small forecourt already clogged with three police cars and a milk-float. The front doors, with the exception of Swayne's, were all firmly closed. The six 'bijou residences' faced inwards, the third and fourth joining at an angle in the middle of the terrace thus allowing Swayne's house and No. 3 additional space at the rear. Sunshine blazing through the stone entrances lent a Mediterranean sparkle to the tubs and window-boxes overflowing with marguerites and pink and scarlet geraniums.

'Very pretty,' Arnott glumly remarked, flickering hooded eyes to acknowledge the constable's salute as he passed inside Swayne's house.

The light downstairs was still switched on, its glow ineffectual now the entrance and the only other door off the hall stood wide open, permitting the midmorning sun and many policemen unbridled access. Maroon velvet curtaining the alcove looked seedy and theatrical in daylight and motes of dust danced in the beam striking over Arnott's thick shoulders.

Most of the ground floor was taken up by a dining-room linked with a sleekly modern kitchen which led on to the garden. Arnott's gaze slid over the bar counter which effectively divided the dining area from the sweep of steel units, its blind now hoisted to a decorative archway spanning wall to wall. At the dining end the window looking on to the mews was densely curtained and despite the sunsplashed view from the kitchen the atmosphere was gloomy, the polished mahogany table in shadow and, Arnott guessed, rarely used.

Exchanging terse comments with the scenes of crime officers, he motioned them to wait and lumbered up the steep stairs, closely followed by Judith Pullen. A subdued guffaw filtered through closed doors and Arnott glumly imagined the banter of the men awaiting the arrival of the DI and his attractive assistant. Punch and Judy. And they thought he knew nothing of the jokes at the station! He briefly instructed the men to wait downstairs and entered the bathroom, shutting the door in Pullen's face.

Colour blazed in her cheeks and, fuming, she cooled her heels on the dim landing, infuriated by Arnott's obdurate style. Before the rest of the circus arrived, trampling all over the place, Arnott had decided to have the place more or less to himself for a few minutes at least. He quickly emerged, shutting off the sight of the deceased, closing the door firmly and, pushing Judy aside, entered the next room. Her mind reeled with a mixture of exasperation and secret relief: it was difficult to guess whether his manner was offensive or a paternalistic determination to shield her from the worst aspects of the job. Shadowed by Pullen, Arnott prowled Swayne's expensive *pied-à-terre*.

Afterwards, they returned downstairs and he released the

rest of the pack which streamed through the little house, filling the tiny rooms with heavy footfalls and the unstoppable machinery of official investigation.

Arnott stood in the kitchen and, pointing a nicotine-stained finger across the bar counter, said to Judith: 'This little lot would have been the original garage space. Left his car in the mews if he had one. Check that, will you? He might have rented a garage but that's unlikely.' His slurry brown eyes slid over the costly fittings. 'Might've had a driver cum minder. Could afford it by the look of things.'

Arnott pushed past her and peered through a glazed door on to a patio half shadowed by a high back wall. 'Get Benson to fingerprint all this.' He jabbed at the glass. 'And check the locks,' he added. He cast an experienced eye over the paving overhung by the brassy fall of a robinia tree fringing garden chairs and a table. A barbecue half hidden in the shrubbery sheltered a paper bag of charcoal. Social bugger, he mused. 'Ask the neighbours about parties, Pullen. What sort of company he kept. You know the form. Gossipy. Confidential. Get hold of the women if you can.'

Judy stood in the murky dining-room jotting notes on a pad, blonde-streaked baby-fine hair impatiently pushed behind one ear as her head bobbed up to catch Arnott's guttural phrases.

'By the way,' he added, 'where's this blackbird who found the body?'

'Pamela de Cassis, sir. In the pub opposite. And the milkman. He took her there. Hysterical. She won't come back here in a hurry. Shall I have a word?'

His massive head reared up. 'No!'

And then quietly: 'Leave her to me. I just want to poke about here for a bit before them interfering forensic buggers start fouling things up. Tell her to wait. And the milkman. Buy her a rum and beetlejuice or something. I'll be over as soon as I've seen all I want to see. Beats me,' he muttered, 'why anyone with bags of spare like Swayne chooses to live in a fancy bloody rabbit hutch like this. Too small to swing a cat.'

As if on cue, a disdainful Siamese appeared from the shrubbery and stared through the panes of the back door, sapphire eyes unwinking and unafraid. It wore a harness like a small dog, thin strips of red terylene crisscrossing the pale fur.

Arnott's lips twisted in what passed for a smile. 'Don't let the moggy in, Pullen. And check that attic bedroom with a toothcomb before you go over to the pub. See what our dearly departed kept under his pillow.' He nodded meaningfully. 'You catch my drift, Sergeant. Smell out all the nooks and crannies, see if this fine legal brain hanging upstairs enjoyed a bit of sherbet on his night off. You can look in upstairs if you like,' he reluctantly conceded, 'but don't touch the adjoining study to the scene of the crime until I've let Benson run his sticky fingers over it.'

Judith Pullen's eyes widened in mock surprise and she slipped the notebook into the squashy shoulder-bag. 'Back in your basket, Fido,' she murmured as Arnott shoved past and went back upstairs.

Raising a tired hand to a plain-clothes officer in close conversation with a policeman blocking the bathroom door, Arnott passed along the landing. He had been warned to expect Detective-Inspector Erskine. Christ knows why. Special Branch would be in on parking offences next . . .

The layout of the mews house was curious, tailor-made for a bachelor. The bathroom adjoined a small study hung with blue-striped fabric drawn into a tented ceiling, both rooms accessible from the landing and to each other. A single divan strewn with Berber cushions stood against one wall, a Spanish leather trunk heavily scrolled with metal bands commanding the space under the window. Arnott made a mental note to ask the nit-picking brigade to cast their eyes over this little lot. Wrapping his hand in a handkerchief, he tested the drawers of a kneehole desk which dominated the room. All locked. The polished floor was bare, contrasting with the sensuous Arab style of the tented room. And even on this brightest of days the light filtering through the tracery of leaves brushing the window was subdued.

Swayne's house had been expensively modernized, the bathroom and kitchen gleaming with the latest and most stylish equipment. The smallness of the rooms had been cleverly disguised and bore the hallmarks of a professional designer. Part of the kitchen and the toilet area of the bathroom extension directly above it seemed to have been built on, jutting three feet into the wedge of extra space allowed by the peculiarly angled site. Swayne's garden was prettily landscaped, the sheltered patio forming a suntrap on which garden furniture blistered on the paving. On either side of the patio a whitewashed wall about three feet high supported a further four feet of fragile trellis. The wooden slats sealed both sides and rambler roses garlanded the trellis in voluptuous carmine loops, linking the house to a high boundary wall which divided the mews houses from the backs of large stuccoed villas in the next street.

Arnott tapped his teeth with the silver ballpoint Peg had given him for his birthday. He liked to explore every twisted possibility before returning to the obvious. Dicey game, suicide. Couldn't be too careful. An intruder could have scaled the back wall from the end where it joined the stone archway at the entrance to the mews, but no one, for sure, would try climbing that rickety trellis.

The study curtains smelt strongly of cigar smoke. Gingerly, he tried the window. Fastened. And new. He adjusted his bifocals to examine the sill and noted with approval the efficient window-locks in the new metal frame. Pristine. Our friend Swayne, he decided, may have gone in for fancy hangings in this bachelor pad but wasn't fool enough to neglect the locks and bolts. Master bedroom upstairs, presumably converted roof space accessible via a spiral staircase glimpsed at the end of the landing. Check that later.

The rest of the first floor comprised a minute drawing-room overlooking the public house. Rag-rolled walls in tasteful smudges of grey-green outlined gilt frames crowding between rosewood bookcases. Tooled leather bindings jostled with paperbacks, the books interspersed with a collection of Staffordshire figures. Robert Peel. Wallace. And surprise, surprise: Grace Darling in her rowing-boat.

Arnott's jaundiced eye skimmed the festoon blinds at the window and the desiccated buds of crimson Baccarat roses hanging on withered stalks in water, the stench of which permeated the sealed room. The drooping flowerheads brought Arnott's attention abruptly to the matter in hand.

'Doctor's here, sir.'

Reluctantly he shambled on to the landing to join the duty constable.

'Well, well. Here we go again. Let's see what sort of tangle our barrister got himself tied up in, shall we?'

CHAPTER 2

The milkman was getting restless. He circled the pokey saloon bar alternately peering from the dark interior at the frantic activity in the mews and leaning over the bar whispering earnestly to the licensee and his wife. Outside, the gay window-boxes and brightly painted doors formed a sparkling backdrop to the continuous arrival and departure of police cars. It occurred to the publican, Leslie Weston, that Sherbourne Mews would be on the map after this and no mistake. But would it be good for business? Once the press moved in and the nosey-parkers made a beeline, the regulars would give the place a wide berth. Suicide was one thing. But perverts were no draw in a quiet neighbourhood, what with all this AIDS lark on the rampage.

'Whole lot'll be curdled in this heat.'

'Curdled?' said the barman, startled from his anxieties.

Kevin Bates pointed dramatically through the open door at the milk-float hemmed in by Panda cars.

'Can't they send someone else to finish the round?'

He dismissed Les's remark with a contemptuous shrug. 'On a Monday morning? In August? You must be bloody joking! Short of drivers as it is with holidays.'

Pamina slumped at one of the small tables, immobile, apparently deaf to the conversation, entirely withdrawn into her own stunned recollection of the appalling events.

'What did they say when you phoned the depot, Kev?'

'Manager can't see why I've got to hang about at all.' He wiped a moist hand over his T-shirt. 'Nor me, to be honest. I seen nothink.'

The landlord jerked his head round, nudging his wife. 'Hang on. Looks like they're coming over.'

She continued polishing glasses and warily eyed the small procession: Arnott, Judy Pullen, a constable and a man in a lightweight grey suit somewhat detached from Arnott's entourage.

Kevin Bates stepped forward.

'Look, mate, can I go?' He blocked the entry, a crescent of dark sweat staining his armpit as he gestured towards the black woman slumped in the shadows. 'I brought her in here because she was having a fit. But I didn't see nothink. I'm miles behind with me round as it is,' he finished lamely.

Arnott's response was laconic. He pushed past, adjusting his eyes from the brightness outside and stood squarely in the middle of the saloon. 'Got a watch, son?'

' 'Course.'

'What time did you bring her in here, then?' Pamina had not moved, seeming unaware of the questions ranging beyond her as if she were indeed part of the dark interior.

Kevin looked confused, running freckled fingers through his gingery crew-cut. 'Can't say exactly. Just after nine, I reckon.'

The landlord moved round the bar. 'Ten past,' he said.

'We'd just opened up to give the place an airing while Lou cleared up.

'Knew Swayne, did you, Mr Weston?'

'By sight,' Les conceded. 'Sometimes popped in for a quick one but not regular.'

'Alone, was he?'

'Mostly.' He frowned, dredging his memory. 'Used to meet a thin blond chap whose face looked familiar—Josie'll remember—but not recently. Otherwise he just had a jar with whoever happened to be in. Matey sort with his own kind, he seemed to have plenty to say for himself all right.'

'This regular boyfriend of his you said, from round here, was he?'

'No. I recognized him from the telly. At least Josie did. In one of those soaps. Josie likes it.' He smiled apologetically, indicating his wife.

'*Odyssey*,' she said flatly. 'He played the marquis part. Good-looking,' she agreed, 'if you like the type. Bit feeble, if you ask me. But he's been in lots of things. Came in here first a couple of years ago with a real star. Nicholas Farrow. Caused quite a stir in the bar, it was when Nicholas Farrow was in that Evelyn Waugh series the Yanks went wild about. Mind you, he was better-looking then, more like Robert Redford.'

'You mean Farrow or this other actor? You don't know *his* name?'

She shook her head and continued wiping ashtrays.

'Lots of film people live round here. Actors come and go . . .' She spread the damp cloth on a brass rail under the bar, irritability seeping through her blank expression as the hands of the clock moved towards opening time and the forecourt became increasingly clogged with police activity. Murder was one thing—there were pubs still coining it from Jack the Ripper—but this! This could only give the mews a bad name for queer goings-on. From what the black woman said . . .

Arnott nodded to the constable taking notes, who moved

in to check the details while the DI turned back to the
milkman. Judith Pullen sat beside the dead man's cleaning
woman whose dazed expression unwillingly focused on
Arnott and Kevin Bates. She seemed spellbound, unconscious of her surroundings.

Eventually the milkman was allowed to go, glad to make
his escape into the mews where already the heat bounced
off the cobbles promising another scorcher. Arnott turned
to Les Weston and they talked in a huddle at the bar, the
note-taking constable straining to catch their remarks, the
plain-clothes man quietly observing from the inglenook.

Pamina's flat features were a mask, the skin subtly
drained as if scoured from within. Opaque. Arnott dispatched the landlord to fetch tea all round and lowered
himself on to a velvet bench seat under the sunbright
window, a few feet from his pretty young detective and
the black woman, his face an etching of fine unreadable
lines.

'Mrs Pamela de Cassis, sir,' Judith said. 'Worked for
Swayne for three years, three mornings a week.'

'Pamina,' she stressed, speaking for the first time.

'What?'

'Pamina. Pamina de Cassis. Not Pamela.'

Judith's confusion brought the first smile of the day to
Arnott's sagging features.

'Daughter of the Queen of the Night, Detective-Sergeant.
The Magic Flute.'

Arnott's wry reproof raised Pamina's eyes to his and from
her stiff acknowledgement a germ of complicity was born.

'My apologies, Mrs de Cassis. This young woman has
little time for culture.' He leaned forward, placing heavily
veined hands on the pub table. 'Now slowly, in your own
words, tell me about Mr Swayne. Nice man, was he?'

Gently, and with little prompting, Arnott released the
emotion churning under Pamina's apparent inertia. Judith
Pullen marvelled at the torrent of information which, first
gradually and then in tumbling phrases, revealed her

employer as, quite simply, a gentleman. 'And nothing will make me believe, sir, that he did that thing.'

Her colour had returned, the flesh now shiny and live, the anger in her eyes snapping from face to face crowding the bar parlour. 'He wasn't supposed to be there. Mr Swayne paid me my month's wages on Friday before he went.'

'Oh yes?' Arnott leaned forward, his pouchy cheeks like a bloodhound's. 'Didn't pay you to take time off yourself, for instance?'

'I had me holiday. Went to see me sister in May. You inferring I poke about while the man's away? Why should I come to work if he pay me to stay home?' Her voice became louder and stubbornly she shook her head. 'No. I clean the house when he's on holiday. Right through.' Majestically, Pamina de Cassis got to her feet, her mind set.

'Then why the milk?' Judith snapped.

'Milk?'

'Yes, you said Bates was delivering milk as usual.'

'His mistake.' Pamina was mulish. 'In August Mr Swayne go away and in August I clean all through.'

Arnott shot an angry glance at Judith, his hand motioning flatly under the table to her to stop ruffling his witness. The constable looked round inquiringly, pen poised, and Judy subsided in her seat. In the shadows Detective-Inspector Laurence Erskine lit a cigarette, the rasp and flare of the match magnified in the charged atmosphere.

Arnott brusquely directed Judith to collect Pamina's handbag from the house and get a signed statement before arranging transport. Cups of tea, barely touched, stood on the table. Thoughtfully, Arnott relaxed, stroking his chin. The constable moved in with his notebook. Arnott sipped the lukewarm tea.

'Get all that, lad?' he said. 'When you've got it typed up, tie up the loose ends with the lab brigade.' Arnott caught the gleam of amusement passing between the constable and Erskine. Too late for me to start messing with all the newfangled gear, dictating into tape-recorders, all that lark, Arnott thought. Too late by a long chalk.

Briskly, he continued. 'Tell Pullen I want to see her at the station by dinner-time, say twelve, we should have some preliminary medical report by then and—' He stopped abruptly as a uniformed sergeant appeared in the doorway, temporarily cutting off the bright rectangle of sunshine bisecting the bar floor. The sergeant approached his DI and leaned confidentially across the teacups. He spoke in a monotone, his back to the man by the fireplace.

'I checked with Swayne's chambers like you said, sir. The clerk wants to send someone to collect some legal papers but I told him he'd have to speak to you about that.'

'Next of kin?' Arnott barked, aiming a fierce glance at the barmaid who sullenly moved in to clear away the cups.

'Younger brother, actor calling himself Nicholas Farrow. Married, lives in Islington. That's all, apart from a sister mostly resident in Hong Kong, but Swayne's secretary says she's probably staying in Yorkshire at present. Comes home every summer to spend a couple of months with her in-laws apparently.'

'Give Sisley here a list of their addresses and telephone numbers and come back to the house with me. I want to hear more about these legal papers they want to grab from the poor stiff. Tell me more about these chambers . . .'

Their gruff exchanges faded as they moved towards the door, Arnott waving absently to the landlord as he pushed the men ahead of him into the mews. Judith Pullen passed them as she returned with Pamina's handbag. She leaned across the table, speaking quietly to Pamina before leading her outside, the silent figure in the shadows following behind, apparently uninterested in Arnott's circus.

They almost collided with Arnott's men who suddenly stepped back in their path in response to Arnott's lunge to pull back the Sergeant to add further arrangements to the schedule. Arnott frowned as the fourth man stepped aside. 'Oh, Erskine. Forgot you'd been dragged in on this one.

Not much to it. You'd better come into the house and check it over when the pathologist's through. Just for form's sake. You can go through Swayne's desk when I've located the keys,' he added expansively. 'Got to shuffle that lot before this clerk of chambers bloke starts shouting the odds. Bank statements would be interesting. Nothing like debts to show who a man's enemies are.' Arnott's watery eyes shifted to the newcomer. Tall. Sinewy under the smooth suit, the eyes gravely intelligent. He stood his ground waiting for Arnott to continue, the pause in which his silent anticipation lurked jerking the older man into a flurry of explanation. 'You never know. The silly poof must have left some sort of letter before he strung himself up. Save a lot of time, that would.'

Arnott propelled the uniformed sergeant ahead, exchanging curt phrases, the sun striking down almost without shadows directly into the well of the mews, accentuating the wispy grey hairs lying along the collar of Arnott's well-worn jacket.

Judith Pullen strolled behind, the straight fall of her bob swinging neatly across thin shoulder-blades. After steering Pamina into a car she turned aside just as Erskine fell into step beside her.

'Is he always like this?' he muttered.

'Retires soon.' Judith grinned at her lanky companion. 'Makes him nervous. Arnott,' she whispered, 'would much rather have a nice quiet few weeks to see himself out. No aggro. No messy unsolved cases and definitely no weirdos.'

'Let's have a drink when you're through.'

They paused, nearing the late Francis Swayne's front door.

'Sorry, I've got to get the cleaner's statement and see she gets home. Arnott wants me back at the station by twelve.'

'Will you be here later?' Larry Erskine's persistence was legendary.

'Maybe.'

'Sixish, then. Here at the pub. I want to have a few words with the landlord when he's mellowed a bit.'

Judith shrugged, absorbing Arnott's shouted directions as he disappeared into the dark hallway of No. 4 Sherbourne Mews.

She hurried to catch up, leaving only Erskine to engage the unwinking scrutiny of Pamina as she sat in the waiting car.

He threw down his half-smoked cigarette and strolled into the house just as the doctor breezed past.

Erskine waited in the hall, killing time, chatting to the young constable on the door. Then he wandered round the ground-floor rooms, examining the layout of the strange little house, filling in until the first wave of police experts had departed.

He was sitting in the garden enjoying the sun when, half an hour later, the clatter of several pairs of feet on the stairs and the cheerful banter of the medic and his team signalled a general exodus. Hearing the revving of cars in the mews releasing him, Erskine straightened his tie and went back inside. The tiny rooms now empty seemed shopsoiled, the air oppressive with the faint smell of human sweat.

Upstairs, Arnott sat at Swayne's desk, systematically emptying the drawers on to the floor. Larry Erskine appeared in the doorway.

The older man looked up, irritation mottling his flat cheeks.

'It's sanctioned, Erskine,' he said. 'And the fingerprint mob have OK'd everything.'

'No note, then?'

'Not so far.'

'Are you releasing the body?'

Arnott leaned back in Swayne's chair, a slow smile mischievously breaking through. 'Thought I'd hang on for the next of kin to get here. Swayne's brother. Any minute now. Might as well see how he takes it, don't you think?'

Erskine's response was vague. 'Suppose so.'

Stepping carefully round the piles of typewritten sheets on the floor, he looked into the gaping drawers.

'I shall need to check the details here, I'm afraid. Indepen-

dently. Just routine, Arnott. For my files. But as far as the
men are concerned you can pass me off as "narcotics". I
don't want any loose talk.'

'Be my guest.'

'Where did you find the keys to the desk?'

'On a ring with the others. In the alcove downstairs. Sort
of curtained-off cloakroom affair. Must have dropped out of
his pocket when he hung up his coat.'

He raised a stubby forefinger, jiggling a bunch of keys.
'No car keys, though. The brother may have an idea about
that when he gets here. Pullen tells me he's quite a star.
Goes under the name of Farrow. Not much of a one for the
pictures meself.'

'Nicholas Farrow, the film actor?'

'That's him. Forty-seven, mostly "resting" by all accounts. Still turns heads in the street, it seems. Quite a boyo
in the hippy era, so Pullen tells me.'

'How would she know?' Erskine laughed, his face crink-
ling with amusement. He started rifling through the engage-
ment diary at Arnott's elbow.'

'Don't know much, I grant you.' Arnott leaned back and
slowly winked a reptilian eye. 'But the girl fairly soaks up
all these gossip columns. Dempster, *Tatler*, *Harper's*—all the
tittle-tattle. The Swaynes enjoyed a gilt-edged package tour
through life, according to our Judy. In the early days, that
is, a bit threadbare now, death duties caught them on the
wrong foot maybe. Eton for starters, though.' Then, slyly:
'But I don't have to fill you in about that. Why's your mob
nosing round?'

'Perhaps Eton's where Swayne got his taste for dressing
up.' Erskine nodded towards the adjoining bathroom. He
had a facility for playing it close to his chest, giving nothing
away. Even the Met had its moles.

Arnott grunted. Sweeping the elaborate inkstand to one
side, be began to sort the papers into piles. 'Nothing
much here,' he remarked. 'What's your angle? Not another
Anthony Blunt, was he?'

'I'll just check through that lot, if you don't mind.'

Erskine removed the papers to the divan. 'Before the legal documents are returned to chambers. Is there a safe?'

Arnott shook his head. Setting the inkstand back in place, he slid the stiletto blade of a letter-opener under the paper in the leather blotter and peered underneath.

'By the way,' Erskine continued, 'did you establish what lights were on when the cleaning woman arrived?'

'Says she didn't get this far. But the desk light, this angle thing, was on when we got here. Hot. Been on all night. All ruddy weekend most like. Oh, and the one downstairs,' he added, 'in the hall. But the cleaner says it was always dark once the door was shut. She must have put that on herself like she said or she would have been on her guard before she got upstairs.'

Arnott beckoned to Larry Erskine in a comic gesture of conspiracy. Erskine rose from the divan and sat on the corner of the desk.

'Doctor reckons it's perfectly straightforward,' Arnott whispered. 'Swayne died early Saturday morning between three and five. No evidence of any break-in. No hanky-panky from outside, anyway. Faint rope marks round his chest and upper arms, nothing serious. Funny how being tied up turns these buggers on! I sometimes think there's a whole world out there the rest of us couldn't fathom in a month of Sundays.' He tapped his nose with a silver ballpoint. Then, after a moment's thought: 'And as far as we can tell, nothing's missing.'

Erskine jabbed at the open diary. 'Last Friday night. According to this Swayne was attending a private perform-ance of *Rigoletto* at Somerset House. Charity do.'

'Very exclusive, Pullen reckons. Small audience hand-picked to raise funds for the new Courtauld. It got some space in one of the Sundays, she says. Something about one of the sopranos passing out with the heat while she was on stage stuffed in a sack. Last act. But the average age of the audience was about fifty and no royals present, so not much mileage for the press. There was a supper party afterwards in the old rooms which had been tarted up for the occasion, I'm told. And the whole thing broke up about midnight.'

'Where was Swayne after that? Was he alone?'

Arnott shrugged. 'Not a clue. Sort that out in due course. Pullen's having a word with the neighbours and his secretary may have some idea if he was making up a party.'

'Not my idea of a night out.'

Arnott's laughter bellowed, filling the confines of the tented study. 'Surely not deadly enough for you to hang yourself, though?'

Resuming his low confidential tone, Arnott drew Larry towards the window, breathing hard. He took a single key from his pocket. 'Take a dekko at this lot,' he muttered, unlocking the Spanish trunk.

Inside scores of pornographic magazines, video cassettes and a few expensively bound books were neatly stacked. To one side clear plastic folders enclosed what appeared to be lingerie. With distaste, Erskine looked in, lifting the transparently parcelled lace and chiffon with the tip of his pen.

'Bumper funbox.'

The older man grinned like a cartoon fox, his dentures unnaturally white. 'I suppose your squad knew all about Swayne's little hobby.'

Erskine shrugged.

Arnott relocked the trunk with a flourish.

The constable's head appeared round the half-open door.

'Mr Farrow downstairs, sir. And a chap from the *Record*'s sitting round outside. Asking awkward questions. Wants a statement.'

Arnott jabbed the air in angry disbelief. 'How do these bloody press blokes smell a dirty story so quick? This film star brother's the only titbit. They must be scraping the barrel, by 'eck.'

The constable's expression was carefully blank.

'Yes, sir. By the way, sir, a set of car keys has turned up. And more house keys. All mixed up with bags of shopping in the hall. Sergeant Pullen should have taken the shopping when she collected the cleaner's stuff. I should have mentioned it.' He dropped two bunches of keys on to the desk. Arnott fingered them and sat down.

'Silly cow. Ask Mr Farrow up.'

Arnott closed the desk drawers and Larry withdrew to the corner of the room. Almost immediately Nicholas Farrow entered, the pallor seeping through suntanned cheeks giving his good looks a jaundiced, sickly quality.

Rising from the thronelike chair, Arnott waved in Larry's direction.

'This is Inspector Erskine and my name's Arnott. My condolences, Mr Farrow. I take it you prefer to use your professional name.'

The man ignored Erskine and blurted out, 'Is this true? Francis dead? I don't believe it.'

'Prepare yourself for the worst, Mr Farrow.' Erskine's voice insinuated itself smoothly and he moved forward to guide Swayne's brother to a seat. 'It may have been some sort of ghastly accident.'

'Murder? You mean someone was here?' Farrow's tone was shrill, unstagey, unprofessional. Arnott relaxed: he recognized genuine shock when he saw it.

'Not that we know, Mr Farrow. Did your brother have any special friends? Entertained here, did he?' Arnott's tone was implicit.

'No!' Farrow snapped, half rising. 'Tell me the truth. Has Francis had an accident?'

'Hanged himself,' Erskine bluntly replied.

Arnott moved with surprising agility round the desk. 'In poor health was he, your brother? In debt? Blackmailed by any chance?'

'Suicide! That's a bloody lie. I shall insist on a private post-mortem.' He threw off Arnott's hand and made for the door.

'You'd best see the body. An official identification will be required. I take it you are prepared for that?'

Nicholas Farrow nodded, his thinning hair flopping boyishly across his forehead, the handsome face now kindling dim recollections in Arnott's brain of a smoother jawline, a film star smile. Farrow's bloodshot eyes drawn with fatigue contrasted bleakly with the carefree jeans and sweat-shirted image he affected.

'Does my sister know about this?'

'No,' Erskine said. 'Is she in London? We shall need to have her address for the record.' His manner was affable and Farrow's unspoken assent hardly registered in the mêlée of distracted thoughts which seemed to jerk and spin behind his twitching eyelids like a faulty reel of film. Highly strung, Arnott reflected. All the bloody same, the silver spoon brigade.

The phone jangled on the desk between them and Erskine lifted the receiver, listening intently as the Inspector propelled Farrow into the next room. In the leaden silence Farrow's gasp audibly summed up the horror of the hideous cadaver now stiffening under the girder from which it was suspended.

Erskine took off his jacket and draped it over Swayne's chair. Kneeling by the desk he carefully removed each empty drawer, examined it minutely, peering under the kneehole with the aid of a small torch. Satisfied, he rose and, drawing a miniature toolkit from his pocket, unscrewed the telephone and poked at the jumble of wires. Reassembling the instrument, he slowly toured the room, twitching aside pictures and draperies and beaming the torch into every cranny. Then he moved back to the papers spread about the divan.

Erskine heard the heavy steps of Arnott and Nicholas Farrow descend the stairs and the rattle and squeal of a car leaving the mews. The men on the landing relaxed and shuffled along the short strip of runner, talking and laughing in muted undertones.

Soundlessly, Erskine closed the door and settled at the desk with a notebook and a small camera. After ten minutes he twisted round and, taking a pack from his jacket, lit a cigarette. He leaned back, faintly perplexed. Sauntering through to the bathroom, he gazed at the grotesque figure lolling like a fairground Aunt Sally, its tongue poking almost comically at the succession of viewers on this bad, bad Monday.

He glanced round. The curtains, drawn back now, admitted bright sunshine into the bathroom, its gay tile patterns and burnished brasswork far from sinister. The wide sill of the triangular bath was furnished with a selection of colourful jars and bottles, and above the elaborate shower fitting a corona supported the shower curtain looped gracefully through a lion's head fitment on the wall.

Erskine moved closer to the body, drawing deeply on his cigarette under the bored gaze of the constable who had sidled in with a report sheet which the Inspector accepted without comment before dismissing him with a curt nod. Swayne was a small man with the spare build of a jockey. In fact, the women's clothing fitted well.

Righting the upturned bathroom stool, Erskine climbed up and stared closely at the knotted rope, thin and efficient. It bit deeply into the flesh on a slip knot secured overhead to a steel beam which supported a sloping ceiling surfaced with the same Moorish tiles surrounding the bath.

He stepped down and edged round the corpse to peer at the lavatory pan, a decorative item boxed in mahogany like a Victorian commode. A palm in a blue and white china pot half screened the toilet area from the bathing end, its elegant fronds arching upwards towards the noonday sun whose brassy rays bore down on poor Swayne decked out like a fairground hussy. Erskine subdued a picture which sprang to mind of the curvaceous charms of Annie Miles

from his home town, chosen specially for the Tip the Lady
Out of Bed stall at the Red Cross fête where fifty pence
bought the chance to pitch the sparsely clad Annie on to
the grass.

The constable and he exchanged rueful grins and Erskine
sauntered back into the study to fetch his camera, then
carefully positioned several shots of the body. The ghastly
thing is, he reflected, the poor sod's tragedy merely looks
farcical.

He was just settling down to scan Swayne's address book
when the constable urgently rapped on the door. Before
Erskine could speak he entered.

'What's up?'

'Not exactly sure, sir, but—' The man moved awkwardly,
his fresh face eager but held in check: determined not to
make a complete fool of himself. 'It's Mike Smith, he's on
duty with me, see. And when Inspector Arnott went back
to the station Mike said we might as well have a cuppa and
see what's doing in the kitchen. We've been here since
half-nine, sir,' he muttered defensively, 'and not had a
chance to get so much as a drop of tea. Not a bite—' he
elaborated.

'Get on with it, man!'

'Well, sir, Smith thinks he's found a bomb.'

CHAPTER 3

It took a frenzied half-hour for Nicholas Farrow to locate
his sister's ex-directory number in Yorkshire, his bureau a
shambles, the accumulated clutter of letters and bills in
marked contrast to the immaculate order of Swayne's desk.
He poured a shot of whisky and refilled the glass as he
listened to the mechanical buzz, infuriatingly prosaic.

'Sabina!'

'Nick, how wonderful. Did you get that part in the new—'

'Sabina, listen, for God's sake!' He gripped the receiver, pressing his elbow hard on to the table in an effort to still the tremor which gripped him like influenza.

'Sabby. I've dreadful news. It's—'

'Not Sandy? The boys? Oh, Nick, what's happened?'

'No. It's Francis. Sab, it's terrible. Brace yourself, darling.' He floundered for the right words, his mind in a turmoil, then hiccoughed. 'He's killed himself,' he blurted out. He emptied the glass.

'Francis?' Her reply was husky, the merest whisper. 'That's impossible. A car accident? Or the boat? They've made a mistake. It's someone else. Who told you this?'

He took a deep breath before continuing in careful, measured phrases.

'Listen, Sabby. Just listen. I got an urgent call from the police to go to the mews. Christ, what a bloody nightmare!' On a choked indrawn breath the bald facts spilled out. 'Francis hanged himself in the bathroom on Friday night. It wasn't discovered till this morning.'

'Hanged himself? Francis? Oh no . . .' Sabina groaned, dropping on to the hard hall chair, long sun-brown fingers raking her hair.

Nick's words rapped out, shrill, staccato as machine-gun fire, sparing her nothing. He paused, adding as a wisp of comfort, 'The body's been taken away. We'll know more tomorrow.'

'I'll come down.'

'What about Sybil?' A woman entered, regarding Nicholas almost with indifference as she lit a cigarette and passed it to her husband.

'Aragon's here,' Sabina answered. 'She can pull her weight for once. Sybil's very capable despite her blindness. She's an old woman, of course, but . . .' Sabina floundered, mind reeling. 'There's always Mrs Carter.'

'The housekeeper? Could you, Sab? I'm all to pieces. I just can't believe Francis would do it. When did you see him?'

'We lunched together last week but he was terribly busy. He was due to come up here for the weekend when I get back from Florence in September.' Sabina's voice was firmer now. 'I can't take it in, Nick. He wasn't even depressed. Overworked. But spry as ever.'

'It's true all right. I had to make an official identification. There's worse.' He paused. 'I can't talk about it on the phone. Can you get a train right away?'

'I'll drive. Where are you?'

'At home. The police are coming back tonight to check some details. The solicitor's already on my back, not to mention Francis's chambers. And the press have been hounding me since I left the mews . . . don't say anything when you get to the house, there's one guy out there now . . . Sandy's been marvellous.' He reached out to clutch the sleeve of the woman standing behind him, his voice stumbling in rapid, broken syllables. 'Just get here as soon as you can, darling. Don't listen to the news, for God's sake. I don't think I can take any more . . . It's all so vile and—'

'Stop, Nicky! There's no time now.' Sabina's thoughts swam and like a drowning woman she clutched at practicalities. 'I'll come straight away. About seven, I suppose, but that depends on the traffic. Did you see Francis before . . .?' She faltered. 'He told me there was to be a reconciliation.'

'That's what's breaking me up, Sab. It's all so bloody unfair. We'd all agreed to forget about that old row. Sandy organized it. She's a tower of strength, that girl. No one knows her as I do. She was going to fix a party for all of us, you, Harry, Francis, us, the boys . . . And now it's too late! How can I live with that? The last words I spoke to Francis were so cruel, so horrible.'

'Don't blame yourself, love. Francis spoke to me about it. We talked about the boys. I'll tell you about it as soon as I can get there.'

Soundlessly replacing the receiver, Sabina Morland sat

in the chilly Victorian splendour of Fernside, knees pressed together, the absolute stillness of her pose imprisoning the bird of terror which flapped and shrieked inside her skull. Francis had hanged himself?

She stared down at her suntanned feet in sandals placed together on the tessellated floor, the red, blue and gold lights filtering through the glass door panels staining her legs as unnaturally as the dreadful act of which her brother was accused. Suicide? The taste of tears dissolved her shocked inertia and, jumping up, she ran upstairs into the sunny room overlooking the garden.

An old woman seated by the window was fumbling with a tape-recorder, her arthritic hands jabbing a cassette into the machine. Without looking round she flung her words back at Sabina entering the room.

'This bloody thing'll have to go back, Sabina! It's crackling and hissing like a Christmas goose.'

'You're too rough with it, Sybil. I'll get Aragon to have a look at it.'

Irritably the old lady pushed the machine aside and inclined her head, alert as a starling. 'Is there something wrong, my dear? Was that Harry on the telephone?'

Sabina clasped her hands, locking the fingers in a painful knot in a desperate attempt to keep her voice level.

'No, darling. It was bad news. But not Harry. I have to go back to London immediately. Francis has had an accident.'

'Your brother? The barrister? Oh, you poor dear. Francis was not one to drive dangerously I would have thought. Step off the kerb without looking, did he?'

Sabina gulped. 'Not a road accident.' Then she blurted out. 'At home. He's dead, Sybil.'

A rug on the landing flew sideways as a long-legged girl in paint-stained jeans skidded into the room, her thin arms shooting out for balance, heavy silver hoops swinging at her ears.

'I heard the phone,' she panted, stopping short at the sight of the two women uncharacteristically clasped together. She backed off, muttering, 'I thought it might have been Rick.'

The old woman pursed her lips, nodding vehemently. 'Rick. Rick. Rick. I'm tired of hearing nothing but Rick! Sabina's had tragic news.'

Blowing her nose, Sabina stumbled to her feet. She faced Aragon. 'I'm so sorry, darling, but I've got to go back.'

'And me?' The girl's response was eager, immediate. She was beside Sabina, clutching her arm. 'Can I go with you? Please!'

Sabina brushed off her stepdaughter's fingers and, choosing her words carefully, said: I'm afraid not, Aragon. Sybil needs you here. I can't take you. It's business.' Harry's magic phrase. Even as she uttered it Sabina heard his voice in her mind. The glib, all-purpose excuse for any eventuality.

'Shit!'

'Stop that, my girl.' Sybil's tone was final, her empty eyes drilling the space between them. 'Sabina's brother has died. You are to stay here and help Carter. Never mind about this Rick. Your father has some views on that subject, I have no doubt.'

The girl's lip drooped sulkily and, drifting about the room, she mentally shuffled the new permutations of her summer exile in Yorkshire. With Sabina out of the way . . .

Suddenly, she sprang forward, touching Sabina's arm, 'I'm sorry, Sabby. Poor Nicholas, he was such a lovely bloke. All the girls at school used to—'

'Not Nicholas!' Sabina impatiently pushed away the girl's hand. 'Francis. You won't remember him.'

'The old one? Of course I do. Oh dear . . .'

'I must go straight away. I'll drive down,' she added briskly. 'Will you be all right?' The question was directed at Aragon, the unspoken implications well understood.

Turning aside, Sabina kissed Sybil's dandelion puff of white hair. 'I'll pack a few things and go now, Sybil, if you don't mind. I'll ring you this evening when I have more news. Can you explain to Mrs Carter?' Her voice faltered. 'I don't think I can bear to talk about it any more.' The old woman rose and they held each other for a moment.

Sabina fled, slithering on the oak treads of the staircase, footsteps quickening to a rush as she reached the hall. The two left in the bright sitting-room moved together into the pool of afternoon sun fading the carpet.

Later, the girl sprawled on the chintz sofa next to her grandmother, they registered the muted sounds of Sabina's departure. Aragon reached out a scrawny arm bridging the space between them and laid her dirty palm in the hands of the blind woman, absorbing the faint scent of verbena which clung to her cashmere wrap. The cassette whirred in the recording machine and they listened to *Washington Square* read aloud in the smooth honey accents of a Texan movie actress.

Sabina drove directly to Wetherby and joined the stream of lorries and cars heading for the metropolis. The Porsche was stifling, the sun searing her bare arm as the miles flew under the tyres, the windscreen spattered with hundreds of minute black flies, speckling the glass with flecks of blood. She watched the tiny insects smash into the screen, then briefly struggle before becoming merely another black smear. Sabina shivered at the thought of poor Francis's body putrefying in the shut-up house over the weekend, hanging like some bedraggled game bird killed out of season. Tiny beads of sweat broke out on her upper lip.

As she neared London clouds were massing above the city, the air humid and leaden with the threat of thunder. She dared not turn on the radio news in case the dramatic death of Nicholas Farrow's brother destroyed her subconscious conviction that Francis was really alive, that it was all a terrible mistake. Was Nick's name still worth a headline even in the doldrums of a dull August? The silly season?

Since her marriage Sabina Morland had lived in Hong Kong and the star rating of her handsome brother was unclear to her. When she came back for brief holidays, England seemed a world apart, she herself a different person, almost a stranger, out of touch with family feuds and gossip. Nick seemed to be acting in rather dreary things on TV and was always short of money. Not that she told Harry about their little private arrangements. Acting was like that, Nick said, up one moment, dredging the bottom the next.

And there was Francis's own brief illumination under the media spotlight only this year. When he got that Irishman off. A legal miracle, they called it. Sandy had sent her some cuttings with her own brutal commentary on Francis's involvement, tinged with a grudging approval. But surely a court case, even one involving a so-called terrorist, wouldn't render poor Francis newsworthy for ever?

No, Nicholas was the weak link. If the news agencies latched on to the kinship of Nicholas Farrow with the suicide of a QC there might be something in it to make the headlines, but surely not Francis himself. Why was Nick being so paranoid about publicity? Yet there was something he had hinted at, something else, something he didn't want her to hear before they met. Could someone else have been involved, some sort of scandal, a double suicide?

She shook her head, mentally shifting the kaleidoscope of nightmare thoughts multiplying by the minute. If the papers did get hold of it, so what? Nothing could hurt Francis any more, the hurt could only touch herself and Nicky. It was selfish to worry about any of it. Sabina swallowed hard and put her foot on the accelerator. She thought the misting of the road ahead was a mirage of the burning air and raced on, heedless of the tears.

As Sabina Morland, still unaware of the tawdry details of Francis's death, was tacking across the city towards Islington, Larry Erskine was ordering a cool pint of bitter in the Ring of Bells.

The bar, in contrast to his morning visit, was now

crowded, the small saloon packed with braying young executives and their girls, some grouped outside in the mews talking excitably and laughing in whooping brittle yelps like a pack of foxhounds. A couple of seedy-looking press photographers stood gloomily by the window sipping gin. A middle-aged couple with their dog, evidently local, stood at the bar complaining loudly to Les Weston.

Larry Erskine stood at the corner of the bar, his jacket slung over his shoulder, his tie loosened. What a day! He tapped the ash of his cigarette on to the floor and glanced towards the door. Half past six and no sign of Arnott's girl, Judy Whatsit. He doubted she would show up at all after this afternoon's fracas. He sighed and, ordering another bitter from the stony-faced landlord, pondered the hospitality rating of publicans he had known. He put Les Weston about 95th on the list. Erskine became aware of the clammy smear of his shirt sticking to his shoulder-blades and, sipping the froth off his beer, pushed his way through the crowd and out into the mews. It was scarcely cooler and storm clouds seemed to clamp down on the triangular forecourt, giving the brightly coloured window-boxes a lurid clarity.

He stared over at Swayne's house, closed up now and already seeming abandoned. Only a slight movement behind the upstairs blinds betrayed the continued police presence. Flicking his cigarette on to the cobbles, Erskine decided to go home.

He felt a hand on his shirtsleeve and was jerked out of his reverie.

The middle-aged woman had followed him outside, her nervy Irish setter gasping against a choke chain.

'You're with the police, aren't you.' It wasn't a question. Her shrewd glance took in his crumpled suit, tie awry.

'Detective-Inspector Erskine.' That surprised her all right.

'I'm not sure who to ask about this. We're not a neighbourly lot, you understand. But it's about Tai-Tai. Something must be done.'

'Oh yes?' Not another complaint about some new heroin derivative he hadn't heard of? Erskine mentally flicked through Drug Squad terms, dredging his memory.

'Tai-Tai,' she repeated. 'The cat.' Irritably snatching at the dog's chain in disbelief at the sheer obtuse stupidity of the force these days, she slowly enunciated, 'Mr Swayne's Siamese.'

'Oh yes. Of course . . . Ah well, Mrs . . . er . . .'

'Morrison-Carr. Kate Morrison-Carr. From Number Three. I've already mentioned it to Miss Pullen and she promised to ring back this afternoon but—'

'We've been rather busy,' he interposed in his smoothest manner. 'But—'

'Well—' she nodded at the tankard in his hand—'you're not busy now.'

'I'm quite sure Sergeant Pullen will get back to you as soon as she can. But it's not really my department,' Erskine said, his tone now frigidly polite. 'Madam,' he added.

'Animals can't be filed away like parking tickets, Inspector. I could report this to the RSPCA.'

The setter danced at their feet and salivated affectionately over Erskine's Gucci moccasins.

'Alfie!' she snapped. 'Sit. Look here. Tai-Tai has been hanging about and nobody seems to be taking the least notice.' Kate Carr's lips clamped in an uncompromising snap. 'It would seem the police are more interested in the dead than the living.'

Erskine conceded she had a point there.

'I'll tell you what I'll do, young man,' she said. 'I shall keep Tai-Tai at my house. Put that in your report, Inspector. And you may tell Mr Swayne's poor brother to call on me. Tai-Tai's a champion, you know. A valuable animal.'

Without waiting for an answer, she jerked the chain and dragged Alfie back inside the Ring of Bells.

The astringent retort died on his lips as Mrs Morrison-Carr's backside retreated. He shrugged. Erskine had had enough tiptoeing round everyone's sensibilities on this case.

Glancing at his watch, he drained his glass and decided to call it a day. Forget the whole thing. Leave the whole nest of worms undisturbed.

But Fate in the unlikely form of Judith Pullen intervened. Her recently MoT'd runabout entered the mews and scuppered his resolve.

CHAPTER 4

The green Volkswagen, a well-worn beetle, rusting but with one new and glistening door, threaded its way through the parked cars blocking the mews. Judy Pullen's face, strained and serious, peered through the windscreen, scanning the jolly group of yuppies outside the Ring of Bells. Erskine waved and, smiling broadly, moved forward to open the door.

'I can't stay,' she tossed at him, her glance stinging. 'Christ knows why I'm here at all. I'm off duty and you're not even on our side. But you should know. I've just come from the station.' She threw her linen jacket on to the back seat. 'Get in.'

She made no sense and even if she did it seemed to Larry Erskine a funny way to talk to a senior officer. He shrugged. Leaning into the car, he started to argue about leaving his own vehicle. She cut him short. 'We can't talk here. Just get in.'

He did as he was told. Perhaps it was the way she said she was 'off duty'. No wonder she and Arnott were known as Punch and Judy.

The car picked its way through the archway and into the welter of Gloucester Road.

'Go towards the park. Left here,' he said.

Sluggish, the traffic crawled towards Kensington Gardens, tempers frayed in the humidity of a torrid afternoon in the city, the wasted air of exhaust fumes and human exhalation pressing in all round. Larry found himself staring at the sharply defined profile of the girl beside him, the clearly angled tip of eyebrow and chin softening into the delicate roundness of her cheekbones. Bit frail-looking, he decided, to be much use in any practical police work. Even so . . .

She parked the Volkswagen at a meter near the park.

He indicated the disc stuck to her windscreen. 'Why don't you use your residents' parking over there?' His bantering approach did nothing to soften the grim set of her mouth as she locked the ageing beetle.

'Doesn't apply here. Residents can park for miles round Knightsbridge and Notting Hill but this bit's another zone.'

'Living in the Royal Borough's a bit expensive on a sergeant's pay, isn't it?'

'Any of your business?' she snapped.

Unperturbed, Erskine took her elbow and led the way through the unbroken ribbon of traffic and into the park. A canopy of trees shading the broad avenue created a cool tunnel, the first breath of green all day. Judith Pullen drew apart and stepped out, drawing in the pollen-drenched air like a draught of clear spring water.

Erskine matched her stride and after a hundred yards she slowed down, walking towards the Round Pond. In the early evening it was the quietest part of the gardens, the children and their toy boats gone, nannies with their high perambulators home for tea, only a few tourists still plunging on, guidebooks clasped like passports through the maze of sights to be seen.

Her pace slackened and Erskine remained silent, anxious not to rekindle the inexplicable rancour before she said what was evidently on her mind. She dawdled at the cement rim of the pond looking across the unruffled steel surface of the water.

'I've just come from the station,' she said. 'Arnott's asked to be taken off the case.'

Erskine's head jerked up and he started to speak but she

had moved on. A few yards ahead she turned, glancing over her shoulder in cool appraisal of the lean detective in the expensive lightweight suit, calculating the effect of her announcement. He stood immobile and called out to her, 'Why should he do that?'

'He likes to do things his own way. He's been at it too long to change his methods now. That bomb business, calling in the explosives mob without asking him and then—'

'Let me say it just once more.' He spoke carefully, choosing his words. For his own reasons he needed to have a foot in the other camp. 'I had to act immediately. I had my orders. The men I called in behaved very discreetly. I didn't clear the mews, call out the bomb squad, instigate a full alert. I had already examined the device myself. I know a bit about it, you know,' he added sarcastically. 'It was obviously not set to go off. There was no immediate danger. It wasn't even a professional job.'

'Kids' firework?' she sneered.

A dog-walker approached, circling the circumference of the pond, his mild interest taken by the young couple obviously having a row. Lover's tiff presumably. He whistled to a cross-bred labrador which defiantly plunged into the shallow water, scattering the ducks.

Irritably, Erskine took her arm once more, propelling her across the grass towards a massive chestnut tree.

He resumed his appeal. 'Arnott had absolutely no cause to kick out like that. Keeping that sort of information out of the report is merely politic. The device was an amateur effort, effective if activated but in fact an interesting toy, a sort of scientific DIY job.'

'Why wouldn't you let Arnott deal with the thing officially? I suppose the fact that this pervert was a QC had something to do with it? Friends in high places.'

Erskine smiled thinly, opening his hands in disbelief. 'Sergeant Pullen. You have entirely missed the point. A piece of machinery was found on the premises. Not hidden away. Placed clearly on view in a cupboard with the tea and sugar. Take my word for it, it was not set to explode and—'

'It had plastic explosive, fuses, the lot.' Her small white face was whiter now, stiff with petulance.

'Yes,' he agreed. 'But, believe me, nothing would be gained by disclosing all that at the inquest. Representing O'Laughlin put Swayne in the headlines and the discovery of a bomb in his kitchen would bring the whole business back on the public's conscience. We don't want that. We may be dealing with terrorists here. O'Laughlin got off on a clever technicality Swayne was swift to grasp. It's best forgotten. He'll slip up again and we'll nail him up for ever next time. It doesn't take much to antagonize the Unionists, especially at this critical stage of government negotiations.'

'Legal expediency I suppose you'd call it!' The contempt in her voice rekindled Erskine's exasperation.

'Getting O'Laughlin off that rap was legal. And what did that prove? The law's an ass.'

He drew a deep breath. 'Let's be constructive about this. All Arnott was instructed to do was to shut his eyes to one tiny bit of evidence. No one had broken in, murder isn't at issue, no blood, no government secrets have been lost. What the hell's he making such a holy litany of it for?'

The girl shrugged, sharp collar-bones lifting under the thin cotton blouse in brittle accord.

'You would never understand. Personally, I don't even like Arnott. He's lazy and stubborn. He's antediluvian in his methods and has a threadbare set of prejudices. But he's honest. And he cares about justice. He's had his share of barristers talking villains out of court, and presumably a QC with all the right connections whose sordid suicide is whitewashed into the bargain was the last straw.'

'Whitewashed?' Erskine's sardonic laughter rang empty as a cracked bell on the evening air. 'Tarted up like a drag queen, then hanging himself, can hardly be glossed over. The evening papers have had a ball already!'

'Haven't you heard? It's not suicide.'

A sudden breeze from the lake raised the blonde hairs on her arms. She shivered. 'A ghost over my grave' rose to her mind and she fixed Erskine in a cold stare.

'I didn't think it was,' was all he said, his eyes sliding aside in speculation. 'He was a Catholic,' he added.

'That explains it!' She hooted with derision. 'He can even be decently buried now. Forget the sordid little details just so long as he didn't actually *intend* to string himself up.' She drew aside, looking back the way they had come, and started back to the car.

Erskine relaxed and lit a cigarette, apparently no longer affected by her bitterness. He quickly caught up, hands thrust deep in his pockets. They matched long strides towards the frivolous outline of Prince Albert seated in majesty within the elaborate gilded memorial. The sun, engorged by thunderclouds, swiftly disappeared, strong rays accentuating the billowing cumulus in baroque and vulgar splendour.

'The pathologist has been persuaded,' she went on, 'that it was an accident. Swayne tied himself up for a thrill and slipped.'

Erskine stopped dead. 'Are you inferring,' he said, gripping her arm as she tried to walk away—'no, listen to me, Judy! Are you inferring that the pathologist is lying?'

'That hurts!' She shook free and set off at a run. They reached the Volkswagen together and breathlessly she glared at Erskine, two spots of colour staining her cheeks. 'And you can find your own way back.' Even in her own ears it sounded childish and the angry exchange between them assumed the fatuity of staged moves in a mock battle. Who really cared anyway?

She laughed, pushing him aside to unlock the car.

'Just a minute, Judy. Are you having me on? About the suicide. It was accidental?'

'Apparently. See the report yourself in the morning. As you didn't know,' she added with sly amusement.

He let her go and stood in the empty parking space watching the green car speed away. The heavens suddenly opened, slow drops of rain remorselessly turning into a deluge. Erskine stood bleakly on the pavement, his suit drenched and not a taxi in sight.

Sabina Morland awoke in their London house, a stuccoed villa backing on to Holland Park chosen by her husband as a gilt-edged investment, a foothold in the escalating London property market, a hedge against inflation. Sabina liked it too but for all the wrong reasons. The pretty ironwork canopy sheltering the verandah was charming: Harry considered it a security risk. The proximity of the park was nice too, especially the Orangery, where often one caught sight of wedding parties behind the glass like glimpses of a silent movie.

But best of all she revelled in her own tiny, sunless garden, densely verdant and often dripping, a place where minute ferns and lichens sprouted from the wall and between mossy flagstones. It was all so different from Hong Kong, even the wet Augusts which were so often the setting for Harry's long leave were a delight to her. On the brightest morning the thrust of greenery against the drawing-room windows was like being at the bottom of the sea, cool and dark.

She crept downstairs and made some coffee, the bubbling percolator and strong aroma imposing sanity on this tragic homecoming. The overnight storm had raged for hours, lightning searing the outline of the bedroom window on her sleepless brain like a white-hot brand, the crack and dying roll of the thunder passing, it seemed, directly over the house.

Sabina poured black coffee into her cup and sat at the kitchen table watching a broken branch of the fig tree sway backwards and forwards against the window, its rain-slashed leaves glossy and thick like jungle foliage. The dreadful first evening with Nick and Sandy had brought it home to her. Francis was dead. Horribly, horribly dead.

She stirred her coffee, tearless now, the anguish crystallized from sap to amber. Dear Francis, always the strong one of the three. Now carelessly dead.

The police had been kind. That policewoman—Sergeant Pullen was it?—had phoned Nick to say that the pathologist had ruled out suicide. Accidental. One blessing at least.

Poor Nick. The press had besieged his home: the flip side of being a television actor. It had been difficult to force her way through and presumably the papers would be full of it all week, or so Nicholas thought. Even so, Sabina was shocked to discover the extent of his complete disintegration . . . She poured a second cup and involuntarily drew back from the window, wondering for how long Nick would be badgered.

The policewoman said she would call today. She had some questions about Francis just 'to tie up the loose ends', she said. Sabina took her cup into Harry's study and after scanning his secretary's typewritten itinerary booked a person to person call to Tokyo.

Later, just before twelve, the doorbell rang and Sabina Morland came face to face with Judith Pullen for the first time. Eyeing each other at the top of the short flight of steps leading up to the door, they were mutually relieved that just two women were involved. Francis Swayne's undignified exit was a delicate wound to probe from both points of view. Judy could scarcely imagine either Arnott or Erskine putting this reserved young woman at her ease.

'Won't you come through?' Sabina stood aside, ushering Judy through to the small drawing-room. 'Coffee?'

'No, thank you, Mrs Morland. I won't keep you long. Just a few questions. Mr Farrow—er Swayne?—couldn't tell us a great deal. But he mentioned you had seen the deceased recently. Had they quarrelled, your brothers? Mr Farrow seemed out of touch considering they both lived in London. Confused by the shock, I expect. You—er—both have my sympathy,' she added as an afterthought.

Sabina indicated a seat by the empty fireplace and Judy

sat down, drawing a notebook from her bag. Glancing up
at the tall woman in the black linen slacks leaning against
the mantelshelf, it occurred to her that the dark curly head
reflected in the overmantel was more like a boy's. The two
women were about the same age and height but in every
other respect poles apart.

'Oh, Francis and Nick didn't always see eye to eye. It
caused problems. My sister-in-law has strong left-wing
views and Francis teased her, you know how lawyers are.
Arguing just for his own amusement, really. Francis had
no firm political affiliations himself.' Her hand fell open
expressively, flopping from a loose wrist, a gesture both
elegant and unaffected. 'As a matter of fact,' Sabina continued, 'Nick and Francis quarrelled quite seriously two
years ago and haven't spoken since. Harry and I hoped to
bring them together somehow this trip but . . .' Her voice
trailed away and then in firmer tones she went on: 'But they
were blood brothers under the skin, if you know what I
mean. Our parents were killed. A car crash. Francis,
being the eldest, took over, organized us a good deal. I
am much younger than my brothers and relied on Francis
absolutely. He became more of a father, really. But
Nicholas often resented it. Francis was rather a bully, I
suppose.'

She smiled wryly and paced the pale carpet, hands thrust
deep in her pockets.

'Was there any financial arrangement? Insurance, family
inheritance, anything of that sort? Mr Swayne was un-
married, I take it?'

'Oh yes.' Sabina's step was quick and light and at each
turn in the elegant room her black patent pumps swivelled
soundlessly on the carpet. 'Francis was comfortably placed,
rather careful with his money between you and me. I'm
certain he made a will, he's not a man—was not, that is—
to leave untidy ends. His associates in Gray's Inn will know
more about that, you could ask them, I suppose. But foul
play isn't suspected, is it?'

Judy Pullen swiftly reassured her and pressed on.

'Mr Swayne had a white Renault 5, it appears. Could he have garaged it? It's not in the mews and I gather he was using it on Friday evening. He attended a charity function at Somerset House and the rest of his party saw him leave in his own car.'

Sabina frowned and wondered if all fatal accidents were investigated in such detail. Perhaps Francis's involvement with that Irish business made the police jumpy.

'Who told you that?'

Judy flicked back the pages of her notebook, her baby-fine hair falling like a silk fringe against her cheek. 'A Mr Charles Finbow. Two of the party, including Mr Swayne, went back to Finbow's house for a nightcap after the performance and sat in the garden until two a.m.'

'Really? How spartan of them!'

'It was a very hot night in London. A record in fact. The heat almost spoiled the whole evening, Mr Finbow said. A private performance of *Rigoletto* had been staged in one of the salons, the audience sitting all round and the shutters closed to cut out the evening sunlight. Apparently the heat was so stifling with the floodlights blazing that half the men abandoned their dinner jackets and sweated it out in their shirtsleeves.'

Sabina smiled, hardly able to imagine Englishmen re-sorting to such informalities.

Judy said, 'Could I just check my notes?'

She ruffled the pages of her pad and suddenly looked up, hazel eyes candid and direct. 'You know nothing about Mr Swayne's car? Would he have left it somewhere, too many drinks perhaps after an evening out? He may have walked home deciding he was over the limit.'

'Quite possibly. Francis was fanatical about regulations. Quite a stickler for right and wrong . . .' Sabina's eager phrases petered out and she looked awkwardly away. 'That's ridiculous, of course. I imagined I knew all about my brother. I admired him enormously. Would you believe I knew nothing about his homosexuality?'

'If I may so, Mrs Morland, things are not always clear cut. One of the details in the pathologist's report which will probably be disclosed at the inquest is that Francis Swayne was not an habitual homosexual. A transvestite and presumably a man with deviant requirements, but it was a secret kink of his personality. His friends are as shocked as yourself.'

Judy Pullen paused, unsure to what extent Mrs Morland's sensibilities could be tested. 'A habitual homosexual's anal orifice,' she explained briskly, 'is dilated and keratinized and Swayne's medical report denies this. Also, careful inquiries have not disclosed any homosexual partners or that he frequented bars where such associations are offered. These days such preferences are not hidden to the same extent as years ago, even professional men are not always discreet. Finally, for reasons connected with your late brother's work with political prisoners his background had been quietly investigated, his consideration for a judicial appointment had been vetted.'

'Oh dear, poor Francis. His harmless eccentricity gave the game away in the end. Perrier?'

Judy continued in her dry, matter-of-fact tone. 'I have mentioned all this informally, Mrs Morland, to put your mind at rest on some counts at least. Francis Swayne was not receiving medical treatment, a very fit man by all accounts.' The oblique hint was lost on Sabina Morland or perhaps deliberately ignored.

'My brother sailed a bit,' she continued smoothly. 'We used to have a family house in Suffolk which was let years ago to help Nick at the beginning of his career and to help pay for my education presumably, but Francis maintained his enthusiasm for sailing. He crewed for a friend, Roger Mansell, who took it very seriously. Francis mentioned only last week that he had hoped to sail to Norway with Roger this month but had to change his plans. The boat blew up.'

Judy's startled response spilled water over her skirt and she dabbed at it with her handkerchief. 'Blew up?'

Sabina laughed. 'Something like that. The boat wasn't an old tub! Quite well known in the yachting world. *Seraphina II*. It caught fire only a couple of weeks ago. Arson. I don't know the details. He and Roger had been friends for several years. I introduced them, as a matter of fact. I worked with Roger when I was at university. We were on a research project together which ended rather badly and Francis dragged me out of there and caused a bit of a fuss. Embarrassing. I never got my PhD, which was a pity. Then I met my husband and after a "whirlwind romance", as they say, a scientific career seemed unimportant.'

Judy Pullen scribbled more notes, then glanced up.

'Your brother was due to go off on holiday this weekend. His cleaning woman who found the body insists he was going away Friday night as usual and the friends with whom he spent his last evening say he planned to drive down to the New Forest overnight. He has a cottage near the coast, I understand.'

'Yes. It's just a small place but he liked to get away from London at weekends and it was convenient for the Hamble. And Cowes, I suppose. Francis was rather set in his ways, Miss Pullen. Or do I call you Sergeant? Every Friday evening without fail he went off for the weekend, immediately after leaving the office if he could. Summer and winter. "Mr Metronome" Sandy called him. That's my sister-in-law. She didn't like Francis, thought him too pedantic. Rather pompous.'

'No suggestions about the missing Renault, then?' Judy persisted.

'I'm so sorry, rambling on like that. I'm waiting for Harry to fly home. It's been a relief to talk to someone. I'm afraid I've taken advantage of your politeness.'

Sabina's smile was apologetic and she fumbled with her glass. 'No, I can't help you about the car. Francis didn't rent a garage, I know that. That's why he bought small cars. Expensive cars left in the street in London every night are broken into with dreary regularity. But of course you know all that! My brother usually left his car outside the house. Easy parking was one of the things he liked about the mews and he had a residents' parking permit, of course. He boasted he was the only man in London who had never had a parking fine or been clamped—the sort of boring remark that irritated Sandy almost to violence. He *would* go on about minor misdemeanours like that.'

'It would be an odd coincidence if the car had been stolen over the weekend. It'll probably turn up. I'll put out a call.' Judy checked the last few pages of her notes and looked up. 'Just one other thing, Mrs Morland. Mr Swayne's cat.'

Sabina's large brown eyes widened and Judy thrust into the back of her mind the recollection of the same huge eyes popping in Francis Swayne's head as it lolled under the harsh illumination of the photographer's flash.

'Tai-Tai! Good heavens, I'd forgotten all about her.'

'Mrs Morrison-Carr, a neighbour, has been looking after it but she rang the station again this morning. She can't cope any longer, her dog won't leave it alone.'

'More likely the other way round!' Judy grew reflective. 'Francis adored that animal but poor Tai-Tai's no fluffy pussycat. I can't leave her in England for Tan to look after. He has the garden flat in the basement, a Chinese architectural student, the son of a friend of ours in Hong Kong. He stays here while he's studying.'

'It must be convenient to have someone to look after the house.'

'Absolutely. He's a charming boy. But I couldn't saddle him with a cat.'

'Might eat it?'

Sabina smiled wanly and said, 'Nicholas is allergic to animal fur—or so Sandy says—and I'm abroad so much.'

'Mrs Morrison-Carr is being rather persistent. It could go to the animal rescue place in Battersea, I suppose. Family pet—?'

Sabina laughed. 'Heaven forbid. Tai-Tai's a tiger. Not everyone's cup of tea and probably vicious with children. No, a family pet she is not.'

Sabina gathered up the empty glasses. 'I'll take her back to Yorkshire with me. My mother-in-law lives in the country. It's a large house. Tai-Tai would probably fit in quite well. Shall I telephone this woman, Francis's neighbour?'

'I shall be at Sherbourne Mews about five. If you could meet me there I'll arrange for the cat to be ready for you to collect. If you feel up to it I would like to go over the house with you. Just to make sure everything's in order. You may notice something we've missed.'

'Hasn't Nicholas checked all that?'

Judy hesitated, recognizing Sabina's understandable reluctance to go to the house but someone from the family must be involved. And she didn't need Arnott to point out that women were often more observant. Except he didn't phrase it as kindly as that. From what she had seen of the actor brother, Judy Pullen guessed he would be no use at all.

'I thought you said Mr Farrow was not on close terms with the deceased?'

Sabina winced.

'That's true. Nick hasn't been to the mews for ages. Till this happened, that is. What about Pamina? She would know exactly what is supposed to be there.'

'The cleaner? She's in a state of shock. Wouldn't even go back inside the house for her things yesterday.'

'Poor soul. She's helped out here occasionally. I'd better go and see her, pay her what's due and so on. What a terrible shock for her to discover . . .' Sabina shuddered.

They walked into the hall.

'This afternoon, then?' Judy persisted.

'Yes, of course. I'll be there about five.'

'You'll need a box for the cat. There doesn't seem to be

a pet basket. Mrs Morrison-Carr has had to keep it in her spare room because of the dog.'

'Tai-Tai went everywhere with Francis at weekends. Even to the boat sometimes. He put her in a harness thing for travelling and led her about like a dog. He attached the lead under the driver's seat and Tai-Tai travelled beside him.'

'Lucky pussy.'

Judy hitched her bag on to her shoulder and waved cheerfully as she got into the car. Seagoing cat on a lead, she muttered to herself as she fumbled into gear. Now I've heard it all.

CHAPTER 5

The reverberations following Arnott's explosive reaction to Erskine's part in the investigation stunned everyone at the station. The atmosphere was razor-thin and normal noisy clatter reduced to awkward whispers and the scrape of metal chairs.

He had complained officially to the Commissioner and laid unfortunate indictments on the subjects of ethics, truth and the dignity of the law. In consequence Arnott was placed on two weeks' leave and advised to cool his heels until after the inquest.

Working between Arnott and Erskine, Judy Pullen was, to say the least, awkwardly placed. Arnott was right, of course, but expediency, she reluctantly admitted, had to be taken into account. Political considerations shaded what might once have been a black and white issue and men like Larry Erskine flourished in an ever-expanding grey area.

Judy Pullen had survived an ill-tempered lecture from the Superintendent on professional loyalty and the importance of government security, etc. etc., and baldly directed that the case be wrapped up and no messing.

Erskine kept away from the local station but coolly pur-
loined all Arnott's files, thus forcing Judy reluctantly to
share the temporary headquarters he had set up at Sherbourne Mews. Here Erskine took over Swayne's desk, his
cheerful disposition soon establishing an exclusively male
coterie.

Judy Pullen worked alone in the kitchen at a narrow
breakfast bar, making do with a wall telephone. Preparing
the facts for the coroner was now merely routine and since
Arnott's self-ejection Judy dourly admitted she would be
glad to move on to something else. Glumly she flicked
through Swayne's mail and, extracting the free soap coupons
and special offers, secured the rest with an elastic band. The
death of Francis Swayne QC left a sour after-taste all round.

The overnight storm had cleared the air making the rear
of the mews a pleasant oasis away from the constant stream
of pressmen and police messengers who passed upstairs.
Erskine, seated importantly behind the desk held court in
the manner of a royal guest, seated at the lawyer's high
backed chair.

Judy stretched, flexing her cramped fingers and went
outside. At four-thirty on this bright August afternoon the
garden was inviting. She paused on the threshold, staring
up at the backs of the peeling stuccoed houses which overlooked the mews, the high wall offering no privacy from the
upper storeys. A medley of ill-assorted curtains suggested
that the imposing houses the mews had originally served
were mostly now divided into flats and bed-sits, the roles
reversed: the rich occupying the servants' mews and the
poor sharing the substantial villas. She strolled under the
robinia, admiring the match of old bricks in Swayne's
extension. Only the slick pointing betrayed the building
line, the roof level rising to merge with the original, the new
slates masked behind a double parapet planted with yellow
ivy.

'Judy! Fancy a cup of tea?'

Startled, she spun round, irritated at being caught out,

apparently idling. Erskine's affability was difficult to counter. And constantly catching me on the wrong foot, she thought, making it impossible to retain any sort of working relationship. Anyway, I'm not the tea girl.

'No, thanks. Mrs Morland will be here shortly.'

He leaned against the door, his brown hair overlong, the casual manner softening the undeniable efficiency summed up in the crisp shirt and neatly pressed trousers, as sharp Judy guessed, as the click, click, click of his logical brain. She edged past him, back to the kitchen and the pile of official forms.

'If you've got a moment could you give me a hand? A little experiment.'

Judy waved vaguely in the direction of the littered breakfast bar. 'There's all this paperwork to finish and—'

'It'll only take a minute. Out here.' He backed into the hallway, pulling her into the street. 'I want to see if you can reach the catch if I shut the door. Put your arm through the letter-box.'

Her laughter was brittle. 'You're kidding! I may be skinny but getting my arm through a letter-box is a monkey's trick.'

Erskine's eager insistence was inextinguishable. 'Just take a good look at it, sweetie. It's a big wide flap, impossible for an adult, but a girl or a kid could possibly open the door by putting her elbow through to reach up to the catch on the inside. Go on, have a go. Please.'

She eyed the door with suspicion. 'And who prizes me free when I get stuck?'

He pushed her out and shut the door just as Swayne's neighbour was returning from a walk with her dog. Embarrassed, Judy smiled briefly, drew a deep breath and crouched on the pavement under the undisguised scrutiny of Kate Morrison-Carr. She inserted her hand into the flap. It was a wide brass fitting, handsomely polished and capacious for a lawyer's mail, ideal for the excesses of Sunday newsprint. Slowly advancing her forearm, Judy gingerly insinuated the elbow. So far, so good. Ruching up her sleeve, she adjusted her position, twisting her shoulder to push her arm through to feel about for the latch on the inside. Success! Swayne's front door slowly swung inwards, Judy crawling after, her arm still trapped. Erskine's howl of delight audibly expressed Kate Carr's open-mouthed astonishment. Bending down, he grasped Judy's wrist, lightly kissing each finger before allowing her to extract herself. She flushed, eyes bright with achievement and irritation.

'I told you it would work,' he crowed. 'Bloody thing's too wide. I can't think why the locksmith didn't suggest a letter-basket behind the door while he was fitting all those fancy bolts on the windows.'

'Good God,' breathed Kate Carr, visibly shaken. 'If I hadn't seen it myself I'd never have believed it. Ours is the same.'

'Quite.' Erskine drew Judy inside and, dismissing Swayne's neighbour with a curt nod, shut the door.

Judy relaxed, smiling. Such a silly experiment. But he was right. Anybody could open that door. Anyone with thin arms. Or a child. She opened her mouth to speak as the doorbell rang. They were confronted with Sabina Morland, her perplexity compounded by their laughter echoing in the small hallway.

'I was watching from across the street. That was simply astonishing, Sergeant Pullen.' She followed them upstairs into the sitting-room.

Judy introduced Erskine.

'It was the Inspector's idea,' she said. 'Strange when your brother went to such a lot of expense getting a security firm in and no one guessed that the door could be opened without a key.'

'But it couldn't,' Sabina retorted.

'We've just demonstrated that it could, I'm afraid,' Erskine countered.

'Oh yes, in theory. But in practice Francis was extremely careful. He locked the door from the inside when he came in. Every time. Most methodically. He'd heard of people burgled while sleeping or watching TV, the thief slipping the lock. This house was sealed like a tomb even when Francis was at home. We used to pull his leg about it. If there had been a fire in the night, for instance, he would have to find the keys in the smoke and confusion before he could unlock the door from the inside to get out. A deathtrap, actually.'

Judy was crestfallen. 'She's right, sir. I took the cleaner's statement myself. She didn't say anything about Swayne locking himself in but he impressed upon her the importance of double-locking when she left the house and it was always bolted up securely when she arrived in the morning. The door was double-locked when she got here on the Monday, just as usual. It couldn't be done.'

'Unless he forgot. Coming home after a night out, hazy after a few drinks, anxious to get off again as soon as possible.'

'He was supposed to drive to Hampshire that night and—'

'To avoid the summer traffic,' Sabina interrupted. 'Saturday travel in August infuriated him. Francis would prefer to lose a night's sleep and arrive at the cottage at dawn than be caught in holiday jams.'

'But he could have just shut the door temporarily. He was in evening clothes, hot and uncomfortable after a sweaty night at the opera. Presumably he rushed back home to shower and change before starting straight off again.' Erskine lolled against the cushions and lit a cigarette. 'From your description of your brother's careful planning, Mrs Morland, do you think he might have already packed, stowed his suitcase in the car ready for a swift getaway, perhaps?'

Sabina paced the room pausing to finger an ivory netsuke on the mantelshelf. She turned to face them, her brows drawn like soft charcoal strokes under the crest of short hair.

'Quite probably. What puzzles me is why you are probing

his movements so carefully.' She held out the exquisitely carved piece in her palm. 'Francis has many valuable things here and on the face of it nothing's missing.'

'His car's missing,' Erskine said.

'That's no problem,' Sabina snapped. 'He parked it somewhere close by. There are hundreds of parked cars within a stone's throw of here. Perhaps arriving back so late that night he was anxious not to disturb his neighbours by slamming car doors in the middle of the night. Sounds echo in the mews and with so few people living in close proximity I dare say they are sensitive about noise.'

Erskine dropped the subject and pressed on to something else. 'One thing bothers me,' he said. 'Initially we assumed it was suicide. But the last stub in his cheque-book indicated the withdrawal of a large sum of money . . .' He paused. 'It seems your brother arranged to withdraw £5000 in cash on Friday afternoon from the Law Courts branch in Chancery Lane, and did so. There's no sign of that money here and we have searched most assiduously.'

Sabina's expression bore an extinguished quality, an inner ache which numbed her to further blows. She slid into one of the brocade chairs.

'He was going on holiday.' Judy's tone was sprightly. 'He could have paid an outstanding bill of some sort. To his chambers, perhaps. Petty cash?' she suggested wildly. She sympathized with Sabina Morland. She had lost more than a brother, a lifetime's admiration made farcical.

Erskine dismissed Judy's remarks with a raised eyebrow. The urgent peal of the doorbell was a welcome interruption. All three sat silent, straining to catch the shrill words half-audible from downstairs. Shortly a policeman knocked and entered. 'A Mrs Morrison-Carr downstairs, sir.' He grinned. 'Says she's got a cat for you.'

Erskine rose to shake hands with Sabina Morland before escaping to Swayne's study, leaving the others to deal with Mrs Morrison-Carr. He'd had more than enough animal talk with the late Francis Swayne's loquacious neighbour.

Kate Morrison-Carr was wearing a crumpled frock, a
Liberty print cut unfashionably short, revealing sturdy legs
planted squarely on the Persian rug. Placing a large cardboard box behind the door, she shouted cheerfully at the
yowling beast trapped inside. The noise ceased abruptly
and Mrs Carr glanced round the room. She stepped forward
to commiserate with Sabina who sat dazed, bewildered by
Erskine's latest disclosure. In cash . . . It must have made
a sizeable package . . .

They sat down. Sabina roused herself to address this
additional stranger invading Francis's house.

'It was good of you,' she said, 'to rescue Tai-Tai. I can't
think how it could have slipped my mind. You live next
door?'

'At Number Three. The other side, the Prewitts, are
always in Scotland for August. Lucky them! London's un-
bearable in the summer. Stifling.'

She rose suddenly and made for the door. 'I must go now.
Alfie will be whining for his evening romp. Not much brain,
that dog, but his timekeeping's spot on.'

Judy scrambled up, stumbling over the bulging folder,
spilling loose papers all over the rug.

'One moment, Mrs Carr!' She kicked aside the papers,
grabbing anxiously at her receding witness. As Arnott used
to say: 'One nosey neighbour's worth a parcel of distressed
relatives.' 'May I have your phone number? Just in case . . .'
she lamely added.

Kate Morrison-Carr looked gratified and strode back to
the sofa to help retrieve the official forms and typewritten
statements. She held them out, including the unsolicited
advertising material from Swayne's mail, all efficiently
stacked together with her capable square-tipped fingers.
Then she began to search her handbag for an address sticker
to affix to Judy's report.

Sabina relaxed, her gaze abstracted. Judy proffered the
postcard from Rome delivered with the Monday morning
mail and placed in the hall by Pamina.

'It's signed Dominic, Mrs Morland,' she said. 'Does that ring a bell?'

Sabina glanced at it, then handed it back, shaking her head.

'The rest is just bills and so on. The usual guff that comes through the letter-box, half of it waste paper.' Judy separated the soap powder vouchers, circulars, decorators' and plumbers' business cards, placing them on the coffee table.

Kate Carr swooped across the room, pointing to a bright yellow printed handbill. 'We get stuffed up with this sort of junk all the time. That one for instance. St Laurence's Hospital Fête. July 20th. That was over even before the idle delivery boy got round to circulating it. I only hope no one paid him.'

Judy studied it, Sabina lost in a private reverie, her head inclined towards the tracery of lace curtain outlined by the sunlit window.

'I get bloody incensed with that sort of thing,' Kate Carr exploded. 'The Hospital Friends go to enormous expense getting handbills printed and then the effort's wasted because delivery's inefficient. I've seen wads of these handouts just dumped in lobbies, outside empty houses even. Free newspapers, even those glossy magazines the estate agents bring out.'

'Well, thank you for your help, Mrs Carr. If you'd just let me have your phone number—just stick it on here—' she held out her notebook—'I'll be in touch and—'

Judy's attempt to stem the flow was ignored. The Morrison-Carrs are not so easily deflected.

'Money down the drain! But whereas the estate agents can afford it, it makes my blood boil when charity efforts are wasted like that.'

She snatched up the yellow handbill, vehemently waving it under Judy's nose.

'I actually saw this one come through the letter-box. Sunday morning, a fortnight too late at the very least. I showed it to Jeremy and he feels the same. I went straight out to the mews to collar the little blighter who was pushing them through and give him a piece of my mind.' She slapped the handbill back on the table in disgust. 'But when I caught up with him I let it go. He was a cripple. Well, he had a limp, walked with a stick and not young at all. It seemed a bit rough to pitch into the old boy when he was doing his best. Ironic, really, to ask a chap who can hardly struggle along to deliver hospital charity bumph.'

'Perhaps he was earning a bit of pin money.'

Mercifully, Sabina seemed to rouse herself at this point and leapt up, holding out her hand to Swayne's neighbour.

'Thank you so very much for looking after Tai-Tai. I bought a cardboard pet carrier but it looks as if she's settled in the box.'

'Shouldn't try transferring her if I were you. It was the devil's own job getting her in and I've made a couple of holes so she's got plenty of air.'

'It will only be for half an hour. I'm going back to Holland Park now and I'll free her when I get home. Has she eaten?'

Their voices receded downstairs. Judy Pullen sat thinking about the conversation. Weird listening to Kate Morrison-Carr talking as if Swayne had still been alive over the weekend. Nasty surprise when she learned her predictable neighbour had been hanging just the other side of her bedroom wall for nearly two days. Undiscovered until Monday. Ugh. As she started scribbling in her notebook Judy heard the front door close and at the sound of Sabina's quick step on the stairs Tai-Tai took up the extra-terrestrial yowling once again.

She hurried in, slightly flushed, and snatched up the box. 'I'll be going, Sergeant Pullen.'

Judy jumped up, taking the pet carrier from her hands and replacing it behind the door.

'Before you go could we just go round the house very slowly, and make quite sure there's nothing missing?'

Sabina reluctantly agreed and they moved back to the

fireplace both surveying the surfeit of carefully chosen objects set about on dusty surfaces.

The door burst open, crashing into the box. Tai-Tai fought back, spitting and scratching like a demon in its cardboard prison. It was Erskine.

'Just got a call. They've found the car.' He laughed, ignoring Sabina, speaking directly to Judy, her pen poised awaiting Sabina's observations.

'Bloody thing's clamped, not five hundred yards from here, on a yellow line. Left overnight apparently. Probably since Saturday morning. Silly bugger presumably dumped it when he got back from the opera jaunt, intending to move it first thing Saturday morning. I'm off.'

'Hey, wait for me!' Judy grabbed his arm. 'I can do this later,' she said to Sabina, whirling round to catch Erskine before he disappeared. But he was already clattering down the stairs.

'No, stay,' he shouted. 'I've got to get my squad to look it over before it's moved. There's a suitcase on the back seat.' Without waiting for a reply he slammed the front door.

The two women stood by the window and watched him drive off, several customers already relaxing with their drinks outside the Ring of Bells, fascinated by the constant coming and goings in the normally stagnant Kensington backwater.

Picking up her notebook, Judy shrugged and mutely trailed Sabina as she dredged her memory of Francis's precious things. Even the cat had given up. It was as if all those left behind in the wake of Erskine's exuberant exit had subsided into their own gloomy considerations of the mysterious end of Francis Swayne QC.

'Maybe he dare not drive back into the mews and disturb the neighbours twice in one night.'

'But whatever was he up to?' Sabina croaked, her throat thick with tears. 'Did Francis rush out again to meet someone, pay them money, blackmailed do you think? I thought

I knew Francis through and through. Dashing about London in the small hours carrying all that cash, dressing up like a drag queen, making fools of all of us. I don't understand anything at all.'

And she doesn't even know about the bomb yet, Judy thought.

'Nor me,' she quietly added.

CHAPTER 6

The funeral was supposed to be private. At a small church in Suffolk near the Swaynes' former family home, now an impressive girls' school with a lacrosse pitch where the paddock used to be.

Harry Morland flew in from the Far East, snatching a few days from his crowded schedule to escort his wife through the ghastly ceremony, made hideous by the curious attentions of total strangers.

Sabina moved through the ordeal like a spectre, narrow shoulders in a black linen dress brushing those of the other mourners almost unaware of their presence, bareheaded as the men in the funeral procession. This fragile elegance was a foil to her brother's anguish, his vitality reduced to crushed shabbiness as he shied away from the crowd of reporters who had somehow got wind of the interment. Even a television crew had invaded the village, attempting to pad out the story with shots of the girls' school, abandoned now for the summer holidays. It was an empty month for news of any sort, even government scandals, and the chance to film a well-known actor caught up in genuine distress was a straw to clutch at. Re-runs of the scenes outside the Dublin courthouse in which Francis Swayne had briefly eclipsed his brother's starring role were flashed across the news, allowing viewers a chance to contrast the skimpy build of the barrister with his handsome siblings.

The lawyer had attracted his own influential friends, including useful political connections, but most sent anonymous floral tributes and prudently stayed away. The titillation of his bizarre end was liable to taint everyone pictured at the graveside—even the women.

Inspector Erskine and Judy Pullen hovered at the edge of the crowd pressing in on the family plot, standing quietly together like acquaintances of the deceased, too polite to push themselves forward.

'Nicholas Farrow looks ghastly,' Judy muttered. 'Much older than I'd imagined. The designer stubble doesn't help.'

Erskine's eyes narrowed and he shifted his position to study a late arrival at the graveside. An incongruously colourful club tie struck a wrong note: presumably one of Swayne's sailing fraternity.

'The glamour boys are always disappointing in daylight.' Erskine grinned. 'Stick to policemen, Ju.'

She hated being called 'Ju', always had and guessed he knew it.

'Why did we drag all the way up here? Swayne's car was "clean", wasn't it?'

'As the driven snow. When we got it back to the pound after establishing it wasn't wired for a big bang, it checked out fine. Swayne's suitcase packed full of weekend gear, reasonable junk in the boot—sailing wellies and so on. All smelling like roses.'

'No lacey nightwear, then?'

'Kept for private relaxation after a busy day at the law courts. Off with one wig m'lud and on with the new. I've come across these cupboard fairies before. The women's stuff is strictly for personal entertainment. You have to find one well down the line, committed to a sex change, into therapy, the lot, before he plays dressing-up games away from home.'

'Then why are you still hedging? Not banking on an open verdict by any chance?'

Erskine took out a pack of cigarettes. 'Is this bad taste,

would you say? In a cemetery and all?' He lit up with a wry smile.

'No worse than all these TV yobs in their anoraks puffing away and housewives straining to catch a glimpse of Nicholas Farrow. It's sick the way everything has to be served up as public entertainment. Go ahead, nobody will notice.' Her eyes were challenging, the uncertainty of the role she was expected to play in Erskine's scheme fuelling an irrational irritability. 'Do you have to smoke so much?' His enigmatic flippancy was getting on her nerves.

He grimaced, inhaling deeply as he regarded the tense figure beside him, the beige skirt and jacket enhancing her heightened colour.

'No. Accidental death suits me fine,' he answered. 'Not that I believe it. There are some photographs for your own private viewing, but that can wait. Did you discover anything about our actor friend on the lines I suggested?'

'A bit short of decent roles but some of his old films re-run on the box lately have revived his popularity. And there's this historical "soap" still churning out which is well up in the ratings. God knows why. But nothing special in the pipeline apart from a telly ad for aftershave or men's perfume, I'm not sure what. But this actors' cooperative he set up with his wife seems to be flourishing. Plenty of well-known names are willing to join the bandwagon. A sort of fashionable kudos has gathered momentum since he persuaded some stars to direct and the publicity's been generous. They've got bookings in Edinburgh during the Festival and Birmingham over Christmas. And his agent hinted something about an Australian tour in the offing.'

'Nicholas Farrow certainly attracts publicity. Pity it's not always for performances,' was Erskine's dour response. 'Does his wife act?'

'Sandra Sullivan? A bit. But she trained in Italy in stage management and design. Opera and big screen epics. A first-class reputation for special lighting effects but she's lost several jobs for political troublemaking. She's intense, sharp-witted, one of the theatrical Trotskyites. I can't imagine her left-wing harangues endearing her to her late brother-in-law, especially as I hear on the grapevine he was angling for a seat on the bench.'

'Who can tell? Perhaps he was a secret sympathizer like Anthony Blunt?'

'Farrow's agent seemed to think it's mostly Swayne's money financing the actors' cooperative, but I can't see it myself. The sister's married to the industrial wizard, Harry Morland. But the Swayne family money all went to the elder son, Francis copped the lot when the parents were killed in some sort of accident.'

Erskine made a conscious effort to concentrate on the proliferation of twigs on the Swayne family tree despite the fascinating amber flecks in Judy's eyes.

'—and my guess,' she was saying, 'is that the family—apart from Harry Morland of course!—haven't got much in the way of personal fortunes. Except Swayne himself, who seemed to be a bit tight-fisted by all accounts.'

'Put it all by as a nice little nest egg for the old age he never enjoyed.'

'You're a sardonic swine. This is his funeral, you know.'

'Don't worry, Ju-Ju. He can't hear. And even if he could, poor old Francis could eavesdrop on any one of a dozen conversations here and find plenty less indulgent than myself.'

'It's the sister I feel sorry for. Nicholas Farrow seems only half aware of what's going on.'

'Too right!' Erskine threw down his cigarette and carefully ground it into the turf. 'Notice his pretty blue eyes? All that sniffing isn't tearful emotion either.'

'Drugs?' Judy conjured with this possibility and watched Erskine's laconic appraisal of the funeral party.

'Booze too, probably,' he continued. 'Whoops, here we go, the crowd's moving back to the cars. All over, thank the Lord.'

They followed the mourners and assorted hangers-on

drifting back to the lych-gate. Erskine studied each one, mentally recording the familiar and unfamiliar faces assembled in the village churchyard. The limousines slid away, immediately followed by the noisy departure of the reporters and disappointed sensation-seekers. After seeing the priest leave by a side door and hurry away, Erskine and Judy were left alone in the quiet lane observing the gravediggers cheerfully begin to complete the day's work.

'Have we been asked back to the hotel?' Judy queried as they approached the car.

'What you might call an indirect invitation.'

'We can't just barge in,' she spluttered. 'I draw the line at that!' He started the car, staring up at the taut figure by the open passenger door.

'Suit yourself.' He revved up, leaning across to close the door.

She slid into the seat beside him like a sulky schoolgirl, snapping back the straight fall of yellow hair.

'I'm not just passing the time, Sergeant Pullen.' His mock severity was even more difficult to counter than the familiarity. 'There's a small matter of £5000 still missing. I thought it might be packed in the suitcase we found in the car but that was a very unlikely longshot. His clerk at Gray's Inn is totally baffled about the money. I tried tackling the sister but got the big brush-off from Morland. Nicholas Farrow's incommunicado and his shrewish wife, who I thought would be raising the roof about every item including police misuse of Swayne's teabags, told me to mind my own business. So pick the bones out of that, Sergeant.'

The car sped through winding lanes, the big empty sky bleaching a wide horizon.

'But we won't discover a wad of notes at the Fleece, will we?' she pleaded. 'It seems in pretty poor taste to intrude after the burial. The TV coverage was bad enough.'

'It's our big chance to see them all together. Funerals are very revealing. Everyone beady-eyed waiting to put in a bid for granny's best tea-set. This will be on a more subtle level but the ingredients are the same. Swayne's solicitor is here. The will interests me. And I want to have a quiet word with Swayne's yachting chum, Roger Mansell, wasn't it? The one whose boat blew up.'

The Fleece presented a convincing façade, drawing tourists all year round. Attracted originally by its authentic mediæval beams, they were comforted by the high star rating and twentieth-century water-beds. Guests' fantasies of a former Viking existence—even when crudely interrupted by the scream of Tornado jets from the nearby airbase —were oddly strengthened by this modern equivalent of violence and threat.

The funeral party filed into a private suite, their hushed conversations perfectly encompassed by the linenfold panelling and mullioned windows. The main room was a permanent stage set as photographed in the brochure, immune from weather or season, invariably dim and scented with pot-pourri, a log fire flickering in the inglenook, only the variation of daffodils or chrysanthemums delineating the time of year. Perfect for a wake.

Larry Erskine smoothly circulated, avoiding the family enclave protecting Sabina Morland and her brother Nicholas. Judy Pullen hovered just inside the door, self-consciously sipping her sherry. She recognized no one apart from the brother and sister but presumed the suave character acting as host was Morland. Nicholas Farrow stood immobile as if he had merely a small walk-on part in this particular drama. One presumed the fabled quarrel between Swayne and Farrow's wife extended beyond the grave: she had apparently stayed at home.

'Are you a relative? Or a friend of Sabina's, perhaps?'

Judy Pullen turned quickly, adjusting her shoulder-bag in a nervous gesture. The man beside her was thirtyish, thick-set with an amiable bear-like hugeness, a defiantly garish tie announcing a determination to make his own rules. The muscled frame under the dark suit and a tanned complexion set him aside from the other mourners who were in the main, elderly.

'I know Mrs Morland slightly,' Jane said. 'But I'm afraid I never met the late Francis Swayne.'

'Poor old Francis. Rotten luck, an accident like that. I take it you hold no feminist views on the subject?'

'I'm not sure what you mean,' Judy parried, 'but I'm not here to congratulate perverts if that's what you're inferring.'

His bland friendliness dissolved. The shrewd reappraisal was, in fact, more attractive and Judy revised her own first impression.

'That's where you are quite wrong,' he said. 'Francis wasn't gay, I'd swear to that. My name's Mansell, by the way. Roger Mansell. I've known the family for years.'

'You were his sailing partner?'

'Sailing. Nothing more. Francis was a good friend, a sensible worthwhile human being, whatever rot the tabloids choose to make of it. If his brother wasn't a film actor I doubt whether they'd bother to send the press bloodhounds in.'

'But even Mrs Morland is confused. She thought she knew him better than anyone.'

'On the bottom line, what was Francis's crime? Tying himself up for thrills. Lots of people dress up and aren't condemned for it. The legal profession's riddled with it, robes and wigs—not to mention the bishops.'

'But traditional vestments are not part of a sexual romp, are they? Francis Swayne may have been a very nice guy but preening himself in a chiffon negligee isn't normal.' She tried to move away but Roger Mansell blocked her escape.

'There you go again,' he persisted. 'It all hinges on sexual prejudice. Dressing up is OK so long as you don't get a kick out of it, eh? What's the harm?'

'AIDS for a start.'

He grasped Judy's arm, steering her away from the eye-popping incredulity of a waitress patiently offering a plate of vol-au-vents.

'Once and for all, woman,' he said, 'Francis was not homosexual. He liked women, flirted a good deal, as a matter of fact. The very last time I saw him, the night he died, he was having a tête-à-tête with a fruity looking piece at the Savoy.'

'You've got a vivid imagination, Mr Mansell. Francis Swayne was at the opera all evening and dining with friends afterwards. All highly respectable music-lovers. I've checked.

'Are you calling me a liar? What's your name, by the way? Not one of those press bastards, are you?'

'Judy Pullen. And you're mistaken, Mr Mansell. It must have been another night you remember. I've plenty of witnesses to prove Swayne was attending an exclusive party at Somerset House.'

'Well, that's not a million miles from the Strand, is it,' he said contemptuously.

Judy's confidence wavered. He had a point there.

'What time do you think you glimpsed him with this girl?'

'I don't "think I glimpsed him," as you put it. I know Francis. We were mates. I'm married, happily married as far as a sailing man ever is, so don't smirk in that spinsterish way. I'm telling you I saw Francis with a girl that Friday night. In the piano bar. Fiona and I were meeting friends, she'll tell you if you don't believe me. It was about nine o'clock. They were a bit late and we were hanging about when we noticed Francis tucked away in a corner having a drink with this Chelsea bird, all spiky hair and black leather. He was in a dinner jacket and looking thoroughly chuffed, but she was obviously furious. He saw us and waved us over. We sauntered up to their table and I started to natter about the weekend's racing. I've borrowed a boat for the rest of the season. Francis didn't introduce the girl, who was glaring at us like a harpy while poor old Fiona stood about like a spare oar. After a few minutes this punky bird of paradise grabbed something from the table and without a word to Francis flew off.'

'Did he attempt to stop her?'

'No. I apologized for butting in, spoiling his fun, but he laughed it off. Said he was due elsewhere and was only saying a final goodbye anyhow.'

'He wasn't angry?'

'No way! From the look of things the girl was getting the old heave-ho and knew it. He wasn't bothered in the least. Afterwards we all strolled back to the lobby and when my guests turned up Francis got a taxi and presumably dined elsewhere. I've already told all this to a bluff old Yorkshire bobby—Arnott—a name straight out of Wisden! And he wasn't in the least surprised. Old enough to refer to gays as "poofs" but far less narrow-minded than the feminist brigade.'

This last remark had an edge which made Judy bite back an unladylike retort.

Roger Mansell replaced his empty glass on the waiter's tray and took another, staring gloomily into the crowd, augmented now by a louder, younger set.

'And why are you here?' he asked.

Mercifully, she was saved from a reply by the arrival of Larry, who introduced himself baldly as Detective-Inspector Erskine of the Special Branch. So much for the low profile!

The impact on Roger Mansell was electric, his instant reassessment of the fair girl at his side unprintable. Judy melted away, edging towards the exit, embittered at her own discomfiture. To be suspected of gatecrashing was bad enough: to be cast as a police infiltrator seemed unforgivable. And true, which was the rub. She longed to escape and slipped out of the hotel to join the gang of press photographers drinking on the croquet lawn where it was possible to have a clear view of the parked cars and all the exits. They seemed to mistrust the front entrance.

It was nearly two hours before Erskine came to look for her, his smug confidence now oiled by a satisfactory lunch and, Judy guessed, more evidence to fuel his mysterious terrier-like harassment of the bereaved family.

'Where've you been, Judy?'

Without waiting for an explanation he handed over his car keys. 'Take the car back to London, will you?' A Phantom jet split the sky, obliterating her reply.

'I'm going back by train with Swayne's solicitor,' he shouted. 'I'll fill you in later. How about dinner?'

Her furious mimed protest as she waited for the fly-past to vanish over the horizon was wasted on Erskine.

'I'll pick you up about nine-thirty from your place. Don't look like that, Sergeant. All in the line of duty. Orders, if you like. There's something I want to ask before I leave.'

'Leave?'

'I've been taken off this job. I'm flying to Brussels in the morning.'

He walked away, turning only to sketch a mock salute at the slight figure left speechless by yet another totally unexpected withdrawal from the case.

CHAPTER 7

It was getting on for eleven that night before Judy Pullen's buzzer announced Erskine's arrival. She took her time, washing a coffee mug in the sink before approaching the intercom. A gesture wasted on Erskine who merely gave the bell a prolonged second blast.

She lived at the top of a large Edwardian house, the hall wide and smelling of polish and ancient dust. The mahogany staircase creaked authentically under the worn carpet as Erskine bounded up whistling a piercing, unrecognizable tune. Judy leaned over the rail three floors up. The low wattage of the single light-bulb absorbed the pale folds of her cotton dress as she lingered on the landing like the ghost of some long-departed maidservant.

'The woman under here has a baby,' she hissed. 'Have you no thought for anyone but yourself?'

'No. Life's too short.' His smile was warm and his jauntiness maddeningly undiminished by the long day in Suffolk.

'Ready?' He held out his hand for his car keys, a document case clamped under his arm.

'It's a bit late for dinner!'

He shrugged, resumed the whistling and followed her through to the main room, a bedsitter termed 'studio flat' in the agent's window. The room was wide and uncluttered, floor cushions constructed from old Persian carpet strewn invitingly about a balding Indian rug. A curtainless dormer window was open to the rooftops and warm night air. But there were no stars.

Judy rummaged in her handbag and produced the keys. She softened. 'It's late. Let's take a rain check on dinner.'

'I already owe you lunch. I suppose you got nothing at the Swayne wake?'

She laughed, shaking her head, and Larry Erskine was caught up in the amber flash of her eyes for the second time that day.

'Come on. Let's get some fresh air. I know a curry place near here. I've had enough of the "funeral meats" for one day.'

They walked along Gloucester Road, the exotic smells seeping from a medley of restaurants blending with the balmy temperature, spicing the air.

'Did you sleep on the train?'

He laughed, grabbing her arm to steer her down a narrow alley between two shops. 'I was with Swayne's solicitor. He'd been liberally sampling the sherry and then relaxing in the Pullman, topping up. I had my work cut out keeping *him* awake.'

They passed through a doorway flanked by a screen of palms, the darkness of the restaurant sparsely illuminated with brass hanging lamps, the damson-coloured walls almost obliterated with sepia photographs of rajahs and overcrowded tiger shoots.

Judy's eyes narrowed in the smoky atmosphere and she allowed herself to be propelled between the tables and pushed on to a velvet banquette.

She made a small *moue* in response to his satisfied glance and they sat silent for several minutes examining the menu.

Eventually, it seemed simpler to let Erskine choose, the turbanned waiter seeming to know him very well indeed. She amused herself wondering whether familiarity with Moghul cuisine was part of the training in the rarefied environment of Erskine's squad.

Much later, they ordered coffee and Judy, lulled by a procession of delicious dishes and wine, smiled dreamily as Larry Erskine lit up his umpteenth cigarette. It had been a nice idea. It seemed extraordinary that she had found his manner so irritating. The trouble with this job was, she conceded, it made you defensive.

'About Brussels,' she said, staring fixedly into the swirling liquid in her cup. 'How long have you known?'

'Never mind that. I'll be away for two or three weeks and afterwards I'm due for a spot of leave. It'll be October before I'm back in London.'

Judy forced herself to look up brightly, the evening tarnished. 'I'm pretty busy myself,' she said quickly. 'And goodness knows what's happening about Arnott. There's a rumour he'll take early retirement. I suppose they'll put someone in. He wasn't easy to work with but better the devil you know . . .' her voice trailed off.

'Liqueur? Brandy?' The words sounded far away, fading. Or perhaps it was the increasing buzz of conversation under the huge old-fashioned fans slowly rotating overhead: the restaurant was now full. After-theatre parties, Judy supposed. Her head felt as if it were wrapped in a hot towel.

Gulping down the scalding coffee, she attempted to finish the whole thing before becoming as mesmerized by the

fabled charm of Detective-Inspector Erskine as all the rest.
'I wish you wouldn't smoke so much,' she said.

He leaned forward, stubbing out his half-smoked cigarette
and began speaking in a low monotone, not conversation-
ally, but in a continuous urgent stream.

'I was on to Swayne before. Just routine. He was being
considered for a judicial post but nobody liked his slick
handling of the McLaughlin case. But they had to go
through the motions and frankly it was a relief all round
when he was found dead. Accidental. A last frolic in his
fancy dress before going on holiday, where presumably he
would have to behave himself for several weeks. He'd had
champagne cocktails at the party and was pretty chirpy by
all accounts when he left his friends. Perhaps he got careless
with the sailor's knots. Anyway, what looked like suicide
was accidental and the coroner and everybody else were all
greatly relieved.' His mouth twisted sarcastically.

'The trouble was,' he went on, 'the homemade bomb in
the kitchen . . . Also, I didn't like this sailing lark. Swayne
could go anywhere in that ketch with Mansell and be up to
all sorts of naughties. But my lot weren't keen to stir the
mud and naturally it was simpler all round to let the
pathologist's decision stand. Ignore any complications. I
had to sort out the family interest too, just to make sure I
wasn't looking at it from the wrong angle. Who might
benefit from Swayne's death? And the solicitor, dear man,
laid it out all nice and clean like washing on the grass.'

'Wills aren't secret, you know. Anyone can look them
up.'

'Just a week before he died Swayne had completed an
educational trust for his two nephews. Joshua, ten, and
another one—Luke or Jake or Jack, some name like that—
who's eight. Very nice of Uncle Francis, wasn't it? The only
peculiar thing about it was he hadn't spoken to their parents
for a couple of years and hadn't even sent the kids birthday
cards, or so my loose-lipped solicitor says. Our film star,
Nicholas Farrow, is in no position to educate his two sons

in the family style and his wife pretends to be ideologically opposed to private education. Hypocritical cow. These upper-crust Commies want it both ways. The solicitor said that when Swayne offered to put the boys through the gilt-edged educational hoop the political objections were immediately tossed aside.'

Erskine cleared his throat and continued in staccato bursts as if dictating a complicated memo. 'Presumably to cement the deal, nasty old Francis insists they sign a formal agreement which is tied up in such a way that he alone directs the boys' education and apparently had already vetted a very expensive prep school near Oxford and arranged for the two nephews to start this autumn. Boarding. Out of earshot of Mummy's bolshevik bawling and ensuring that the heirs to Malhams Court, the family seat currently posing as a Suffolk St Trinian's, are brought up as proper little English gentlemen.'

'That would cost thousands! The rent from a school won't pay all that.'

'Funded by agricultural land including three farms run very commercially by our late St Francis, plus advisers of course. He wasn't as hard up as he led the family to believe.'

'Does the trust still stand after Swayne's death?'

'A belt and braces job. Swayne had sealed every loophole. He wanted to make certain neither Nicholas nor the sister-in-law could tamper with the arrangements or get their hands on the capital.'

'What about the will?'

'Swayne left the cottage to Roger Mansell. Doesn't sound much, just a weekend place in Hampshire, but the area's a honeypot for the sailing crowd and pretty exclusive. Makes you wonder if he owed Mansell any favours, doesn't it?'

'Swayne didn't commit suicide! The poor devil hardly anticipated anyone was going to benefit for years and years.'

Erskine stared at the face before him, chin cupped in her

hand, hair ruffled, the fine strands gleaming like gold mesh veiling the extraordinary tawny eyes.

'Has anyone ever told you your eyes are the colour of very expensive sherry?' he quipped.

Ignoring this, she dragged him back to the matter in hand. 'When was the will signed?'

'A couple of years ago. It could have coincided with the family row, except nobody's admitting there was one! Only the educational trust is new.'

He paused, frowning, his fingers creasing an empty matchcover into a sharply pointed arrowhead. Suddenly he beckoned the waiter and ordered more coffee. He continued.

'Apart from the weekend cottage and some small donations to a legal charity and to some sailing club, the residue of the estate, except the money put aside for the trust, was to be divided, half to the sister, Mrs Morland, and half to the two boys. In a nutshell, after death duties, etcetera' Nicky gets the big house in Suffolk but with hardly any financial leeway apart from the rent from the school and only until his elder son is twenty-five. Nicky and his wife could turn out the girls' school and live in Malhams Court themselves if a country squire lifestyle appealed. But he doesn't strike me as the type. It all sounds legally watertight to me. Francis had weighed it all up very shrewdly and the theme of his will is "Keep my brother and his wife financially handcuffed until the boys are old enough to handle the estate". Probably wise but spiteful, don't you think? Francis Swayne obviously had a mind like a corkscrew apart from being bent in other ways.'

'Poor Nicholas,' Judy murmured. 'Hamstrung first by his brother and ultimately by his son.' Her thoughts slid in meandering byways like the random trickle of a depleted stream.

'. . . cunning old weasel had it all worked out,' a distant voice was saying. 'Poetic justice that it was messed up at the end.'

Judy grasped at her flagging attention like a lifebelt and

plunged in. 'I found out about the milk,' she announced
with smug satisfaction.

'The milk? What milk?'

'The cleaning woman said Swayne was on holiday but
the milkman was still delivering milk.'

Larry Erskine stared at her in disbelief but, undeflected,
she pushed on.

'I caught up with him next day and asked him straight
out. I thought there might have been some sort of mix-up.
But it was all quite simple. The milk had been cancelled for
four weeks, Pamina—the cleaner—told him on the Friday
when she paid the bill. But the milkman had seen the cat
hanging about over the weekend and thought she'd got it
wrong. Swayne only had deliveries for the cat, they used to
joke about it: milk, and a chicken every week. All for the
cat! So when the milkman saw the cat over the weekend he
left a pint as usual. He thought Pamina had made a
balls-up.' She giggled. 'He has a low opinion of women and
especially black ones.'

Larry guessed he had probably overdone the wooing of
Sergeant Pullen. Her brain seemed to be dissolving before
his eyes.

Irritably he patted her hand. Drawing a large envelope
from his briefcase, he slid it along the velvet banquette.

'Without wishing to stir anything up, I'd like you to keep
an eye on the Swayne family for a few weeks and keep me
informed. Don't mention it to anyone else. This is just
between you and me. The bomb hasn't been tied in with
anything, £5000 has disappeared, Swayne's mysterious
sailing trips across the Channel are under suspicion and
I'm still investigating the explosion on Mansell's boat.'

He leaned across the table, taking her hand. 'Judy, listen
to me,' he whispered. 'This is important. I don't want to
start a landslide and there isn't anyone else I can trust to
help me. I've got to clear up some business in Brussels and
I may have to slip out to Cyprus but I'll phone. At your
place. When you've got your wits about you—' he grinned

—'examine the photographs in the envelope.' He painfully
tightened his grip on her fingers, forestalling any movement.
'Not now!' And then, resuming the quiet tone, 'You'll see
what I mean. And try to purloin the bit of rope Swayne
used. Nylon. Probably from a ship's chandlers.'

He raised her hand to his lips and they sat in silence.
Deep within Judy Pullen's muzzy brain there rose the
illusion of two people holding hands over a candlelit table,
whispering not of the bizarre death of a rather unpleasant
barrister but of kisses and romance under a Bombay
moon.

He took her home in a taxi. It seemed the best idea at
the time.

CHAPTER 8

Judy moved all her work to Swayne's study after Erskine
had left and spent the rest of the week searching the house.
Since the funeral she had had the mews house practically
to herself and even the press had lost interest. The heat had
gradually diminished and skies assumed the dappled grey
of a normal English summer.

Since Arnott's application for early retirement had been
accepted the vacuum in the Division had provided an opportunity for Judy to spin out the business of tying up the loose
ends, and the Chief, presumably following hints from Above,
seemed more than anxious to allow the Swayne case to peter
out naturally.

At the station opinion was divided: the WPC organizing
a collection for Arnott's retirement party found the task
unexpectedly smooth, generosity flowing both from those
glad to see the back of Arnott and his foul-mouthed prejudices and also from those experiencing guilt at the lack of
support for his bull-headed protest. Very few knew exactly
what secret information had been suppressed in the Swayne

case but the supremacy of Erskine's brand of detective was an indication of things to come.

The homemade bomb was still unexplained and the shadowy presence of Special Branch still exerted sufficient leverage for Sergeant Pullen to drag her feet. In the confusion prior to the appointment of Arnott's replacement her ability to prolong the investigation went unchallenged.

In fact, she was mystified. Drew a complete blank. It was far from clear what exactly Erskine had had in mind on that last evening together. Not only professionally . . . And her clouded recollection of his account of the case did not help.

Judy Pullen sat at Swayne's desk puzzling over Erskine's enigmatic appeal. What was she supposed to be looking for? Would she recognize it even if she tripped over it? She pored over the photographs he had handed over, mostly his own and stomach-churning in their clarity. A dozen views of the body hanging from the joist, some full length, some close-ups, all horrific. She forced herself to study them at home and was as nonplussed as before. Trouble is, she grumbled to herself, there's no one to ask. And to be brutally frank, Sergeant Pullen was reluctant to admit even to herself that the secret of the photographs remained totally incomprehensible.

She sighed and returned to the laborious business of sifting Swayne's private papers. His secretary, a Miss Mackenzie, was becoming increasingly vocal regarding her own access to Swayne's affairs and could hardly be put off for much longer. The solicitor had already written formally requesting a date for the handover of the property of the deceased.

Judy resisted the waves of panic which threatened her temporary isolation. The only people not pestering her were members of the family, which struck her as being a bit odd. Sabina Morland had flown to Italy with her husband and stepdaughter immediately after the funeral, and the Farrows had gone to Edinburgh with a brand-new play which was so avant-garde as to receive reviews, albeit unflattering, in the quality press.

Next morning there was a postcard from Erskine. A colour reproduction of a liberally blood-spattered Renaissance painting. Leaning across a naked male body, a lovely creature with the countenance of a madonna and the cleavage of a harlot held aloft his severed head. Hardly 'wish you were here' stuff! Judy stood in her yellow kimono against the pearly light of her rain-splashed bedroom window and turned it over. Rome. *Judith Slaying Holofernes*. Underneath, Erskine had scrawled: 'Just as well I didn't take advantage, wasn't it?' And then: 'Can't telephone just now but how about joining me in Cyprus? Middle two weeks in September? My treat. Be in touch. L.' She slid on to the window-seat, suddenly limp, and grinned. The rain didn't seem to matter after all.

Thereafter a postcard arrived every few days. No forwarding address and no telephone call. This one-sided romance —and romance was just about the only word for it—left her with no way to respond to his jokey suggestions—or repel them for that matter. It was a chaste Victorian courtship: no kisses, no words of love and, in the abrasive 1980s, a very peculiar method of enticement. Perhaps he imagined she had heard it all before; certainly the postman was intrigued—and no wonder.

In Florence Harry Morland received a telex and urgently returned to Hong Kong. Sabina and her stepdaughter stayed on, ten days later still listlessly fulfilling the quota of 'sights' Harry's itinerary dictated.

Aragon had been particularly obdurate for the whole holiday. Her sulky presence was a bleak reminder to Sabina of her limitations as a stepmother. The obliging twelve-year-old at the wedding had been transformed into a taciturn young woman whose sole aim in life was to share a disagreeable lifestyle with a married artist called Rick. Harry's confident assertion that keeping his daughter well away from London would cure her of this desire was, in

Sabina's opinion, totally out of touch with reality. Sifting her own adolescence for a similar passionate intransigence, she dismally admitted that the seventeen-year-old Sabina Swayne had entirely lacked Aragon's single-mindedness. About anything. Frankly, after several weeks as gaoler, Sabina was more than ready to throw in the towel. If Rick desired this teenage gorgon and he was really as appalling as Harry made out, it occurred to Sabina they were a couple ideally suited.

Then Fate took a hand. They, too, had an urgent summons. To Yorkshire.

PLEASE COME STOP MOTHER FALLEN STOP IN HOSPITAL HARROGATE URGENT STOP BETTY CARTER.

Guiltily aware of their mutual delight at this legitimate escape route, Sabina and Aragon hurriedly packed and caught the first flight home. The gates were open at last and seated on the plane they each breathed a sigh of release as the Tuscan landscape disappeared below.

Arriving at Heathrow after ten that evening, they drove straight to the London house, surprising the Chinese student living in the basement in the throes of a very peculiar party. Tossing aside the remnants of her role, Sabina cheerfully allowed Aragon to mingle, shutting off her imagination from the exotic scents drifting up through the house. After Rick, the unemployed action painter, Tan Yau-Hang's friends could only be an improvement.

Sabina flung herself on to the sofa and breathed in the blessed silence of her own house. Bliss. Reaching for the telephone she called Betty Carter. Only a broken collarbone, thank God. Poor Sybil. But she would be allowed home tomorrow with Sabina's approval. After more assurances on both sides Sabina rang off and sat in the darkness of her drawing-room listening to the steady swish of traffic on the wet road. Pausing only to pick up the pile of mail in the hall, she ran upstairs, showered and lay in cool sheets planning her next move.

Tomorrow: Yorkshire. With Aragon, of course. But

somehow she seemed less bloody-minded at Fernside. And to give the girl her due Aragon adored her grandmother. Oh yes, everything could only get better.

Idly sifting the letters, one small package looked interesting. It was from Francis's secretary and contained several bunches of keys labelled 'car', 'house', 'cottage', etc., presumably spares from his chambers. She tossed them in the drawer of the bedside cabinet and glanced through the rest of the mail.

One envelope caught her attention, the precise handling of the handwritten address horribly familiar. Sitting bolt upright in the lace-canopied bed, she stared unbelieving at the postmark, already three weeks old. Leeds? At last, opening the letter, she read: 'Dear Sabina—'

—No date, no address, only a telephone number. Truly a bolt from the blue.

The shock of seeing you on the TV coverage of the funeral gives me courage to add my own words of sympathy to the many you are doubtless receiving. Indeed, it is ironic, is it not, that Francis who would have done his legal and illegal best to keep us apart should be the one to bring us together? Over his dead body one might say. Forgive me. That was tasteless.

But until the newspapers disclosed your name in the course of reporting the funeral I had no means of contacting you again. Francis Swayne was indeed thorough in his arrangements to place his sister beyond my influence, in connivance with Mansell, it would seem.

I bumped into Mansell at Lord's in June and after fruitlessly searching out the old team I was determined to broach the question and asked him for your address. Perhaps he told you of his cautious reply?

Sabina flinched, amazed that Roger had kept this to himself, and wondered if Francis had intervened. She read on, the small copybook script neat as a graphologist's sample.

I felt that after so long there was a chance we all might agree to some sort of contact being re-established. We had a few drinks in the pavilion—holy of holies for me, of course, knowing as you do my passion for The Game. Peculiar that Mansell should grant one longed-for consummation and deny me the other ... But I digress.

Sabina smiled, hearing Geoffrey's faint accent through the stilted phrases. She turned the page.

I have had enormous difficulty reassembling the project we all struggled so hard to achieve. Much of my own source material was retained by the investigative team and my most earnest endeavours have had little success in reclaiming what is essentially my life's work. Could you help me? I dare not approach Fisher, and Mansell is as you say 'sitting on the fence'.

Is it possible you might lend your influence to soften the implacable heart of Academe to release my files? I have laboured unceasingly to save something from the chaos but I need hardly explain the impossibility of duplicating our research. Computer facilities to back up the data are vital if I am to have the smallest hope of attracting a grant.

Would you consider turning over your own data to me? Or, better still, assist me to re-shape the scattered fragments? Surely, all our work should not be tossed aside for others to reap the rewards? We were so close to a breakthrough. Mansell declines to take any initiative and Fisher is bitterly opposed to my reinstatement. You are my last hope.

In order to allay any embarrassment on either side may I suggest this letter remains a secret between us? I should

prefer that in view of Mansell's obvious determination to
let sleeping dogs lie my tentative contact be private. I am
in the process of packing up here but this number in
Leeds is valid for the present. Please, Sabina, do not
throw away this chance which is not only my last hope
but may be yours.

We have much to discuss. I need to see you.

With affection,
Geoffrey.

Sabina let the pages slip from her fingers, tense with
the shock of the old spectre emerging from the shadows.
Geoffrey's was a subtle and dangerous invitation: the more
so because it expressed a half-formed desire thrust from
her mind, a regret which flickered repeatedly across her
subconscious like a recurring dream. Forcing her to abandon
her research was the cruellest decision Francis had made
for her. For the noblest of motives, naturally. She had been
a fool to allow him to direct her life. But now he was
dead . . .

She shivered. Quickly gathering up the scrawled pages,
she thrust them away in the drawer with the keys.

CHAPTER 9

Ralph Arnott refused to attend his retirement party. And
Judy Pullen was the obvious target when it became apparent
to the Chief Superintendent that a 'volunteer' must be
dispatched to Mortlake with the gift. Everyone had been
openhanded and a wholesaler was invited to supply at cost
price. Cooperating with the police, it was called.

Judy Pullen drove over Putney Bridge, dreading the
reception she might receive at Arnott's home. His career—
after almost forty years—had come to an abrupt and
unsatisfactory end and a man who had never been friendly

was unlikely to welcome her appearance on his doorstep. 'Beware Greeks bearing gifts' seemed about it.

The green Volkswagen trailed with the traffic south of the river, the wide sheet of water sparkling blue and silver like one of Erskine's postcards. She smiled, hugging to herself the thought of the air ticket in her bag, delivered three days ago and offering the first chance to tackle Larry Erskine directly. What about all those postcards ranged now in a festive chain across her mantelshelf like a Christmas garland? Funny sort of romance . . .

Mortlake smelt of hops, malt and beer. A fitting finishing line for the Varsity boat race where the breweries huddled together. She turned into Arnott's street, a pretty row of nineteenth-century houses, some terraced, a few detached. Arnott's house was in the middle, its yellow brick façade set at a bend in the road where it seemed to lie sentinel to the rest.

Parking the car, Judy glanced back at the large carton on the back seat. Arnott had been told to expect her but she felt apprehensive. It wasn't past him to go out anyway and struggling to deliver the wretched thing to his front door seemed to be tempting Fate. She left it on the seat.

She pushed open the metal gate. The neat garden either side of the path looked out of keeping with the shambling, untidy character she had worked for. Nothing original, just beds of marigolds and asters and identical squares of grass either side. But the cottagey effect took her by surprise. She wasn't sure what she had expected, but the bright paint and crisp net curtains at the windows looked cheerful and welcoming.

He opened the door at once and stood back to let her in, a curiously shrunken Arnott from the man she remembered. As if he had shed several pounds and several years of vitality in the weeks since he had stormed out. He wore a handknitted cardigan, dirty white and stained with a medley of blobs and a liberal dusting of cigarette ash.

'Shall we sit outside, lass?' he said. 'I've just made some tea and sunshine's grand.'

She nodded, following him through the kitchen into the little garden where two chairs stood beside an old circular pub table. An elaborate birdbath was set about with hanging nets containing nuts and bacon rinds and unidentifiable balls of something looking for all the world like putty. Starlings and blue-tits attacked all this, seemingly undisturbed by her arrival and, after a moment, Arnott reappeared and put down two mugs of tea.

The silky rayon of Judy's floral skirt, loose and long, slid across her bare thighs in cool folds, almost touching her flat pumps as she sat stiffly in Arnott's garden sipping strong tea. It was difficult to know where to begin and Arnott's politeness had caught her out. Madness to imagine she would ever have welcomed Arnott's familiar abrasive style, but she would have done so now. Retirement seemed to have robbed him of his famous rudeness and the man sitting quietly beside her watching the birds was a stranger. She gulped her tea and blurted out, 'You should have come to the party. It would have been great. We all miss you.' That was true enough.

His gimlet eyes peered under shaggy brows and she half suspected a twinkle there. Or was she getting paranoid about being laughed at? She had rarely felt uneasy before this Swayne business, awkwardness was new to her. She had found herself behaving stupidly with Erskine and here she was doing it again. The trouble was, everyone had changed places.

'No point,' he said.

'I've a parcel for you in the car. We all chipped in. Jilly Pitts organized it, chose it really. You could exchange it . . .' Her words petered out, seeming inconsequential and clumsy.

Arnott grinned in his old foxy way and leaned back in the canvas seat.

'Don't take on so, Judy lass. You drew the short straw

bringing it here. I'm not bitter with that lot at the station. It's me. A combination of rage and disappointment.'

'Disappointment?'

'That Swayne lark. Fancy a cunning old bugger like me letting that rotten case get under my skin. Wasn't worth it, was it? I wouldn't have minded if it hadn't been my last investigation. Lousy finish after all these years. Stupid to make such a song and dance. Peg wouldn't have let me show off like that!'

'You're entitled to your principles.'

'I knew I had only a few weeks left. It seemed to make all them years on the force such a bloody farce. Hushing up this and that, keeping the bomb business off the record, letting the Special Branch put their oar in.' He spread his hands wide in a gesture of defeat.

Judy scrambled up. 'Hang on. I'll get your present.'

He followed her to the car and after a tussle he carried the bulky thing himself. She trailed behind, a thick folder which she had recovered from under the passenger seat clamped to her chest. He made straight for the kitchen, and Judy glimpsed a spotlessly neat lounge on her way through, each vase and doiley meticulously placed. He unpacked the box straightaway and they stood back, the gleaming piece of machinery looking for all the world like a token from outer space. A microwave oven.

Judy glanced at Arnott, half expecting one of his foul-mouthed expletives. But he was grinning away, pleased as Punch. Punch and Judy. She wished he had come to the party.

'You like it?'

'Smashing. Just the job. Poor old Peg would've been over the moon if she'd been here.'

'I'm sorry about your wife,' she muttered. 'I heard—'

'Cancer. Inevitable, but a shock all the same. Only last April.' He paused. 'I'm glad she didn't know I'd buggered it up at the end.'

'Of course you didn't. Why don't you come down to the

station for a handshake all round? Informally. You never
said goodbye to anyone. I can understand you dodging the
party but I'm leaving too. We could go together if you like
and take them all out for a drink. Jilly and the others. After
my holiday, that is.'

'Leaving? You been promoted, then?'

'C6. The Fraud Squad in Holborn. Quite different from
the blood and drama of the Royal Borough.'

'Pleased?'

'You're not the only one who left with a nasty taste in the
mouth after that Swayne business. I haven't the stomach
for it. I've always been good at figures and you don't need
any previous accountancy training, they tell me.'

'Did you apply for a transfer?'

'No. The Super called me in. Said he thought it would
be a good idea.' She smiled. 'I'm looking forward to it. I'm
not really cut out for murder investigations.'

'Swayne committed suicide.'

'Not according to the Coroner. It was an accident.'

'Balls!'

Arnott slumped into one of the kitchen chairs and rolled
a cigarette with a small machine. Fascinated, Judy watched
his clumsy nicotine-stained fingers making heavy weather
with the delicate fag paper and a pinch of tobacco. The
result was thin and bent like a peeled stick. He lit it trium-
phantly.

'Bloody performance, this. But I thought the palaver
would make me cut down and I've got time for it all right.'
The caustic edge was back. Judy sat at the table, feeling
herself on firmer ground with this craggy old devil.

'Listen, er—sir,' she added with a laugh. 'I need your
help.'

She opened the folder and spread Larry's photographs
over the table. Arnott's eyes narrowed and he drew back,
singed by the repellent pictures rendered even more obscene
in this scrubbed little kitchen.

'I'm at my wits' end with this lot. Larry Erskine—the

Inspector they sent over, you remember—took these and told me not to show anyone on the force.'

'That lets me out, ducky.'

'Not really. But I know you'll keep it to yourself.' She caught his eye, desperation in her own. 'I'm out of my depth completely.'

Shuffling the glossy prints, she laid them out neatly in rows. The hand-made cigarette was already half spent, its delicacy disintegrating between Arnott's fingers.

'Erskine said they showed something the pathologist had missed. I've been studying them for weeks and I'm none the wiser.' Delving into the huge shoulder-bag, Judy drew out a plastic envelope containing a length of blue rope. 'And this I've acquired on the q.t. but I don't think anyone's bothered now the case is closed.'

'The actual rope?' Arnott's gruff prompting re-established the familiar relationship and Judy rushed on, the words tumbling out.

'And I've also kept back a few other things. I've copied out the details from my notebook and a whole lot of guff about Swayne's will which may interest you.' She placed a shorthand pad on top of the photographs, together with the yellow handbill advertising the hospital fête which had riled Swayne's neighbour.

'What's all this about, Pullen?'

'I'm going away. Tomorrow.' She hesitated. 'I might as well tell you. I'm meeting Larry. Privately. In Cyprus. We struck up something—I'm not sure what—and he asked me out there for a couple of weeks.'

Arnott let out a slow whistle and leaned back in the kitchen chair. 'Well, well, well. Slyboots.' He spoke with a rough kindness and then, banging the table with his speckled hand, said, 'Go on, then. Get on with it, girl. What's Erskine fishing for with all these dirty pictures?'

'That's it, Arnott. I don't know. I can't keep it to myself and once I start this new job it'll just get shoved aside. I don't like to leave all this hanging about in my flat, my sister has a key and sometimes crashes out there if she misses the last train. The whole thing nags me. I can't sleep. There's a lot unexplained and Erskine dare not stir up anything because his people want it hushed up. I went to see the cleaner yesterday, Pamina de Cassis. The one who found the body, you remember.'

'Of course I bloody remember. I'm not senile, Pullen!'

'She's still off work. She's been ill. Delayed shock, the doctor said. She's on all sorts of tranquillizers and won't leave the house. She's lost her other job and just sits about in a state of terror. She seems to think someone's going to get *her* next.'

Irritably he stubbed out the puny cigarette and, unearthing a brand-new pipe from a drawer, lit up. He prowled about the kitchen listening intently, his bull-like head wreathed in smoke.

'I wanted to check about the keys. You remember two bunches were found with Pamina's shopping stacked against the wall behind the front door? I wanted to ask her why she had two sets of house keys.'

'Clever girl!' Arnott's intensity pierced the nicotine cloud as he drew with distaste on the pipe.

'But when I saw what a state she was in it seemed pointless to ask.'

'Angry, you mean? Or too scared to talk?'

'Neither. She's totally numb. As if she'd been steam-rollered. She's convinced it's all up with her. The husband didn't want to let me in at all, mad as hell he is, saying the police had forced her into this breakdown. Utter rubbish, of course. Nobody suggested she had anything to do with it. Even the mat.'

'Mat? What bloody tangent are you off on now, woman?'

'Swayne's mat in his study.' Judy shook her head, assembling the facts in some sort of order. 'I'll go back to that. But the keys bothered me even more than the milk.'

'Sod the milk. Get back to the keys.' He sat down again,

fidgeting with the new pipe, and in exasperation swept the neatly laid out photographs to the end of the table.

'The funny thing was she's way up in the clouds about everything *except* that Monday. It was as if it was etched in acid in her brain. Indelible. And everything else wishy-washy. She can't seem to let it go, goes over and over it, insisting everything was as usual. I asked her why she had two sets of doorkeys and she flatly denied it.'

'They were found on the floor with her shopping, you say. The stuff she put down when she came in to work?'

Judy nodded. 'Behind the door. She kept repeating she opened the door and the house was double-locked as always. Then she shut it and put her keys and her shopping down while she picked up the letters on the mat. Sisley confirms everything she says. The mail was on the radiator shelf and her carrier bag with shopping and keys—hers with a plastic tag and another set which must have been Swayne's by the wall.'

Arnott relit the pipe, frowning, saying nothing.

Judy said, 'She got very excited, so I changed the subject and asked her about the mat. When I took Mrs Morland round the house the only thing she seemed to think might be missing was a small felt mat, embroidered ethnic sort of thing, not valuable but pretty. And portable. The floor in that room where Swayne had his desk has polished boards but his sister vaguely remembers a mat under the chair, between the leather trunk and the desk. It could have been sent to the cleaners while he was away. I wasn't accusing her. I just wanted to check if Pamina remembered it being there on the Friday. It was the only thing missing,' she added lamely.

'And the husband says you're inferring she stole it?'

'Stupid! With dozens of really valuable things in the house, she'd hardly make off with a mat, especially when she was in hysterics after finding the body. She even forgot to take her own groceries. Mike Sisley took the carrier bag round later. It was only when he moved the shopping he realized there were two sets of keys on the floor.'

'But that's fucking rubbish!' In exasperation Arnott threw the pipe across the room. 'I remember Sisley reporting all this just before that film actor chap, the brother, arrived to identify the body. The keys found with the cleaner's shopping were car keys.' He stared across the table at Judy, appalled. 'Why ever didn't I think of that? The bloody cleaner wouldn't need car keys.'

'But the others? The keys found in the alcove with the coats?'

Beating a tattoo on the table to underline every syllable, Arnott spelt it out to her. 'The keys on the floor under the coat-hooks in the alcove were house keys. Swayne's. We assumed they'd dropped out of his pocket when he came in from the opera. He'd had a sweaty evening, flung off his coat as soon as he got inside the door and raced upstairs for a shower before he drove down to the cottage.'

'But if that's true,' Judy persisted, 'why wasn't his coat in the alcove? And he wasn't in all that much of a hurry. His dinner jacket was hanging in the wardrobe upstairs and the trousers were in the trouser press. He was very methodical. We've several witnesses who saw him wearing the black tie outfit and there's even a neighbour who heard him come back. *And* drive off again.'

'You've lost me now, girl. What the hell are you on about? Swayne drove home and then off again?'

'It must have been in my report after you were off the case. Swayne's neighbour saw him go off early Friday evening and actually saw him arrive back alone in the early hours.' Judy described the conversation with Kate Morrison-Carr and Sabina Morland.

'Regular night owl, this witness of yours.'

Judy flicked through her notes and found the page.

'Mrs Morrison-Carr. She'd got up to see to her dog, been kept awake by a party in the flats at the back and as her kitchen's at the front of the house she saw Swayne come home from the opera and says he was alone.'

'Good witness, this Mrs Carr?'

'Excellent. Bit of a busybody. Organizes the Neighbourhood Watch Committee.'

'I know the type,' Arnott sighed.

'Then after an interval, she doesn't know how long, she heard his car drive off to the country for the weekend as usual. When she saw the cat—Swayne's Siamese—hanging about the garden on Sunday she assumed he was back.'

'But the car wasn't there?'

'She didn't go into that. When she was telling me all this she obviously didn't know that Swayne had hanged himself before dawn on the Saturday.'

'Give her something to think about!' he chuckled. 'Perhaps Swayne came in late from the party, changed into casual clothes and went straight out again. To meet someone. Pass over the missing £5000, perhaps? Any chance of the people holding the party at the back seeing anything?'

Judy shifted awkwardly and admitted nobody had thought to ask.

'Hot night like that, all the windows open, someone might've seen Swayne's quick-change act, swapping dinner jacket for casuals to go out and then eventually coming back to prance about in his wig and nightie.'

Judy cut him short. 'There's no evidence to suggest he changed out of his dinner jacket before going out. In that district nobody would remark on formal kit in the middle of the night. Anyway, the curtains were drawn, sir.'

'You'd think some nosey bugger would notice something!' Arnott was becoming petulant. Giving up cigarettes had not sweetened his disposition, she decided.

'It's a funny area, sir. People move in and out of those furnished flats all the time. Even the parties are open-house. It would be impossible to find out who was there that night, especially now that the case is officially closed.'

'This Mrs Nosey Carr from next door,' said Arnott. 'Can't she help?'

'I'd go and see her again if there was time. But I don't think she can tell us any more. She made enough fuss about this leaflet—' Judy pulled out the yellow handbill from the pile—'so I don't imagine she'd miss any juicy details.'

'What's wrong with it?' He stabbed at the paper.

'Nothing really. It was delivered late—after the date of the hospital fête it was advertising—by a disabled person, which is the only reason she didn't create a stink at St Laurence's about it.'

'That the AIDS place in Fulham Road?'

'Er, yes, I suppose it is. But it's an ordinary hospital too. It's just that the AIDS patients are the ones who catch the headlines.' But this new slant sounded promising. 'Could it have been a hint?' she said. 'Some crackpot getting at the gays?'

'A bit far-fetched,' Arnott jeered. 'You would have to spell it out clearer than a printed handout and there were no threatening notes found in the house. Anyway, they all had one, you said. Every house in the mews?'

'I suppose so. Anyway, I'm sure it's not important. Just filling in the details so you know everything that cropped up after you walked out.' Arnott looked up sharply. Judy wished she had put it more tactfully. But then—what the hell? Arnott *had* walked out on the case, there was no denying it. And tact wasn't high on *his* list of priorities.

'They dropped the inquiries about the bomb?' he said.

Judy nodded. 'And there's still the missing cash, but even the family are not complaining so it's difficult to pursue that line, I guess they've all had more than enough of the spiteful publicity and just want the whole thing to blow over. Larry Erskine's satisfied the bomb didn't conform to any he'd seen before. He thinks it's a homemade affair, efficient and scientifically constructed but not an obvious terrorist device. It wasn't set to explode, you know. Wasn't even hidden.'

'Perhaps it was a little toy Swayne put together like

Meccano, just to see if he could do it. After dealing with the
moronic O'Laughlin I bet he thought making bombs must
be a piece of cake if an Irish clod could do it!'

'His sister says he was totally cackhanded. She's got a
scientific degree of some sort and reckons her brother could
barely mend a fuse.'

'He was a sailing man, though. He'd have to have a bit
of nous to race a boat like the one he shared with that friend
of his. What was it called . . . ?' In exasperation Arnott
banged the table, sending several of the photographs skim-
ming on to the floor. '*Seraphina!* I had an Isle of Wight
holiday once, Cowes week. Peg got quite carried away with
it all. *Yeoman, Seraphina* and *Passing Cloud* or whatever that
Prime Minister's boat was called. I remember *them* all right.
Beautiful.'

'I thought Passing Cloud was a cigarette.'

Arnott was not amused.

'Anyhow,' Judy continued, 'it's gone up in smoke.'

'What do you mean—gone up in smoke?'

'It caught fire. This summer. The boat Swayne sailed
with—' she flicked through her notebook—'Roger Mansell.
Arson apparently. A disgruntled fellow competitor tossed a
fire bomb maybe.'

'No sailing man would sabotage a lovely boat like that.'
Arnott's voice was almost a whisper and thoughtfully he
moved round the table, picking up the photographs and
stacking them neatly at Judy's elbow. He bent to retrieve
the broken pipe and put the pieces in a waste-bin. Placing
the shorthand pad on top of the pile of pictures, he regarded
her shrewdly.

'Are you doing all this just to patronize me? What's the
game?'

Judy rose, pulling her car keys from her bag and forcing
herself to stay calm, not to be flustered by Arnott. 'I am
trusting you, sir, to look through all this.' She vaguely
gestured the pile of paper. 'And when I get back in two
weeks' time to tell me what it all adds up to. If anything.

I'm not at all happy with the way it's been shoved out of sight and a lot of people on the sidelines, including Pamina de Cassis, have suffered by Swayne's death. Everyone who had anything to do with the investigation, including Sisley incidentally, has been transferred or—' she faltered—'retired. Erskine knows more than he dares to spell out and I feel the whole thing's like a bundle of dirty washing no one's prepared to sort out.'

Arnott followed her out to the car and stood on the pavement as she tried to revive her flagging battery. A breeze had risen off the river, a breath of autumn in the air which blew Arnott's thinning strands of grey hair into a wild halo.

'By the way,' he said, 'did they ever find the car?'

'Swayne's Renault? Yes. You'll never believe this! It was under our noses all the time. Just behind High Street Ken. Clamped. It's still in the police pound since Erskine had it through his net looking for more explosives. Clean as a whistle, locked up properly but parked on a yellow. He wasn't all that law-abiding, our late barrister, was he?'

Arnott straightened stiffly as the Volkswagen shot off and in her rear-view mirror Judy Pullen recognized the bow-legged gait of the cantankerous old devil she remembered.

Arnott whistled through his teeth in a breathy tuneless wheeze as he tidied Peg's kitchen. He always thought of it as Peg's kitchen, Peg's dressing-table , Peg's curtains. And since she'd gone, leaving it all for him to deal with, keeping Peg's house in some semblance of the apple-pie order she had seemed so effortlessly to maintain had kept Arnott sane.

But eternal tidying was no substitute and he guiltily realized that even his best efforts would never qualify for Peg's seal of approval. He sat at the kitchen table and ponderously made another fiddle-arsed cigarette.

It took him twenty minutes to unpack Pullen's microwave and another hour to read the instructions and set it up. It sat on the counter top like a squat cyclops awaiting instructions. Undeniable: he couldn't go on for the rest of his life tending Peg's bits and pieces. He would put the house on the market—just as soon as he'd extracted himself from this mess. Swayne's quicksand had almost swallowed him up as greedily as that poor black woman who had stumbled into more than she knew.

Reluctantly drawing Pullen's files and notebook towards him, he found himself churning with dread and anticipation. But the set of his jaw was obdurate. Proving he'd been right all along about this would be one in the eye for the lot of 'em. Judy was right. There'd been a lot of pushing under the carpet one way and another. It was a bad business and he didn't see why that tricky bugger Swayne should get away with it. What accident?

By nightfall, Arnott had made his second undeniable discovery. You'd got to hand it to that clever sod Erskine. He'd seen it all along. With all the pain of extracting a splinter from a festering ego, Arnott had to admit *he* was the one who'd been wrong. Swayne's death hadn't been accidental. It wasn't even suicide. Francis Swayne QC had quite clearly been murdered.

Next morning Arnott washed, shaved and put on a suit for the first time in weeks. After knotting the tie, his breath laboured as he leaned over Peg's dressing-table to see himself in the mirror, he ran a thick forefinger along the hooked nose.

'Ugly customer, Mr Punch and no mistake.' His foxy grin tilted at the reflection in the glass.

He shambled through to the kitchen and made breakfast, slowly crunching through his usual two slices of toast, not taking his eyes from the pile of photographs and papers stacked by the evil eye of the bloody microwave.

He'd been wrong about Swayne, no doubt about it. But it was still not too late to see it right. He'd nothing to lose. And ruling a line at the end of this business—even if only to his own satisfaction—would release him. He'd prove it for Peg. Put it away all neat and ironed like her bloody sheets, all the edges nice and crisp. He'd lay nearly forty years aside easy in his mind and not have to spend the rest of his days gnawing away at it, knowing he'd fouled it all up with his own arrogance. A man's work was his life: it deserved a decent burial.

CHAPTER 10

Sabina Morland and her mother-in-law sat together under a ramshackle arbour at the end of the terrace fronting Fernside. Within the tangled arches of a climbing rose the warmth of the sun striking low from the horizon conjured up the unseasonable benevolence of early October. Much of a crumbling balustrade edging the terrace had been removed, the lip softened with a narrow planting of pansies. The remains of the broken stonework remained at each end like decaying molars, fortuitously lending the Victorian gothic house an authentic touch of ruin.

The younger woman lay on a cushioned chaise, an old teak lounger of the sort laid out in rows on the decks of pre-war cruise ships. Her eyes were closed, the fading tan stretched ivory-pale over cheekbones like those of a mediæval damsel.

Geoffrey's letter had lit a fuse which smouldered in the dismal aftermath of Francis's death, igniting Sabina's latent dissatisfaction with her comfortable lot. Apparent listlessness shrouded secret resolutions like underground fires carefully damped down. The prolonged visit to Yorkshire dictated by Sybil's accident provided the shelter in which the spark kindled. Next week Aragon would be safely dispatched to Glasgow to begin her drama course and Sabina would be free to contact Geoffrey. He could help her. Why had she not thought of Geoffrey Tallent before? It was obvious. All that old scandal was dead and buried. She sighed in quiet satisfaction. Yes. Geoffrey would help her begin again.

'Are you awake, dear?'

'Just daydreaming, Sybil.'

The mediæval damsel opened her eyes, instantly twentieth-century. 'Would you like me to make some tea?'

'That would be nice.' The old lady's hands fidgeted in her lap, her right arm strapped to her chest under a mohair stole. 'It's Wednesday. Mrs Carter goes into Harrogate every Wednesday to meet her sister.'

Yawning, Sabina swung her feet to the ground in one smooth unhurried gesture. Sybil irritably considered this languid quality excessive, Sabina's quiet footfall almost sinister: such a contrast to Clumping Carter. Not to mention Aragon. Such 'seamlessness' in a young woman unnerved her, made her jumpy. But then, her shoulder ached abominably. And she longed to be able to *do* something, just to pick up the cat without a nagging reminder of the wretched collar-bone would do. Sybil felt about for her stick and scrambled up, Sabina's hand under her elbow bringing a waft of scent suddenly close.

'I'll come with you, Sabina, my dear.'

'Oh, don't let's go in yet! It's so lovely out here. It may be one of the last warm days.' Sabina touched the old lady's restless fingers grasping the cane. 'I'll bring out a tray and we can enjoy the last half-hour. Can I trust you to stroll about without toppling off the terrace?' she teased.

'Ask Tai-Tai!'

Sabina disappeared round the side of the house. Sybil Morland paced the terrace, the upright carriage and confident step entirely disguising her blindness. She wore sunglasses as much for vanity as comfort. Her failing sight had seemed a dreadful disloyalty on the part of her body after a lifetime's healthy diet and exercise. Hardly fair after more than seventy years of expensive attention. What others might regard as decent wear and tear or even a useful tool for eliciting sympathy was a matter of shame to Sybil

Morland. As if her blindness was the result of a dirty lifestyle, like VD or nits. Her enormous satisfaction in deceiving a stranger unaware of her disability was almost childishly evident and a game in which Aragon was an enthusiastic collaborator.

She would miss the child dreadfully. An insect droned in the rose border, the last bewildered bumblings of the Indian summer. Far away the hum of traffic hurtling towards Wetherby seemed merely amplification of the silly creature's diligence.

Thank God I'm not deaf as well, Sybil congratulated herself. Florrie Mason's a perfect fool these days with her wretched hearing aid. Catches one word in ten and forever getting the wrong end of the stick.

A warm breath off the moors fanned her cheek and, counting her paces on the well-worn flags, she retraced her steps just as the squeak and rattle of the tea-trolley turned the corner. A penetrating miaow announced the arrival of Tai-Tai, already very much at home and anticipating afternoon treats.

Settling back in her garden chair, Sybil insisted on drawing the trolley to her and pouring tea herself. A cup rattled dangerously in its saucer as she passed it to Sabina just as Francis Swayne's Siamese leapt into her lap.

Sabina snatched the saucer. 'Tai-Tai! Get off, you brute.'

'It's quite all right. She'll soon settle.' Awkwardly, with her good arm, Sybil poured milk into the porcelain slop bowl and placed it on the paving. The cat elegantly slid off her lap and lapped the milk, never taking its sapphire eyes from Sabina.

'Are you sure you can cope with Tai-Tai? Perhaps it wasn't such a good idea after all.'

'Nonsense, my dear. She's adorable.' Sybil's head inclined, catching the almost imperceptible purr which now blended with the manic buzzing in the roses.

'It *was* Tai-Tai's fault you fell.' There was no denying it. God knows what Harry's reaction had been when he'd heard. But Harry was inextricably tied up in Tokyo, a syndication of some sort . . .

'Only indirectly,' Sybil insisted. 'The insurance people might call it an act of God,' she added, laughing.

'You mean that evangelist man Tai-Tai got so cross about?' Sabina grinned. 'Holy intervention of some sort, I suppose. Mrs Carter gave me some garbled version, over-anxious to excuse herself, I gather. Guzzling teacakes with her sister, was she?'

'It *was* her day off!' Sybil sipped her tea while Tai-Tai, intent on prey, stalked the weedy undergrowth of the arbour. 'I was sitting here, just like today. But earlier. About two. I had just switched on *Melody Hour* on my little tranny. I heard a car drive right up. Stopped just there,' she said, pointing to the drive below the terrace. 'And he must have been sitting in his car sorting something out because it was several moments before I heard his step on the gravel. It made me a little nervous. Few unexpected callers track us down here.'

'Mm. I've always thought Fernside a bit remote for you these days, darling. You should be in the village, Sybil.'

The old woman frowned at the interruption. 'As I was saying. I stood up and asked him his business. I can guess a whole lot from footsteps. You'd be surprised,' she added darkly.

Sabina stifled a yawn and lay back. Obviously the old girl was going to make a real production number of the incident.

'He said he wanted to know if I read the Bible.' She snorted contemptuously. 'I didn't let on, of course. He clearly had no idea I am blind. Silly man rattled on for a bit, then the funny thing was he called me "Mrs Morland". Just like that. He must have got my name from the village. Said he had thought I was younger. Fancy! Presumably, he had seen Carter at the post office and assumed she was Mrs Morland from Fernside. Or heard her ordering groceries to be sent up. It all made me very suspicious, but I pretended

Betty Carter was in the house.' A slow smile lifted the corners of her mouth and the old lady chuckled. 'Then, would you believe, he had the insolence to inquire if I believed in an afterlife. Asked straight out, no shilly-shallying. What presumption!' Sybil's asperity was legendary. Whoever had directed the unsuspecting Jehovah's Witness to Fernside must have had a laugh; even the vicar from the village kept a safe distance.

'I told him,' she said. 'Young man, the Almighty and I have come to a private arrangement. And when my time comes I will not be standing at the pearly gates whingeing for a place in His many mansions as if He were a celestial estate agent. Oh, I must tell you, Sabina. I heard this marvellous joke from Rosie about the banker who arrives in Paradise and asks St Peter—'

'I've heard it, Sybil. Go on. Tell me about the accident.'

'Well, he went back to his car and I thought to myself: That's put you in your place, coming here uninvited, asking impertinent questions. But not a bit of it! These people have skins like rhinos, my dear. He scrabbled about inside his car and came back with a newspaper. Some sort of religious pamphlet.'

'*The Watchtower*. I saw it in the hall.' And then, sardonically: 'I thought you had Seen the Light, Sybil.' Sabina placed her empty cup on the trolley, and prompted Sybil to continue.

'I said I had no money. I would have to call my housekeeper. I've heard all about old women being mugged for thirty pence and kept my cane ready.' China blue eyes glinted wickedly behind the shaded lenses.

'But he was genuine all right,' Sybil conceded. 'Most charming. Laughed when I said that about getting Carter and I suspect didn't believe one word of it. And while I was standing at the edge of the terrace talking to him Tai-Tai appeared from nowhere, shot through my legs and apparently jumped straight into the hawker's car.'

'And you fell in a heap in the drive. A broken collar-bone. It must have been divine retribution, Sybil.'

'Beastly vindictive, I call it. It was all that Old Testament rubbish put me off religion in the first place.'

'It could have been much worse. Thank goodness the Bible-thumper was here. If Tai-Tai had tripped you up while Mrs Carter was lounging in Betty's Tea Rooms you could have been sprawled out in the drive in agony. For hours. It's not good enough, Sybil. Mrs Carter's got to get someone to sit with you when she's out. What about her niece? Mary, isn't it? From the village. She's unemployed, she tells me. You can well afford it,' she added.

'Clumping Carter's bad enough. Two of them would really send me ga-ga.' Sybil tersely brushed aside Sabina's protests and went on with her narrative. 'The man propped me up against the terrace and dashed inside, found no one there of course and in my painful predicament I distinctly imagined him ransacking the whole house. Not a bit of it! Only goes to show how one can misjudge people. He came back almost immediately with a glass of sherry—clearly got his priorities right,' she snorted. 'And after a devil of a dance getting Tai-Tai out of the car he drove me to the cottage hospital. And left me tucked up while Dr Simcock sent his wife back here to wait for Carter to get back. For a preacher he had very expensive tastes. My dear, the car positively reeked of Havanas!'

'Does Tai-Tai streak about like that all the time?'

'No. Far from it. The darling's wonderfully intelligent. More than Carter, if you ask me. She picks her way round me all day long, as gentle as a pigeon as a rule. I think that evangelist had some fish in his car. Been poaching, shouldn't wonder. I never trust these holy types, Sabina, they all think like Communists, all God's bounty to share and share alike. Anyway, Tai-Tai wouldn't budge and apparently scratched the man to pieces before he could drag her out. Those two-door cars are awkward when one wants to get something off the back seat.'

Sabina laughed. 'How would you know how many doors he had?' she teased. 'If he could afford good cigars he could have been crusading in a Rolls.'

'You stupid girl! A Rolls sounds entirely different.' Sybil paused. 'Actually,' she admitted, 'he mentioned it. Asked if it was painful for me to squeeze into a small car. He was very gentle. I should have got his name and address but he disappeared as soon as Dr Simcock came on the scene.'

'Well, darling, I would have called an ambulance myself. You couldn't have got into the Porsche.'

The sun had gone down and already a thin mist shrouded the lawn. Sabina shivered. October had reasserted itself. Linking arms, the two women strolled back to the house, closely followed by the sprightly Siamese darting ghostlike between them. In the dusk the empty chairs and abandoned tea-trolley remained on the terrace like stage props awaiting the second set.

They entered the house through the open front door and were confronted by a rear view of Aragon whispering into the telephone. Quickly replacing the receiver, she swung round, her dark hair springing up from a topknot and cascading to her shoulders, the ends tinted raspberry red like chenille fringeing.

'Mary,' she muttered by way of explanation. 'Mrs Carter's niece. Can I borrow the Porsche, Sabina? Just for a couple of hours? There's a film in Harrogate . . .'

Without speaking, Sabina shook her head and brushed past, leaving Sybil and her grand-daughter alone in the hall.

'Honestly, Granny,' she fumed, 'Sabina's the bloody limit. She knows I can't stick around here all week. I've driven the Porsche dozens of times at Bracknell. Daddy let me bomb around the factory yard. It's really a tame pussy-cat once you get the hang of it. Truly, I'm a better driver than Sabina will ever be!'

Sybil stretched out a hand, feeling the air, grasping Aragon's black jersey. 'You know very well, my darling, the car's not insured for anyone else. Deliberately so. It's no use nagging Sabina. It's illegal for you to drive it beyond the gates. It was very silly of Harry to let you play around with it.'

She paused, stroking the girl's arm. 'Why don't you ask Mrs Carter if you may borrow the Mini for the evening? She will be back at six o'clock and if you and Mary are going to the cinema together—'

Aragon shrugged off the restraining fingers, tossing the pony tail in an authentic coltish flick. 'Oh, forget it. Mary's a drag anyhow. And a tittle-tattle.' And then, as if a new thought had suddenly bloomed in her head, she cheerfully smacked a kiss on Sybil's cheek and slipped her arm round her beneath the mohair stole. Sybil winced and carefully extracted herself. They slowly climbed the stairs, Aragon chattering animatedly.

'I've fixed your recording machine, Granny. It's all ready. I want you to hear my audition pieces and then we'll put them on tape. It's easier to hear faults that way.'

'Not more of that modern filth, I hope? All that swearing! I can hear that on the wireless without you putting it on my machine.'

'No. Shakespeare. You'll love it. And a funny bit from *The Importance of Being Ernest*. All nice respectable bits. You can play them back to Rosie next time she comes. Rosie's certain I'm going to be famous.'

'Rosie thinks everyone's famous. Even Sabina's brother Nicholas and he hasn't had a good meaty part in years.'

'Naughty! Naughty! I thought I was the only one fed up with Sabina's grotty family.'

They entered Sybil's sitting-room, the lamps warm haloes against the chintz, a small fire crackling in the grate.

'Pull the curtains, darling. I hate to feel the dark peering in.'

Aragon whooshed the drapes across, the brass rings gnashing like false teeth, then vaulted the sofa to switch on the recording machine. Harry Morland's electronics empire had provided the very best equipment for his mother's pleasure, most of it barely understood. Aragon placed a small table at her grandmother's elbow and guided the misshapen fingers across the stops.

'And when we've done this I'll show you how to work it yourself. Then you can send me tapes in Glasgow. Instead of letters. You could record bits here and there, let Tai-Tai have a yowl or two and post it to me when the tape's full. Much more fun.'

'I could telephone.'

'Oh, Granny! You're not antediluvian. That's not the same at all. And anyway, I'll probably be in great demand, not stuck at the end of a phone waiting for calls all the time,' she said, striking a dramatic pose totally lost on Sybil.

'Perhaps when I've got the hang of this we will both be famous,' the old lady tartly retorted. 'I'll be glad to see the back of you. Messing about with all my things. I was perfectly satisfied with those library tapes Carter gets for me.' And with mock severity she added, 'As if we didn't get more than enough of your histrionics without recordings.'

Aragon flopped by the old lady's knees and began reciting. Sybil's hand wandered over the girl's head investigating the top knot. 'What's this?' she muttered. 'Feels like a fly whisk.'

Aragon playfully slapped her hand, continuing with her recitation, her voice swooping dramatically from fluting tones to a throaty whisper.

Sabina quietly entered during this last exchange, standing silently in the doorway observing Aragon's masquerade.

'No, listen, Granny. Be quiet for a minute and when you think I've got it right we'll record it and play it back.'

Sabina disappeared downstairs to telephone Geoffrey before the housekeeper returned. Suddenly, it hardly seemed worthwhile delaying a meeting until after Aragon's departure. After so long the urgency to press on with her plan was undeniable. It was weeks since he had sent the letter. He must think she was ignoring it. She padded through the chilly passage to the kitchen quarters.

CHAPTER 11

It was some time after she got back from Cyprus before Judy Pullen managed to get in touch with Arnott. At first she thought he must have gone on holiday but by mid-October she was beginning to worry. It was with obvious relief she recognized the familiar gruff tones on her office extension. The new job kept her deskbound so far and there was plenty of studying to catch up on in the evenings. And Erskine was still abroad . . . It was, she admitted, a dull patch. How else would an invitation to supper at Mortlake seem so intriguing?

'Eightish? Tomorrow night, then.' She twirled in the swivel chair, smiling to herself. And wondered if the former detective-inspector had yet mastered the new microwave.

Hunched against a steady downpour, Judy hurried to Arnott's front door between the neat dark squares of grass, her hair tucked under a felt trilby.

Heat burst out of the little house like an eager puppy as Arnott opened the door, the large rough hands pulling her inside and quickly closing it again. She shook out her hair as he took her wet mackintosh and wiped her ankle boots carefully before entering Arnott's lair.

'It's grown,' he said. 'Your hair. It looks different. Blonder.'

Judy shrugged, holding out a bottle of Beaujolais. 'It's weeks, Arnott. I've been away.' She followed him through to the box-like lounge, more cluttered than formerly when she had glimpsed it from the hall on her first visit. But cosier. The crochet squares had gone from the backs of the chairs and the rug in front of the fireplace was almost obliterated by a huge glass coffee table, achingly new and as out of place in that dinky parlour as Arnott himself. It was piled with books, notepads, photographs and old press clippings.

He rubbed his hands together in glee, the foxy glance scanning his former assistant. 'A drink, lass?'

'Not now. Some wine later if you like.'

'You're in for a right treat tonight.' Playfully he pinched her arm. 'You need a bit of fattening up, my gel. Beef and dumplings. Best yet. If I do say it meself, Sergeant Pullen, I'm not the worst cook in the world.'

They sat either side of the hearth in which the yellow leaves of a dead poinsettia in a plastic pot hung down like rags. They talked quickly, filling in the details about her new job with the Fraud Squad, gossiping about old colleagues, even touching on the special part Larry Erskine now played in her life.

'Bloody queer that, you falling for one of that mob.' Arnott's eyes slid sideways at her and slyly he added, 'Only bit of good to come out of that sorry business.'

That was the only reference he made to the Swayne case but they knew they must talk it out. But later. After the wine.

He was right. The casserole was excellent: robust gutsy stew, a real widower's brew. After ice-cream and cheese he made a pot of strong tea and carried the tray back to the overheated little lounge. They settled either side of the monstrous coffee table like an old married couple and, relaxing in Arnott's Parker Knoll, Judy accepted her cup and fought the inevitable torpor following supper, a glass or two of Beaujolais and the hypnotic drone of the old man's narrative.

To be truthful, she wanted only to forget the whole wretched business. She wished now she had kept Larry's photographs to herself, let sleeping dogs lie. But from under lazy lids, watching the surer movements of his mottled hands, hearing the eager decisive phrases describing his re-entry into the maze, the part she had played in offering Arnott the chance to bind off the raw edges of his final case seemed inevitable. She roused herself to broach the subject.

'Did you ever sort out those photographs, discover what Larry Erskine meant? He wouldn't speak to me about it. He sees it as some sort of joke between us, a puzzle I must work out for myself. I didn't tell him I asked you to help. Larry only sees Swayne's death as an academic exercise, he couldn't care less. You mustn't dwell on it, Mr Arnott. It's all past, water under the bridge. It wasn't as if he was even a nice man, Francis Swayne. The family is quite content with the coroner's decision.'

Arnott nodded, his big head sunk into thick shoulders, the eyes glinting between the pouchy flesh, his presence dominating the overcrowded little room like that of a Buddha. And then enigmatically, 'Coroner's verdicts can be overthrown.'

He made a cigarette, taking his time with the fiddly little machine, eventually rolling out a passably regular-looking cigarette. 'It was them photographs what started it, all right,' he said. 'Clever sod, that Erskine of yours. I've never gone into all that kinky stuff before but those shots of his set me off down a very mucky track. Went to Charing Cross Road and got some books from Foyles, medical stuff, forensic notes, you know. It seems that tying yourself up for kicks either dressed up like Swayne or naked or maybe with dirty comics spread about while you're half suspended from some sort of noose is the sort of lark these silly buggers get up to. Sometimes it goes too far, the rope slips and then, whoops, it's all over. Not suicide, mind. Misadventure. That's what the coroner thought after considering all the evidence in Swayne's case. But when you look closely at Erskine's pictures the angle of the cord looks funny. There's a faint line rising a bit to one side apart from the actual noose. Look here,' he said, pushing the repellent photographs across to her.

'And study this, my girl, this grazing round Swayne's chest and upper arm. The pathologist put that down to tying himself up maybe in a chair while he looked at his dirty magazines. But I'm convinced there was two of 'em at it. Both together. It's bloody difficult to tie yourself to a chair all on your own. I tried it. A right bugger's muddle I got myself into.' He laughed. 'Perhaps Swayne's little party piece got out of hand, the rope slipped and he was accidentally asphyxiated.'

'And how many times have you told me facts are the only things that count? No crystal balls in a crime kit, you used to say!'

'Mm,' he agreed reluctantly. 'But being retired I can make my own rules now.' He stared down at the well-thumbed photographs littering the glass table.

'We can't prove a thing, I know that. But the more I fix on these photos, the stronger the conclusion that Swayne didn't swing himself from the rafters on his own. It was murder.'

'The pathologist was quite happy. Accidental suicide by transvestites is not rare, Arnott. It's well documented.'

Arnott nodded. 'But the pathologist's like me: at the end of the line. He's seen the sort of caper a dozen times and it scares him rigid these days, touching stiffs who've probably got AIDS, not worth a light in his estimation. He's lost interest in that sort, glad to see one less, if the truth be known. Pathologists are like dentists, love, best when they're young and keen. Us old dogs only want to get back to our kennels.' His cruelty was self-abasing and Judy looked away.

'But if,' she continued briskly, 'you're right, how do you explain someone getting in without a key? Swayne was definitely seen by Mrs Morrison-Carr to enter the house alone. There was no break-in. Not a shred of evidence to suggest anyone else was involved. The walls are pretty thin, she's not the sort of neighbour to keep quiet if Swayne indulged in a struggle in the bathroom which is bang up to her bedroom at the back and on a hot night the windows were probably wide open. And the cleaner, Pamina. She swears Swayne was a nice regular gentleman, and despite the state she's in now I'd take her word that she had no idea he was gay. Pamina was really shattered to find her saintly employer dressed up like that. It wasn't the fact he was dead that upset her, she said, it was the women's clothing. Especially the wig. She still gets nightmares about the wig.

'Bloody comic way of doing yourself in if you ask me.'

'Swayne was extremely careful, none of his friends had an inkling he was deviant in that way. And masochists aren't always homosexuals, after all.'

'And the pathologist's report states quite definitely he was not an habitual homosexual. I know, I know,' grumbled Arnott. 'But I still think he died in some sort of prank with someone else. The hanging was rigged to cover *something* up.'

'And what about all those magazines and books and tapes locked in that trunk of his? Are you suggesting someone dumped all that on Swayne just to make him look bad? Dressed him up like that just to make suicide credible?' Judy's sherry-coloured eyes widened as the ghastly intricacies of Swayne's accident revealed multiplying layers like the petals of a Japanese paper flower unfolding under water.

'How the hell do I know?' His voice rose and then, plunging into the notebooks on the table, he riffled through some typewritten sheets.

'Listen here, missy. I went to see that expert witness of yours, Mrs Nosey-Carr. You're right, she's observant and not the sort to embroider the facts. She saw Swayne come back all right and go into the house alone. And she heard him drive off shortly after. And because the time of death is fixed he must have come back to the mews pretty quick, presumably parking the car elsewhere to slip back with his pal unobserved. My bet is he'd arranged to meet someone when he was cottaging—or even a regular fancy dress partner—and brought him back to the house. They slipped in quickly and while Swayne was doing his drag queen act they have a fight and Swayne's murdered. He's strung up to look like suicide and the other bloke lets himself out of the house and slips away.'

'But how did this mysterious stranger lock up the house again from the outside? Pamina swears it was double-locked as usual and no keys are missing. The security firm only issued three sets and you can't get those special keys cut at any old place. He couldn't just shut the door normally, it had to be secured with both keys.'

'Exactly!' Arnott's breath exhaled in a rasping wheeze, his bloodshot eyes like those of a hound on the scent. Leaning forward, he chopped the air with his hand in a gesture of execution. 'Those bloody keys kept me awake for nights on end. I went back to the house, you know.'

'Down the chimney like Father Christmas?'

'Pipe down, Pullen. I went for a look-see like a regular punter, shown round by the estate agent.'

Not buying, surely?' Now it was Judy's turn to gasp.

'Not likely! When I buy it won't be cheek by jowl with neighbours like that lot. No. Swayne's house is up to rent, furnished, and I just called for a regular poke round. They sent one of those Sloaney tarts to let me in, right prissy little madam, but it gave me a good chance to see it empty. Not crawling with forensics and photographers and people like that poncey boyfriend of yours.'

'Watch it!' Judy laughed.

'I walked every inch of that house and nothing's changed. It's tight as a chastity belt. No one got in or out of that place except with keys.'

'And so? How did your mystery man get out and lock up again if no keys are missing? There were Swayne's set, Pamina's and a spare set locked in his office safe. You're not suggesting his secretary did it?'

'Swayne's keys were found in the alcove, weren't they? Behind that curtain where the coat-hooks are. All he had to do was lock up when he got outside and put the keys back through the letter-box.'

'Pamina could have kicked them as she came in,' Judy reluctantly agreed. 'But I think she'd have noticed.'

'The keys could have been swept to one side as she opened the door, it's draught-proofed, a tightish fit.' In silence Arnott ponderously made a cigarette with his little machine.

'I know!' Judy crowed. 'The letter-box is very wide, he must have put his hand inside and flicked the keys at an angle so they went under the curtain. I tested that letter-box to see if it could be opened from the outside without a key.'

'What?' Arnott pounced on this and excitedly Judy told him about the experiment with Erskine. He jotted notes laboriously in one of the notebooks, ash from the cigarette lodging in the cable stitching of his cardigan. He laid down his ballpoint and looked over his spectacles.

'There's not a single fact to go on, lass. But I just don't think Swayne's the sort to make mistakes. Too bloody careful by half. We don't *know* he brought back a rent boy. It could have been a known acquaintance. That sailing pal of his, Roger something—'

'Mansell.'

'There's still £5000 in cash not accounted for. Mansell's business was on the rocks. He could have come over by arrangement to borrow some cash and something happened.'

'He did see him earlier that evening. At the Savoy. Bumped into Swayne by chance when Mansell was with his wife, he said. That's when he saw Swayne with a woman, a punky-looking girl in black leather. He even said Swayne had let her sweep off with a package from the table. Check my notes. It's on the page about the funeral, I forget the date.'

'I saw that. All hearsay. He could have called at the mews after his own night out to tap Swayne. They seemed to have had some sort of arrangement on the quiet to share the expenses of the boat that blew up.'

'Did the insurance pay out?'

'Can't say. But Mansell's left the country.'

'What's all this about his business being in trouble?'

'So I hear on the grapevine.' Arnott tapped his nose. 'Mansell Electronics, quite a small outfit but very profitable for a few years. Supplied components for surgical probes, a sort of laser. But the Japs have come up with something new, less expensive. Mansell's firm is merging with Pritchard Lang. That's what I wanted to tell you. I'm going to Guernsey to catch up with the Mansells before they push off.'

'Where to?'

'He's bought another boat. A thirty-foot ketch or thereabouts. He and his wife are going round the world, so I'm told. They'll be away for years, out of touch completely. The boat's being fitted out at St Peter Port now and I'm flying over. It's just the place for a secret bank account. A tax haven like that's a perfect hideaway for funny money.' Sensing her alarm, Arnott affected casual practicality. 'Anyway, I could do with a bit of sea air. Kill two birds with one stone.'

'Now what are you up to?' Judy's concern, disguised under a flippant tone was real. It was all getting too involved, there could be real danger in it for bumbling old Arnott. 'Aren't you taking all this too far, sir? It sounds like a busman's holiday to me, picking over an old investigation that's already filed away. It'll be expensive.'

'Just curiosity. That fellow Mansell knows more than he's let on so far. Been in cahoots with the Swaynes for years. He knew the sister, Sabina Morland, before she was married, you know. Too well, I shouldn't wonder. And there was some rum do at the university, all hushed up by old Francis who shipped his little sister off to the Far East to escape some sort of scandal. I've got to look into that as well, so don't be surprised if I'm not around for a bit.'

Judy looked at her watch and frowned. 'It's late. I've got to go, I'm expecting a phone call. It was a lovely supper. Is there anything I can do? Washing up?'

He rose, showering fine ash over the papers strewn on

the table. 'Nay, lass. My pleasure.' He smiled, guiding her out between the crowded chairs and dainty wine tables dotted about the room.

As she struggled into her raincoat she nodded towards the lounge. 'That's new, isn't it?'

'The coffee table? Yes, smashing, isn't it? Got it off a dealer in Putney. Looks brand-new to me but t'chap said it'd come from some big office refurbishment in the City. I got fed up with all them fancy little jobs Peg put in. Keep falling over. And nowhere to spread out all that stuff of yours.'

Judy nodded, smiling back, the shambling bulk of Arnott almost obscuring her view of poor Peg's offending furniture. One thing struck her as odd: Arnott's northern accent, though always discernible, seemed to have broadened since his retirement. As if his isolation from his workmates had drawn him back to his roots. Perhaps he had come to terms with losing his wife. Maybe occupying himself and the unfamiliar leisure hours with the inconsistencies of the Swayne case had nothing to do with Arnott's renewed sprightliness after all.

'I thought I'd have a dekko at his car,' he said. 'It's still in the police pound, you know. I got on the blower to an old mate of mine there, Bill Fittson, and he reckons none of the bloody relatives can agree what to do with it between them. So bloody flush they can ignore a nice little motor like that! Someone's got to fetch it or it'll be auctioned off.'

The rain had stopped but the air was gusty, the sort of night to chill you right through. Judy waved and set off, driving swiftly back towards town. Soon, soon, she promised herself, Larry'll be back in London and she'd be warm right down to her toes again. She wriggled them inside the perky ankle boots.

CHAPTER 12

Sabina Morland agreed to meet Geoffrey Tallent at Knaresborough, a small market town less than a dozen miles from Fernside. It was her own impulsive suggestion which sprang to mind as she stood in Mrs Carter's kitchen waiting to hear his voice, her eye caught by a flyblown print depicting a wide river flowing through a ravine beside a cliff crowned by a ruined castle. Perfect.

Having finally contacted Geoffrey at home, she was relieved Naomi Tallent had not answered the telephone. Neurotic, crazy female. The first awkward exchange was swiftly concluded once Knaresborough had been decided upon. A teashop by the castle, he suggested. Knowing the place slightly, he hesitantly proposed a location which did not infer lunch or, worse, dinner. He had no money to spare, certainly none to entertain Sabina in any sort of style. An English teashop at the fag end of the season would have no implications on either side. Ten-thirty.

Fear churned inside as he silently replaced the receiver. Why must he go on with this? The letter had been a grave mistake, prompted by bitterness, seeing all those familiar faces at the Swayne funeral on his small TV screen. As complaisant as ever, strutting like the pigmy people they really were. Even Mansell! He should never have agreed to meet her again.

Sabina had first to detour to Harrogate to drop off Aragon. She had insisted on a lift; some toiletries to buy, she said. Sabina guessed an attempt to contact the ghastly Rick more likely and shrugged, impatient to shake off the prolonged responsibility of Harry's daughter. It was like trying to cage Tai-Tai. Not for much longer, thank God.

Sabina smiled and drove faster. Even the girl's sulky spikiness must not be allowed to spoil her day. Meeting

Geoffrey again after all these years! It was all going to be quite marvellous, a second chance to pick up the pieces. Every nerve pricked with anticipation, the sheer enormity of the vista sparkling her eyes as she pumped the accelerator and set the Porsche surging through the narrow lanes.

Aragon was nervous. She slouched in the passenger seat staring out. The unusually hot August had slid into an Indian summer which gilded the landscape flying past, the foliage of the beech trees blurred to flakes of gold leaf tacked to a blue, blue sky.

The girl watched Sabina under her lashes, examining the hair curling on the collar of an alpaca driving coat, the neck now unusually flushed, the small ears lobeless as an elf's. Reluctantly, she comprehended her father's infatuation with Sabina, nearer her age than his own. A girl who had presumably been as awkward as herself when Harry Morland had first met her. 'On the rebound,' Sybil hinted, 'from some naughtiness at university.' It was a pity darling Granny wouldn't be wheedled into saying more. Sybil and Aragon were, despite the rift of a generation, loving conspirators under the skin.

Aragon sighed dramatically and, sliding down in the leather seat, sniffed the expensive upholstery. Sabina's birthday present. Aragon grimaced, soft lips pursed under the scarlet gash in the whitened make-up which disguised the unsteady ego. She shut her eyes to the car's tasteful black fittings. Sod you, Sabina.

The Porsche nosed to a kerbside and Aragon leapt out, slamming the door. Striding off across the garish patchwork of the municipal flowerbed, she seemed totally unaware of the tut-tutting of Harrogate's more conventional pedestrians observing her crane-like figure cutting across the grass reservation. This week the stiffly gelled coxcomb was tipped with lime green.

Sabina revved the engine and the car slid into the traffic and pulled out to strike north. Eventually, too eager, she overshot the approach road and entered from the wrong end of the town.

Knaresborough seemed to have a winding High Street which snaked downhill towards the gorge. Sabina was early, the Porsche had eaten up the miles and there were at least forty minutes to spare. Parking looked difficult: probably market day. And crossing the traffic lights, Sabina found she had already exhausted the little town and was on the road back to Harrogate.

Abruptly swinging the steering-wheel, she swerved into a hotel forecourt. A small manor house, smug in its wistaria bower and confidently three star. Sabina uncoiled long legs, locked the car and entered.

It was very quiet. Faint scraping sounds and muted conversations drifting from the restaurant seemed to indicate breakfast was still in progress. The bar was closed, which was a pity as Dutch courage wouldn't come amiss. She exchanged a few words with the receptionist, an anxious body wrestling with computerized accounts. She agreed distractedly to allow the Porsche to remain on the forecourt until lunch-time.

Sabina ordered coffee and waited in the walled garden for it to arrive. The amber air hung warm as honey, stillness wrapped within the dappled enclosure as if time really had ceased to be of any importance.

Dredging her memory, she discovered in one moment of panic she could not assemble Geoffrey's features in her mind. The long fingers, especially his nails—his one vanity, shaped and scrupulously cared for—were clear. But Geoffrey's face was as if under water, the features shifting and blurring, first clearly in focus and then lost again like someone long dead. Poor Geoffrey.

Sabina shivered. Finishing a second cup, she realized she must have been daydreaming much longer than she realized. The sky had become overcast and clouds rolling in looked bilious, their edges saffron with the vanishing sunshine. Glancing at her watch she registered with dismay 9.45.

Stopped! Scrambling up, she shook the watch, holding it to her ear. In haste she scrabbled for coins and, leaving far too much, snatched her things and flew through the hotel and out on to the street.

Big drops now fell, splashing up at her legs as she ran. Pulling a headscarf from her pocket she ran on across the busy junction towards the ruined castle. He'd probably left by now.

As she burst into the teashop she cut a wild figure, filling the narrow doorway, gazing round the assortment of customers sheltering from the rain. Several faces looked up hopefully, momentarily hushed as a flicker of interest flared at the prospect of a newcomer.

She recognized him immediately. He rose, trapped at a corner table, his head brushing the low beams of the teashop, a hand raised to greet her. Geoffrey. How could she have imagined he would be different? In that split second of recognition the years slid away and Sabina relaxed, laughing aloud, pulling the scarf from her wet hair. She picked her way between the tables to take the place he had kept for her. Had always kept for her, she supposed.

But he *was* different. His hair was almost white.

He never knew what it was that dragged him deeper. That letter. It had been a mistake. He had deluded himself that his career was at stake, pretended to himself that work was the essence of the link between them. Geoffrey Tallent despaired of his inability scientifically to analyse the illogical power which drew him on, the emotion Sabina generated a mystery, an undefinable miracle which both exalted and repelled him. He had never meant to come and as he rose awkwardly to his feet in the ridiculous teashop he knew he was totally lost.

Was it really bitterness that had prompted him to put pen to paper, old wounds reopened at the sight of those people attending Swayne's funeral? Paying their respects. Respect? What right had Swayne to respect? But Geoffrey knew the real reason the moment she stepped into the tearoom. He had written to Sabina because at last he could trace her, could tempt her to see him again by holding up her old ambitions like a flattering mirror. How else could a broken man beguile a beautiful young woman?

Sabina and Geoffrey Tallent met almost daily after that first morning. Always in the same teashop where the manageress, a sentimental soul, took a proprietary interest. She saved the corner table until eleven every morning 'just in case'.

The good-looking man reminded her of that chap in the old black and white she'd seen on the telly. *Brief Encounter*, that was it. Not that the girl was anything like the one in the film. He was bigger too, broad across the shoulders like her Tommy. Loading trays with teapots and china in the back kitchen, she wondered about her new regulars. The Singing Kettle was very busy all summer, tourists flocking to the castle and then drifting down the river where there were pleasure boats and ice-cream vans. But late October was very quiet and speculating about the two of them passed the time . . .

They would have been appalled at the woman's fascination, faintly amused to be cast in such romantic roles. Knaresborough seemed an ideal place, not far from Fernside but definitely not the sort of town to attract any of Sybil's friends from the smarter shops and restaurants in Harrogate. The teashop was old. One large room with windows overlooking the ramparts, small oak tables set closely together and old watercolours of the gorge fading on the walls.

Sabina was surprised at Geoffrey's eager acquiescence in their frequent meetings. At first they spoke in whispers, filling in the gaps, tactfully omitting any reference to Harry Morland or Naomi Tallent. Once they lunched at the Singing Kettle but it was merely an excuse to stay on and the urgent need to bridge the intervening years drove away any appetite. They soon fell into a routine: coffee in the teashop, then a brisk walk skirting the church and market square to reach the hotel where Sabina parked the Porsche.

She had been diffident at first about admitting to such an expensive car. Geoffrey's frayed cuffs and worn tweed jacket were no mere trappings of the absent-minded professor. But he was genuinely delighted with the beautiful car, examining its formidable engine, exclaiming with enthusiasm at the precision of its engineering, the sheer excellence of the design. She drove and he relaxed beside her and the words flowed, his faint accent clipping the syllables with an indefinable glamour. He laughingly refused to allow her to see his own 'disgraceful old runabout'. 'Anyway,' he said, 'I would not permit you to smoke in my car, my darling. My little phobia.'

They were both tall, Sabina's stride matching his as they walked by the river. After the clocks went back and the afternoons grew shorter, the talk dwindled and they drove in warm silence exploring the neighbouring villages. It began to get cold.

One day, caught in a storm, they reluctantly entered the famous grotto. The Dropping Well. No longer a miracle to a generation less impressed with geological curiosities who, at the turn of a switch, could summon up all the wonders of the world in flickering television images. Sabina dragged Geoffrey forward.

'Just look at all this stuff!' In the gloom, hats, gloves and babies' clothing jostled with boots and household objects of all kinds suspended in the chemical flow and transformed into bizarre sculptures.

'A petrified draper's shop,' he said.

They wandered along marvelling at the jumble of souvenirs transfigured by the weird alchemy of the water.

He smiled grimly, avoiding her eye. 'Like me,' he said. 'Flesh and blood reduced to stone.'

The mysterious atmosphere of the cave prompted Sabina to touch on something she dared not mention until now. She tugged his sleeve, drawing him aside.

'Tell me, Geoffrey. How has it been since the hearing?

How is it you are able to get away in the middle of term?'

He shrugged and walked away, his voice echoing in the cavern, the damp chill entering his bones.

'Ah now, my own sweet love. There you have it. I had to sell the house, of course. Even I was not brazen enough to stay on after that. Naomi was destroyed,' he added with a sigh. 'But . . .'

He drew a hand across his mouth and then continued, addressing his remarks upwards towards the glimmering petrification which had in a few short years transformed very ordinary things into carvings, both beautiful and terrible in their magical mutations.

'My work continues, of course.'

'I'm glad of that. I was so afraid . . . Did you take it on where we left off?'

'It was difficult. Difficult?' he barked, his mouth twisting in irony. 'The University Council claimed much of my research material for their investigation. It took me years to make good. Kept me sane after you had abandoned me. But it can never be quite the same, can it?' He coughed and then continued in firmer tones, 'I haven't the resources, naturally. A friend at Leeds lets me use his lab on the quiet —I've been working with a research establishment part of the time. Not far from York. A charity. They let us have a cottage in the grounds on a short lease but we're leaving soon. At Christmas.'

'I'm so dreadfully sorry, Geoffrey. It was partly my fault and—'

He brushed her words aside. 'I have a room in Leeds which I use when I get the chance to work in a vacant lab there which a friend put me on to.'

'Are you still allowed access to the old lab?'

'Absolutely not! But it wasn't all wasted. The Institute asked the dean of the faculty of technology to investigate Mansell's allegations, "the academic aspects", as they put it.' The pain in his voice was barely discernible in the lethargic flow of words, as if the razor edges of the indictment

had smoothed in an endless analysis of the official termin-
ology.

'It should never have been raised.'

'I wouldn't go as far as that. Mistakes were made. Mansell
was behaving like a plaster saint but Foster wasn't vindictive. Nor were the other MSc students who jumped on the
bandwagon. It only gathered momentum once your brother
Francis became involved. Up to then it was all just inter-
departmental gossip.'

'Francis was over-protective of me. Roger should never
have talked to him at all. It all started as jealousy on Roger's
part, I think, professional spite, really. Not scientific integrity as they all made out.'

'Mansell never took up the formal procedure, you know.'
Geoffrey spun round, his eyes glittering. 'He threw the first
stone, pulled the University in to investigate and having
dragged my career, my entire reputation, through the mire,
never instituted the formal procedure. Gave me no chance
to clear my name, no opportunity to publish my paper. I've
applied for jobs abroad, of course. But I am still—' he
paused—'tainted.' His mouth twisted in an ugly grimace.
'It's worse for Naomi really. We can't leave and we can't
stay.' He turned aside, staring up at the ghostly souvenirs.
'I'm years behind with my work and crying out for computer time to check three years' backlog.' He strode away
from her.

She caught up. 'I might be able to help,' she whispered.
'Harry has the most up-to-date plant at Bracknell. If you
bring your stuff we could run through it together. I could
arrange it for you. What do you say?'

'Working together?' he rasped.

'We could put it all together again. I have a house in
London. I'm not going back to Hong Kong. I'll file the
research project with the appropriate body. Officially. We
could put everything right, Geoffrey. And I could prepare
my thesis for my PhD.' Her face was radiant. 'Please,
Geoffrey. Give me this chance. We could help each other.'

'Computer time?' he muttered. 'Are you mad?'

He grappled with the prospect and wonderingly he reached for her hand. 'There's a place in London where I could stay, a chap lent it to me while he's on sabbatical. I think I could swing it at Imperial if I could present some fresh data to back me up . . .' Her face swam before him, pale as stone in that terrible place.

'Let's go back to the hotel,' she said. 'I've booked a room.'

Later, in the soft light of the fire in their room, she marvelled at the smoothness of his face as he slept. As if all the anguish had drained away and taken years with it. Sabina ran her hand lightly along his thigh and peered at the jagged scar, barely healed and roughly drawn together with livid stitch marks. A climbing accident, he said. Tenderly she stroked the raised skin tissue and he opened his eyes.

'I've been dreaming,' he said.

CHAPTER 13

At Fernside next day the Porsche skidded into the drive in a swirl of gravel and Sabrina Morland jumped out, running through the house and straight upstairs to Sybil's pretty room. She was sitting in her usual chair, her back erect, bright as a kingfisher in an aquamarine silk blouse.

'Good morning, my dear.'

'Sybil! Were you all right? I hate leaving you overnight like that. I worry. Did Betty Carter give you my message?'

'She said you had called. Staying at Hexham, wasn't it? Burning the midnight oil with your old university friends, I suppose.' Sybil inclined her head, smiling wickedly, her lap filled with a cobweb of fine knitting.

Brushing the old lady's dry cheek with her lips, Sabina bent to peer into the coffee-pot on the tray at Sybil's elbow.

'Ugh. Cold.' Choosing a biscuit, she cheerfully flounced into the overblown roses of Sybil's sofa. Sybil put aside the knitting and chuckled to herself. Not at all like Sabina to bounce about like this, not her usual style at all. She wondered what the minx was up to, pleased to feel the windblown quality which had breezed in with her.

'I'll ask Carter to make some fresh. I would love some myself.' Sybil lifted a small intercom and spoke briefly to the housekeeper in the kitchen and, touching the corner of her mouth with a wisp of lacy handkerchief, cocked her head in that bird-like movement so exactly like Aragon's. 'And so?'

Sabina flushed, avoiding the sightless eyes which puckered with amusement.

'Before I forget, Harry's telephoning this evening. About eleven if that's not too late for you, darling.' Sabina paused before adding firmly, 'I'm thinking of taking up my research again. In England.'

Sybil's smile dissolved. So that was it. 'Won't Harry mind that?' The question put with grave politeness veiled an unspoken reproach.

'We've talked of it increasingly lately. Harry understands.'

'Perhaps Harry would prefer to settle down at last. You could live here, you know. It's high time I moved somewhere smaller, Carter is always nagging to be nearer the village. If you moved to Fernside I'm sure Harry would redirect his energies, be abroad less often. He's always loved this place,' Sybil said, wistfulness creeping in. 'A real home . . .'

'A baby, you mean.' Sabina's retort was flat, unemotional. 'Harry has Aragon. I'm not burning to duplicate her.'

Sybil flinched.

Mrs Carter came in, bringing with her an aroma of fresh coffee, her pace unruffled by the charged atmosphere. A right trio, she sighed. What with the new Mrs Morland squaring up to that saucy chit, Aragon and the old lady egging 'em on for her own entertainment. Ah well, blood's thicker'n water, she'd put her brass on the new madam coming off worst.

'Anything else, 'm?' Mrs Carter substituted fresh cups and, after a brief exchange with Sybil about the luncheon arrangements, stomped off, her heavy footfall gradually fading as she retreated downstairs.

Sabina poured fresh coffee and, fidgeting with gold hoops in her neat little ears, said nothing, wishing she had been less blunt with her mother-in-law.

'There isn't much to occupy you in Hong Kong, I imagine.' Sabina wondered if Sybil's even tone was ironical or was she being oversensitive?

'It's social enough,' she replied. 'Filling in one's time pleasantly is simple enough. But after five years of it with Harry travelling so much I'm running in ever decreasing circles.' Sabina laughed shortly and, stirring her coffee, ruefully added, 'You see how spoilt I've become, Sybil. A silly canary in a gilded cage. Bored and lonely.'

'A child would help, my dear. Babies bring such a lot of happiness with them, after all.'

'And then when it's old enough you pack it up labelled "Not Wanted on the Voyage" and send it home to school. Women much more accommodating than me, Sybil, get quite dotty when the children go back home. And then in the long summer holidays it's easier to stay in England for longer and longer periods where the children's friends are on hand and the weather's not impossibly humid. Husbands take a back seat and one thing leads to another. The exotic Orient isn't all fun and the climate can be really punishing. Sometimes, Sybil, I spend days in the flat cowering in the air-conditioning rather than break out. It hardly seems worth the sweat. Literally. A sort of *accidie* sets in.' She stretched her legs, flexing the toes as if to admire the pretty varnished nails, frowning at her feet as she searched for the right words. 'One gets dreadfully petulant seeing the same old faces. At the cricket club, playing tennis, sitting round the pool, cocktails. Not to mention the eternal traipsing round the shops buying dresses for more parties, more of the club circuit. It's all rather parochial, really.'

'Is there no chance for you to do your scientific work there? Couldn't Harry with all his contacts, arrange something worthwhile for you to do?' Sybil cast about in desperation. 'Hospital work?' she ventured at last.

Sabina shrugged and lit a cigarette, inhaling deeply, her frown etched even stronger. 'I hate moaning like this, Sybil. Harry's marvellous. Money no object. You know how impossibly generous he is. But—' she picked an invisible thread from her skirt as unshed tears glittered—'I've tried, Sybil. One day a week with the refugees, some charity work with a diplomatic crowd, wives, you know—all that sort of thing. But I've got a chance now, a last shot to pick up where I left off.' The urgency was unfeigned and as she began to elaborate the telephone jangled on Sybil's desk.

The old lady crossed the room, steps quick and light, only a hand tremor as she reached for the receiver disclosing her infirmity. Massaging her painful shoulder as she spoke, the forthright tone was as clear as ever.

'My darling Aragon. What a lovely surprise. I thought you said telephoning was old hat? Tomorrow? That will be wonderful. I've been playing your tapes.' She paused and then, 'And Rosie. Yes, my dear, of course I can work it. Perfectly well. Yes, yes. Ah well—' guardedly—'if you say so, darling. Sabina's here, would you—?' With deliberation she replaced the receiver and turned. 'That was Aragon, of course. She's coming home tomorrow and staying over. For five days until after the weekend. A Hallowe'en party in York, apparently. She asked if Carter could pick her up from Harrogate.'

Sabina grimaced, well aware of the grandmother's tactful editing of Aragon's response to any mention of her stepmother. She jumped up and stood at the window watching a chevron of wild geese in their noisy flight, and blew her nose.

Sybil settled back in her chair and took up her knitting.

'Carter took a message for you yesterday. From London.
A Miss Mackenzie wants you to ring her back. She said she
was your late brother's secretary. Something about a car.'

Sabina nodded, her back still to the room and murmured,
'Oh yes. I've had several letters. I asked Miss Mackenzie
to check with the executor about Francis's car. Nicholas
refuses to have anything to do with it. He seems to have
become astonishingly uncooperative since the funeral.'

She turned back to cross the room and stubbed out her
cigarette before resuming her seat opposite the old lady.
Perching on the edge of the sofa, her former gaiety quite
evaporated, Sabina spoke, her voice jarring in staccato
bursts.

'I need your advice, Sybil. About Francis's car. It's
nothing splendid but a perfectly adequate little runabout
and it's been in the police pound for weeks. Ever since he
died, as a matter of fact.' She coughed, clearing her throat.
'Nobody really wants it and legally it's rather a nuisance.
But the police are insisting that we remove it and in the
circumstances the solicitors agree.'

'May it not be sold?'

'Not really. Anyway, Nicholas is refusing to sell any of
Francis's things. The will was horribly complicated. You
see, half the estate, apart from some bequests, goes to
Nicholas and Sandy but is tied up in some sort of trust for
the boys. It's rather a slap in the face for Nicholas. He was
always in hot water with Francis over finances: not the most
accomplished manager on earth,' she admitted with a grin.
'But it puts Nick and Sandy in a bit of a quandary. They
had agreed to allow Francis to take over the boys' education,
you see. The final papers were signed only a short while
before he died, strangely enough.'

'I thought their mother was a kind of Trotskyite. Or is
that an old-fashioned word these days?'

'Mm. Sort of,' Sabina agreed. 'I was absolutely floored
when I heard about it. But I suppose principles fly out of
the window when one is faced with the education of two

bright little boys. Especially as Nick's so feckless and Sandy is constantly getting herself involved in one harebrained scheme after another. Though I gather the latest wacky notion—a sort of theatrical cooperative—is working out extremely well, so perhaps their luck's changed. The solicitor hinted to me that a lot of money had gone into it, so I hope Nick's got his sums right this time.'

'Can't he raise capital through the trust?'

'Hardly. Francis seemed determined to tie up everything so there was no question of the boys' inheritance being siphoned off before they came of age. Francis was tremendously proud of them. Because he had no children of his own, I suppose. He was a great traditionalist under all that silly transvestite nonsense. Oh dear, I'm so sorry, Sybil. It's not a nice thing to talk about. Forgive me.'

'I'm not totally ga-ga, my dear. I probably have more experience of naughtiness than you realize!' Sybil laughed in an easy, unaffected way and said, 'But how can I help?'

'Heavens, I've been rambling! To get back to Francis's car. I've agreed to keep it at Holland Park until Francis's affairs are finalized. The Chinese student who lives in the basement can collect it from the pound if the solicitor gives permission. But I was wondering. Do you think Aragon would like it? Ownership could be transferred, I'm sure, and I could get it re-insured for her. Harry has been so determined to give Aragon no access to a car until this Rick business is under the carpet because he insists the less mobility the girl has the less opportunity they have to meet. He's penniless and Aragon's allowance is strictly regulated. Harry's quite sure everything can be manipulated by finance,' she said with a grin. 'He's probably right.'

'He's only trying to protect the child, my dear. I know it looks parsimonious,' Sybil said, 'but we both understand his motives. If Aragon had not been pushed aside after Lola left him I dare say things would be a lot smoother now.'

'I feel beastly clamping down on her as I've been doing. Harry's safely out of range, it's easy for him to lay down rules at a distance. I thought Francis's car would be nice for her now she seems settled in Glasgow. She would be able to pop down to see you more often. Especially,' she prompted, 'if I'm going back to London. I'd have to put in a great deal of work before I could even approach another lab.'

'She's certainly longing for a little bit of independence. Carter gets very cross lending Aragon the Mini so often. I only discovered yesterday how many times the little minx had wheedled Carter into allowing her and Mary to borrow it. Your idea might be safer than Aragon borrowing strange vehicles from other people. She has wonderful powers of persuasion.' Just like Lola was the thought that flashed through Sybil's mind. 'If you wish, I'll speak to Harry about it when he telephones tonight, Sabina.'

'Would you, Sybil?' Sabina smiled, leaning across to hug her. 'You are an absolute angel. I only hope Aragon doesn't think it a miserable jalopy compared with my Porsche.'

'Tosh! Aragon has her faults and I know I gloss over most of them, but envy isn't in her. She behaves disgracefully most of the time, you don't need me to remind you of that, but she's only greedy for affection. Presumably this Rick person is kind to her and she exaggerates the whole thing. Aragon was sent away to school when she was only eight years old, my dear. Tragic. But it was the only thing Harry could do after he and Lola parted. Aragon's very inexperienced—all that black leather and eye paint Rosie goes on about is just camouflage, of course. And this artist fellow is just the sort of buccaneer to catch a young girl's fancy.'

'At least she seems to be making a lot of new friends at college.'

'Absolutely. Out of sight, out of mind. From these tapes she's been sending it sounds as if she's having the time of her life. Young people just like herself. It was very clever of you, Sabina darling, to suggest a drama course. Rosie thinks Aragon's a real "It Girl" of course.'

'Rosie Peach. Isn't that an incredible name?'

Touching Sybil's shoulder, Sabina made her excuses before slipping downstairs to telephone Miss Mackenzie.

She got through straight away and they chatted about this and that—the weather, the increasingly early appearance of Christmas cards, the awful traffic—before finalizing arrangements for Tan Yau Hang to go to the police pound to retrieve Francis's car. She spelt out his name and confirmed the details.

'The police already have a set of keys from the mews house, car keys, I mean,' said Miss Mackenzie. 'An Inspector Arnott asked the constable at the pound to try them on the Renault, I can't think why. It seems a trifle bureaucratic, don't you agree? Of course, everything's in order and it seems they had to shunt the car around because it has been there so long. Mr Yau Hang will have no problem. They're anxious to get rid of it.'

'Is he calling at the chambers for the documentation authorizing its release?'

'Set your mind at rest, Mrs Morland. It's all arranged, everything is absolutely righty-ho.'

Sabina stifled a giggle. 'Thank you so much, Miss Mackenzie. I'm only sorry there's been so much extra work for you since Mr Swayne's accident—had my mother-in-law not suffered this fall I could have been on hand in London to deal with things without troubling you.'

A sigh at the other end reached Sabina's ear like a rolling wave at high tide. 'Oh, Mrs Morland, I know exactly how it is. It never rains but it pours. Poor, poor Mr Swayne. Tragic. We miss him so very much.'

'How kind you are, Miss Mackenzie. We must meet when I'm next in town, perhaps a small memento . . .' Sabina floundered, 'After so many years' devoted service.'

Miss Mackenzie's wordless sympathy oozed along the telephone line and then, as if an allotted time for sentiment had expired, she prattled on in her normal high-pitched tone.

'By the by, Mrs Morland, that other small matter you asked me to deal with. Mr Swayne's cleaner, Mrs de Cassis. The cheque was returned.'

'Returned?'

'I'm afraid so. Her husband sent it back.'

Miss Mackenzie lowered her voice. 'Rather a rude letter,' she whispered. 'But you know how it is with that sort of person.'

'Never mind,' Sabina said with resignation, 'I'll go to see her myself. There must be some sort of misunderstanding.'

'Please, Mrs Morland, don't do that!' Miss Mackenzie positively squeaked in her agitation.

'You see,' she confided, 'Mrs de Cassis is dead, Mrs Morland. The poor woman was run down just outside her house. In Battersea. A hit-and-run driver in the dark only ten days ago. She hadn't been out in daylight since—well, you know. After finding the body she suffered from some sort of phobia about going out. I tried to telephone, to offer condolences on your behalf, but the husband was extremely abusive. Blames it all on poor Mr Swayne. Can you believe it?'

And Fear, that fish of the dark waters, swam in Sabina's veins. 'I can, Miss Mackenzie. Indeed I can.'

CHAPTER 14

Ralph Arnott was exhilarated by the flight to Guernsey. Peg had always shied off flying without actually admitting to any fear and as he was no sunseeker himself they had been content to take their holidays on the South Coast. But the little aeroplane was something all right.

Arnott strained at the porthole to catch a bird's-eye view as the plane came in to land, the toytown houses and white beaches sparkling in the October sunshine laid out like playthings for his entertainment. As he lumbered down the steps on to the tarmac the champagne air was almost like a breath of spring. By gum, he should have coaxed Peg to try this. And now it was all too late . . . His pleasure collapsed like a pricked balloon.

He had chosen a hotel overlooking the harbour. The room was impressive with solid comfort: polished surfaces, fresh flowers and a TV and bar-fridge discreetly built into a screened-off alcove. He thrust aside any lingering regrets and stood by the window taking in the view, boats catching the last of the sunny days before winter gales closed in. He was lucky to be here out of season and guessed he would otherwise never have secured a booking. Not that he would have preferred it, the heat got him down. A bit of blustery weather livens you up, he thought. The prospect of all that clean air prompted him to pull out a packet of Marlboro. Arnott had abandoned the cigarette machine. For a few days, at least, he would enjoy a decent smoke.

He unpacked, stowing his gear in the handsome chest of drawers, laying his old-fashioned binoculars beside the camera on the bed. He made a careful reconnaissance of all the paraphernalia in the bathroom and to his horror heard himself beginning to laugh out loud. 'Bloody verbena foam bath gel and a shower cap!' Still smiling, he took himself down to the bar.

Before leaving London Arnott had spent many days poring over Judy's notebooks and drawing up his plan of campaign. An afternoon at the police pound tapping every nut and bolt on Swayne's car drew a blank and for the life of him Arnott couldn't begin to understand what troubled him about it. He had also acquired copies of the will and the educational trust Swayne had settled on his nephews. And to the extent of his reduced powers of inquiry Arnott investigated Nicholas and Sandra Swayne. All kosher, a bit suspect on the finance side but nothing to put your finger on.

He even wasted several days looking into the electronic empire of Harry Morland and persuaded Judy Pullen to suss out any financial gossip lurking in the Fraud Squad files. Clean as a whistle. Tramping round the ships' chandlers had produced the only solid piece of new evidence: the rope round Swayne's neck was, in fact, a special type used exclusively for climbing. Well, well, well . . .

When Arnott received a call from Judy with the breathless news of the death of Pamina de Cassis he knew time was running out. To chase up his only other lead he must fly to Guernsey before the Mansells sailed away. Nothing like a world cruise for dodging awkward questions.

After a substantial lunch Arnott picked up his binoculars and took a stroll by the harbour. The sky was uniformly pale like the subtle wash of a faded watercolour. In his Harris tweed jacket and old-fashioned flannels the ex-detective-inspector blended with the thin crowd of holidaymakers taking a final break before the winter closed in. Every ten yards or so he stopped and, peering through the binoculars, mentally noted the disposition of the yachts. The names ran like magic: *Hippocanthus. Fledgling. Zephyr. Spindrift. Mirabel.*

Locating Roger Mansell's new yacht was easy. Thirty-five feet long, a steel hull and built for speed and comfort. It was moored at the quayside. It looked new to his inexperienced eye but workmen were still on board, additional navigational equipment in the process of being installed.

Arnott's comfortable figure and homely accent diffused any suspicion and the men working on deck were easily drawn into conversation. He joined them for a beer at opening time. Arnott's affability was not assumed. The busman's holiday aspect of the jaunt had blunted the professional hard edge and a long-dormant love of the sea and its craft filled like a spinnaker before the wind, blowing away the dust of the city.

In the course of a pint or two Arnott learned a good deal about the astronomical cost of fitting out a new boat like Mansell's, the final eye-opener being the name in the process of registration. Not *Seraphina II*—he would have lost his money on that all right—but *Sabina*. His bluff cheerfulness froze as this was casually mentioned and he listened in silence as the men made bawdy reference to the owner's curvaceous wife after whom they had wrongly assumed the ketch was named. Arnott's brows jutted fierce as a terrier's as he sipped his ale, remembering that other innocent casualty of the Swayne affair. Pamina. No one would ever call a boat after her.

He claimed an old acquaintance with Roger Mansell. Informality shattered, the electricians eyed the Yorkshireman with undisguised suspicion. Reluctantly, the foreman produced the owner's telephone number and, downing their beer, the gang nipped back on board smartish. Arnott reckoned he would get nothing more from that quarter.

He sauntered back to the hotel and stretched out on the bed, the light dwindling now to a dull twilight, filling the warm room with sepia shadows. He dozed off, enfolded in the 'luxe' of a satin eiderdown.

He awoke with a start. It was quite dark. Fumbling for his watch, Arnott discovered he had, in fact, slept for barely half an hour. 'Time I shook myself,' he grumbled and decided to unravel the intricacies of the brass knobs in the fancy shower cubicle. After a steamy confrontation and a lick with his newfangled electric razor Arnott emerged as red as his lunch-time lobster. Dressing in his one dark suit, he sat on the bed to telephone Roger Mansell.

The response was amiable. Yes, of course he remembered the inspector. No problem. What about a drink? At the flat. At seven?

Arnott lit a cigarette and sat in the window-seat watching the lights bobbing on the dark water, the quay still busy with strollers, their pace hurried now, the evening hours firmly apportioned.

His situation on the island was invidious. Having brusquely introduced himself on the telephone simply as 'Arnott', Roger Mansell's instant recall of the craggy police inspector saved a lot of problems. But Arnott was keenly aware of the need for caution, one tactless word could expose the whole charade and see all his weeks of patient sifting laid open to official inquiry. He had his police pension to consider, after all was said and done.

For the hundredth time Arnott cursed his handling of the Swayne case, stupefied by the crass arrogance which had pitched him into early retirement. Feeling like a man in a whirlpool, he dared not look beyond the desperate need to feel solid ground under his feet again. Until he had extracted himself from the morass of regrets, taking up his life again —albeit a meagre existence with neither job nor wife— would be impossible.

Roger Mansell's flat overlooked the harbour on higher ground beyond the hotel with a view of the offshore islands of Herm, Jethou and Sark. His wife opened the door, a pretty girl in jeans, younger than Arnott expected, with silky blonde hair caught up in a ponytail, her smile direct and unaffected. Arnott had knocked on hundreds of doors in his time and had become used to the guarded response, presumably in the same category as the welcome extended to a visiting priest.

She drew Arnott into the sitting area of a large room, sparsely furnished, the sculptured shapes of huge contemporary sofas marooned on an expanse of polished floorboards. The only illumination was from a powerful halogen lamp poised over a chart table. The table dominated the room, its surface littered with maps, books held open with brass weights and an untidy scattering of scale drawings of unidentifiable pieces of machinery.

The hulking outline of Roger Mansell rose from a chair placed between the table and the black window-glass which Arnott assumed commanded a daytime panoramic view. Moving silently on bare feet between the gigantic pieces of furniture, Mansell swept off gold half-moon spectacles and strode towards Arnott, holding out his hand in greeting. Arnott braced himself for a hearty grasp, glad now he had changed from his flannel trousers, the formality of his business suit lending an official air to the visit.

Mansell's wife re-entered with a tray of drinks and placed it on a side table, helping herself to wine before curling up in the corner of one of the enormous sofas. Her pansy-soft eyes regarded the two men with interest and, making no effort to join in, she perched on the edge of their conversation, totally at ease.

Arnott and Mansell had met only once before and the younger man was forced to adjust his former impression. Away from his satellite police back-up Arnott struck him as a more perceptive investigator, less circumscribed by hackneyed lines of official procedure. Used to making rapid personal assessments and analysing scientific evidence, Roger Mansell found himself revising his memory of 'Inspector Plod'. Perhaps the sea air had blown away prejudices on both sides.

Within a few minutes they had cut through the conversational gambits and were probing the edges of their mutual festering wound: Francis Swayne.

Mansell said: 'I'm surprised the CID is still interested. Nothing new since the inquest, I take it?'

Shaking his head, Arnott accepted a whisky and water and after one careful sip relaxed in the embrace of Mansell's all-enveloping upholstery.

'Not a thing. Quiet as the grave, you might say.'

'Then why Guernsey?' Mansell eyed the other keenly.

'Another matter entirely. But seeing I was coming here anyway two birds with one stone's always good policy. And the hotel's expensive,' he added with his foxy grin as if he had a joke up his sleeve.

Mansell laughed. 'Glad to hear the cost of red tape's being accounted for at last. Is it the unexplained bomb in Swayne's kitchen that's blocking the files?'

'Partly,' Arnott agreed. 'But that problem's in the Special Branch folder, you might say. Very funny bunch. They don't take kindly to flat-footed coppers paddling in political waters.'

'Ah yes. I met one of them at the funeral. Urquart, was it? No, Erskine. Erskine,' he repeated thoughtfully. 'Doesn't give a lot away, does he?'

'Now you mention it, he did put a few things my way once.'

Arnott quickly passed on, anxious not to be drawn into revealing the ragged edges of the original inquiry. 'The missing cash still bothers us, for one thing. £5000 drawn in the afternoon before Swayne dies on a day when almost every minute was accounted for. And yet all that money, a considerable package, not the sort of thing to slip in a back pocket, vanishes. All brushed under the carpet without so much as a complaint from the executors of the estate.'

'Why not let sleeping dogs lie, Inspector?' The quiet voice of Mansell's wife slid into the conversation, startling Arnott who had almost forgotten the still presence of Fiona Mansell curled up in the shadows.

'Funny thing, Mrs Mansell. Tiptoeing round sleeping dogs is no recipe for a quiet life. One false move: the dog bites! Oh no, a slumbering beast's not man's best friend if you ask me.'

'The Swaynes are comfortably off,' she lazily persisted. 'And if they're not pressing for results . . .'

She shrugged, a simple childish jerk of the shoulders, infinitely appealing. 'Perhaps it sounds a lot of money to you and me but £5000 doesn't buy much these days. A postage-stamp size bite of van Gogh, a nibble at a race-horse . . .'

'A few nuts and bolts in that beautiful new boat of yours,' Arnott added, a steely glint in the hooded eyes.

'You a sailing enthusiast, Inspector?' Mansell smoothly deflected the innuendo and rose, inviting Arnott to enter the harsh searchlight poised over the chart table. 'These may interest you.'

Arnott stood to one side, sipping his whisky and politely

heard out Mansell's ecstatic description of their proposed world cruise.

'Five years, you say?'

'A voyage of discovery.'

Arnott's 'very nice' sounded positively prim.

'Was it ever discovered who set the fire on board *Seraphina*?' he innocently tacked on.

'How very clever of you to remember the name, Inspector. Beautiful boat,' Mansell said, a note of genuine regret clouding his fervour. 'No. Very simple little bit of anarchy. Paraffin rags, a match in the dark. Why *Seraphina*? That's the only mystery. The method was primitive, the perpetrator presumably some arch-vandal wanting a private pyrotechnic display.'

'The insurance people paid up?'

'Look here, Arnott, is marine insurance your line or missing fivers?' Mansell was rattled, pinning the Inspector in narrow focus above the gold-rimmed glasses.

'Pardon me, idle curiosity got the better of me. My apologies.' Arnott swiftly withdrew, fingers singed, and switched his questioning, aware of the unwinking regard of the woman on the sofa. Resuming a slightly baffled air, he looked across at Mansell who, unable to drag himself away from the fascinating charts, had adjusted his spectacles to jot figures in the margin of a page of technical drawings.

Arnott continued, 'In my notes I see you actually saw some sort of transaction take place on the night of Mr Swayne's accident?'

A choking giggle from Fiona Mansell was quickly suppressed. 'I'm so sorry,' she spluttered, 'but it was the way you said it. "Accident". "Transaction"!' Breaking into hopeless laughter, she untangled her legs and fled the room.

Mansell shook his head apologetically. 'You're referring to the little pantomime at the Savoy when we saw Francis with that King's Road kook with the multi-colour hair-do?'

'My colleague, Sergeant Pullen, reminded me of it. You discussed it at the funeral, it seems.'

'Not knowing she was on duty or even a policewoman! You're right. Well, there's not much to tell, as a matter of fact. Fiona's more observant than me, she could probably give you a more detailed description, but we have picked it over since then, of course. Neither of us knew the girl. Francis made no attempt to introduce us and if it was a "transaction", as you put it, the packet she snatched up from the table might, I suppose, have been the missing cash.'

'But Swayne didn't stop her?'

'Not a bit. They'd obviously been having a little ding-dong, the atmosphere was tense to say the least. But she didn't steal the envelope off the table. Something was clearly understood between them though she may have been wrangling for a better deal. But—' Mansell opened his ham-like hands in a gesture of bewilderment—'It's all guesswork, isn't it? Francis may have been settling up with his travel agent for all we know.' Roger drifted to the window and gazed into the night, now pricked with stars.

Arnott shot a glance of polite disbelief across the pool of darkness which lay between them and pressed on.

'To paint in the background for me, sir, I wonder if you could tell me a bit about the sister, Mrs Morland. You knew her at university, I understand. That was how you were first introduced to Francis Swayne. Am I right?'

'Sabina. Oh yes, of course.' Mansell slid back behind the chart table and seated himself, absent-mindedly shuffling a sheaf of loose papers. 'Great girl, a superb brain absolutely wasted.' He raised his head and Arnott saw the tired lines etching the eyes, creases running from the nose to the corners of the mouth belying the boyish haircut and healthy tan. An underlying weariness was fraying the firm outline Mansell carefully presented to the world.

'Sabina was the fourth leg of a very stable research structure at university. The director of the lab was a man called Professor Tallent and a brilliant biochemist called Fisher made up the team including Sabina and myself.

Sabina was the junior. She was concocting a thesis for her
PhD, but to be honest her aptitude for pure research was
inspirational. It was assumed she had an academic career
mapped out. Fisher got the hunches, I was the practical
chap who made the cogs fit together and the professor led
the team.'

'Then Sabina fell for Harry Morland and threw it all up
for wedding bells,' Arnott grunted.

Roger Mansell stared across the table in bewilderment
and then, with a howl of derision, burst into laughter.

'You romantic soul!' he gasped. 'How wrong can you be!'
Drawing a thick forefinger across his lips, Roger composed
himself to continue.

'The stuff we were on was red hot but the grants were
drying up. Professor Tallent was like a demon, working day
and night, pushing and pulling, dragging the team through
the procedures, trying to beat the clock. I'm an egocentric
sod by nature, flogging my balls off for a self-styled genius
is not my style, especially when we were doing all the
donkey-work and Tallent was likely to reap the rewards.
Psyched himself up for a Nobel prize at the very least.'
Mansell paused and the massive head set deeper into his
shoulders. Suddenly he chuckled.

'His name wasn't even Tallent. It was something unpronounceable beginning with Sz. He was slipped out as a kid
during the Hungarian rising in 'fifty-six and adopted by an
elderly couple in Oxford. He got scholarships and after a
shining degree was set fair for a brilliant career, publishing
papers in every scientific rag he could lay his hands on,
banging the big gong for British research. A one-man brain
drain in reverse!' he said bitterly. 'Our refugee became more
English than the Prince of Wales—even took to wearing
hand-knitted woolly socks like the public school louts—
you'd think he'd been here since 1066! The funny thing was
that it was the very foreignness he was trying to paste over
that Sabina found so mesmerizing. The "odd man out"
effect: the slight edge to his vowels, the perfect grammar, a

dead give-away if your mother tongue isn't English. And
that passionate zeal of his, pure Slav.'

'Were you yourself attracted to Sabina Swayne as she
then was?'

'Absolutely fascinated. She wasn't pretty. Not like Fiona,
for instance. She'd been brought up by Big Brother and
didn't seem to have grasped any feminine wiles in those
days. But there was a ruthless innocence about her which
I must admit set the old hormones tingling. Sabina had a
natural flair for research and was dazzled by the mysterious
professor. He being "older" struck me as half the appeal.
Unfair, I thought at the time. Poor old Sabina's bowled over
by father figures, presumably that's where Harry Morland
scored.'

Arnott vaguely registered the soft closing of a door but
sat still, anxious not to disturb Mansell's narrative.

'Anyway, Sabina and I saw a good bit of each other after
hours, mostly working late on Tallent's projects and Tallent
was cutting corners willy-nilly to get results. The other
chap, Dr Fisher, got fed up with all the unscientific methods
and was unimpressed by Tallent's leadership. Then Fisher
found out that Tallent was inventing data. Wow! A junior
who has the guts to point out that his professor has invented
a series of experiments is shooting himself in the foot.
Academic fraud is no joke and proving it damages everyone
involved. Guilty or innocent. Fisher spoke to Sabina about
it but she wouldn't hear a word against Tallent. Then he
tackled me. We spent a whole weekend checking raw data
in notebooks on which Tallent had based his findings.'
Mansell scratched his head, hunching over the table as if
the scattered papers held a key to the painful episode.

'We even tried to reproduce the results, setting up secret
experiments in another lab. As soon as we picked up one
piece of evidence a whole lot of dependent data collapsed,
like spillikins. Scientific work is based on trust, people accept
published papers as gospel and adjust their own research
accordingly. If you don't play fair, scientists all over the

world are wasting time exploring with dicky maps as you might say.'

Mansell walked over to the drinks tray and refilled his glass, pondeirng the enormity of his disclosure. Arnott stiffened, waiting, beginning to discern the cord which bound these people together.

At last, raising his glass in acknowledgement of the other's presence, Mansell said:

'To cut a long story short, we asked the University Council to hold an official inquiry. You see, the ultimate blow to Fisher was that Geoffrey Tallent had already published under his own name great chunks of our stuff that was OK along with his own duff bits. Fisher was offered a hearing to investigate serious allegations of plagiarism but it was bungled. Even if the council agreed with us, any indictment of academic fraudulence means the whole system's gone off. Where does it end? The sanctity of pure research smelling like old kippers!'

Mansell sagged in his seat, frowning into his glass, the shadows under his eyes etched cruelly in the uncompromising lighting of the room.

His voice rumbled on. 'The pressure on the lab director to supervise PhD students to produce their own research runs parallel to his own need to make a name for himself. The more papers Tallent published, the greater his chance of promotion and prestige. The more spectacular the results, the higher the possibility of attracting grants. University research is as dirty a game as the commercial variety, Arnott. Everyone screaming for results and scientific reputations stand or fall on team effort.'

'And how did this affect Sabina Swayne?'

'Badly. She was attracted by the glamour of Tallent's monstrous ambition and I suspect he was impressed with the sheer Englishness of her background. But I very much doubt whether either of them had the heart for real passion. When Fred Fisher and I tried to get an official hearing for our complaints and the whole thing dragged on for months

I rather lost interest and in fact had practically landed a job in the States. But Fisher hung on and was eventually told to make use of the standard grievance procedure, which would have smoothed it out without too much aggro except that at this crucial point Francis got to hear of it.'

Roger Mansell paused, sifting this early picture of his sailing chum into focus, wondering why he had bothered to spill all this to a nondescript old copper like Arnott. He shrugged. He might as well finish now.

'Francis was always over-protective of Sabina and probably got wind of Tallent putting his grubby fingers up her skirt, so the plagiarism accusation came in handy. He got into a noisy legal huff and puff with the university, throwing the whole scandal into the open. It even made a story in the national press! I was called in to explain myself, while little Sabina was whisked off to Hong Kong by Francis and escaped the whole dirty business. Ironic, because nothing would ever have come to light if Francis hadn't got on his high horse and started proclaiming about "truth and science", "integrity" and "professional morals".

'So Sabina never went back to science?'

'Sabina's appetite for sexy older men had been whetted by Tallent and she was tempted with Harry Morland. As far as I know, she's never picked up a test-tube since.'

'And you? Your connection with the Swaynes?'

'I found it too hot after all that muckraking and had to abandon pure research. Fred Fisher too, which seemed pretty unfair as his work was filched by Tallent and he was the only really dedicated party in the whole team who was also honest. A rare combination. I guessed what Tallent was up to but was busy rowing my own canoe and Sabina would see no fault in the saintly professor even if she'd fallen over it. My job offer in America was discreetly withdrawn and Fisher gave up and joined some research unit at Cambridge. After cooling his head I think poor old Francis felt a bit guilty about his part in exposing the fraud, whisking Sabina out of range when the shit hit the fan and leaving

Fisher and me to catch all the dirt. And Tallent, of course. God knows what happened to him. Not to mention his deadly wife, nagging Naomi. No wonder the poor bugger gave his heart and soul to Science. I've never come across a more poisonous old bag than Naomi Tallent.'

'In what way?'

'The biggest snob in creation. Daughter of a rector of one of the Irish universities.' Roger laughed, slapping his hand on the chart table with a thud. 'Can you beat it? Naomi marries a Hungarian refugee with an unpronounceable name and is clawing and fawning her way up the university ladder as if poor old Geoffrey was sure to end up Chancellor!'

The door slammed and a burst of sea air surged into the room, closely followed by Fiona Mansell hugging a deliciously steamy parcel. She paused in the doorway, her cheeks flushed, eyes sparkling.

'I slipped out while you were going over all that boring old stuff. Fish and chips. Fancy an instant nosh, Inspector?'

Arnott rose awkwardly, clutching his notebook and hastily apologized. He edged to the door.

'I've intruded too long on your hospitality,' he said stiffly. 'I had no idea—'

'Nonsense,' Mansell interrupted, all smiles. 'Do stay.'

After a few half-hearted phrases Arnott gladly put aside his cramped notes and accepted a refill from the tray of drinks at Roger's elbow.

'Just one more thing,' he said. 'Your sailing colleague, Francis Swayne. Did he go in for mountaineering as well?'

'Francis?' Roger hooted with laughter. 'You're right off beam there, Arnott. Francis was terminally lazy. He wouldn't climb a flight of stairs if he could help it.'

In the course of a cheerfully informal fish supper round the ubiquitous chart table, Arnott plucked up courage to question the naming of the Mansells' boat.

Fiona piped up, totally unaffected by what seemed to Arnott a tactless choice.

'*Sabina?* Mm. Curious. But Roger and I were both very fond of poor old Fan.' She giggled. 'Francis Swayne to you. He'd been awfully kind and helped Roger set up the business after the university fiasco.' She shook a finger at Arnott. '*Not* what you're thinking! Francis was generous with legal advice. Words came cheap but he wasn't a man to throw his money about. He did introduce us to the right people and opened up valuable commercial contacts. We did very well out of it.'

'The sailing arrangement was something else,' Mansell chipped in. 'Pure friendship which grew out of his initial kindness in helping to set up the firm. He liked boats but didn't want the hassle of keeping one himself. He offered to subsidise *Seraphina* in a fairly substantial way and in return he shared the fun whenever he felt like it.'

'And left you the cottage.'

'Mm.' Fiona looked pensive. 'That was real kindness. A wonderful surprise. I'd helped Francis furnish and decorate the cottage and he liked to booze there with chums after a day's sport. But leaving the cottage to us was a touch of pure sweetness.'

'He probably enjoyed sharing it with sailing friends and didn't fancy it ending up with strangers. You can get sentimental about a house,' Arnott admitted. 'It becomes a millstone round your neck.'

'He was very fond of it,' Fiona said. 'And it's a base in England for us while we're abroad.'

'A home to come back to,' Arnott mused. 'I'm thinking of buying a cottage myself when I retire. But a long way from here. In the north—it's cheaper. But naming the boat *Sabina*,' he repeated with grave politeness. 'I still don't understand.'

'Well, we got superstitious about another *Seraphina* after the fire and we couldn't call it *Fan*, especially after his dreadful drag queen exit. So we settled for his sister's name.'

'Francis would have chosen it himself,' Roger said. 'He sometimes mentioned it when he vaguely thought of owning his own boat and Fiona and I couldn't agree on any other name. Anyway, anything called *Sabina* couldn't sink, could it? Sabina of the beautiful steel grace lines.' His amusement was barbed.

An hour later Arnott picked his way unsteadily down the hill and back to the hotel. The walk cleared his head. After changing into pyjamas he poured himself a nightcap and settled down to summarize Roger Mansell's story from the jottings in his notebook.

The Mansells were an attractive team, intelligent, humorous and apparently above board. But he'd discovered the new yacht could not be moored in English waters without a tax penalty, which seemed a funny way for a man well known in British yachting circles to skulk away. Guernsey was thickly populated with the wealthy only too anxious to keep funds out of the UK, but they didn't seem like Mansell's crowd.

There was no way he could investigate the Mansells' financial standing without stirring up a hornet's nest. Why not accept them at face value? An attractive couple with a few years to spare from the treadmill of making a living, catching a dream by the tail and sailing the world? How could they be involved with the late Francis Swayne's murder?

And Pamina de Cassis. Did she have some dangerous knowledge? Was her 'breakdown' delayed shock or was she hiding evidence. And if she was hiding evidence was it worth killing her for? Arnott sighed, infinitely depressed.

Fictional detectives never missed clues, misinterpreted evidence, made a balls of an investigation the way he had done. In books everything led to a smooth conclusion, the private eye was never a fumbling old fool like himself.

Abruptly, his dour reflections were rudely jangled by the telephone. Anxious considerations of his off-limit investigation having been discovered flew in urgent sequence through his mind. Gingerly, he picked up the receiver and grunted into it. It was Roger Mansell.

'Arnott! Quick, man! Switch on the telly. First channel. The late night chat show. It's the girl. The one I saw with Francis the night he died. The one who grabbed the money.'

'We've only got the word of you and Mrs Mansell that this mystery woman exists at all, sir. And nobody could prove what was in the package.'

'For Christ's sake, Arnott! Just do as I say. You'll miss it.'

Arnott rose and peered at the dials of the hotel's TV. He switched on. Featured on the screen with the urbane interviewer was a young woman with a peroxide crop and chandelier earrings. With a jolt Arnott recognized the man sitting beside her. Nicholas Swayne.

'Bloody 'ell,' he breathed. Reaching for the phone, he spoke to Mansell without taking his eyes from the show. 'Are you sure?' he croaked.

'Absolutely certain. Of all the sly buggers! The woman Francis was paying off was his own sister-in-law. Sandra Sullivan.'

'Does your wife recognize her? You said it was a punky female in black leather with coloured hair, blue and green or something,' he added doubtfully.

Fiona must have grabbed the receiver as Arnott heard her light voice on the line. 'Listen, Mr Inspector. That's the girl all right. See her left hand? The little finger's missing. I remember it distinctly, it made me shudder at the time. It's the same woman, there's no mistake about it.' She passed the phone back to Roger and the two men talked urgently until the end of the interview.

It was publicizing the latest production of Nicholas Farrow's company on the eve of their departure to Australia. He said very little, leaving his wife to enthuse about their fringe theatre successes but, Arnott swiftly acknowledged, they were persuasive all right, more than a match for the host of the show. But Arnott would put his bottom dollar on the nasty little habit Nicky hadn't been able to kick. And it wasn't dressing up in women's clothing.

A persistent bell was buzzing in Arnott's subconscious. Sandra Sullivan. Sandy. Not an actress. No. Arnott flicked through the annotated file in his briefcase and with a grunt of satisfaction pinpointed the elusive paragraph.

Sandra Sullivan. Politically left-wing. Involved with a Trotskyite theatrical crowd. Acts in own company. Wizard with stage lighting. Trained abroad specializing in stage management and design. Two children by Nicholas Farrow, actor.

A clever little lady like that would have no trouble concocting a bomb for her brother-in-law's kitchen. Looked the sort to harbour a grudge and there was always the prospect of inheriting the money. Presumably she knew nothing about the new will, the restrictions on Nicholas's spending . . . A technically-minded woman wouldn't balk at setting fire to a boat come to that. For spite? She wouldn't be the only one to assume Roger Mansell was owner in name only. The Mansells were notoriously skint. An expensive racing craft like *Seraphina* could well be assumed to be secretly the property of a well-heeled barrister with untaxed income to splash about on a luxury sport.

Arnott lit another cigarette and lay on the lilac eiderdown watching the smoke curl up to the ceiling. The corners of his mouth twitched in grim satisfaction. Not beat yet, old son, he cheered himself. Not by a long chalk.

CHAPTER 15

The last day of October threw aside all concessions to autumn. Wind and rain battered the old house, stripping the last scarlet leaves of the Virginia creeper from the walls.

A consignment of books was delivered from Oxford and Sabina Morland locked herself away in the turret room to wrestle with a word-processing machine on loan from Harry's head office. Fernside suited her mood. The tempo was subdued and none of the old crowd bothered her in

Yorkshire. Sybil had taken on a new lease of life since her accident, relishing the attention of regular visitors from the village, holding court in her elegant sitting-room upstairs and boasting of her clever daughter-in-law. Sabina's collaboration with Geoffrey Tallent was already mapped out and a detailed exploration of his solitary research had been set up at his temporary laboratory in Leeds.

Even the imminent return of Aragon for Hallowe'en could not spoil Sabina's euphoria and Sybil's unspoken foreboding proved unfounded. Aragon burst from the hire car soon after three and bounded straight upstairs. Either the wintry squall had dampened her style or the drama course mopped up the pent-up aggression. The cockatoo's hair-do had subsided to a natural outline and fair skin now shone, unmasked, moist from the rain, the geisha make-up abandoned. The funny black garments were still there but without the freakish paint, the leggings and shaggy purple cloak merely looked frivolous.

Aragon hugged her grandmother with gusto, their mutual delight reduced to wordless satisfaction leavened with hoots of laughter. Mrs Carter hovered in the doorway smiling despite herself, unwilling to join the charmed circle which forgave their 'very own little gypsy' all the tears she had caused one way and another. Turning away to fetch tea and sandwiches, she bumped into Sabina. Alert to every footfall, Sybil's voice fluted across the room.

'Sabina, my dear. Aragon's home, fresh as a bunch of violets.' The old lady patted the seat beside her. 'I've asked Carter to make a snack, won't you stay for a few minutes? You had nothing for lunch, I know.'

Reaching out for Aragon's cold fingers, she squeezed them and went on to explain. 'Sabina's taken up her studies again, my darling. Busy as a little bee up there all day long buzzing with ever more electronic gadgets from Harry's factory.'

'Bully for you, Sabina.' The tone was cheerfully sardonic, merely the banter between friendly rivals.

'You look well,' Sabina agreed and, warmed by the jolly homecoming, consigned all further reading to 'hold'. They relaxed over tea, leaning back in bemused affection, listening to Aragon's vivid account of her first few weeks in Glasgow. At last, after an impromptu dialogue with herself utilizing Sybil's tape-recorder and a good deal of audience participation, Aragon struck her forehead in an exaggerated gesture and fled downstairs to collect her assorted bundles and carrier bags.

'Her friends are calling at six,' Sybil said. 'They are all going to a gig, whatever that is.' She laughed. 'And afterwards to a party. Hallowe'en. Fancy dress, I imagine.' Nervously she added, 'I gave her permission to stay overnight, I'm sure Harry wouldn't object.'

'I'm sure he would!' Sabina grinned. 'But what Harry fails to appreciate is that he is not confronted by the full blast of Aragon's desires like the rest of us. Anyway,' she added, 'it seems a bit odd to withhold permission to stay out when she does whatever takes her fancy when she's in Glasgow.'

'At least it's got her away from that Rick person.'

'Oh, forget Rick.' Sabina waved her hand dismissively. 'I shouldn't lose any sleep over Rick, Sybil. He's taken care of.' Ignoring Sybil's quizzical lift of the chin, Sabina escaped back to the turret room and to her calculations, needing no warning bells from Harry to guard Sybil's inability to keep secrets. Especially where Aragon was concerned.

After an early supper Aragon persuaded her grandmother to receive her college friends in the old drawing-room downstairs. Betty Carter had obviously been dragged in on the scheme and had directed Jack Pierce, the gardener, to lay a fire. The whole house was centrally heated and, at Harry Morland's insistence, draught-proofed as far as an old house will allow. The leaping flames in the grate made the panelled room oppressive.

Aragon was delighted. She led Sybil into the little-used salon and they circled the carpet, the old woman fingering

half-forgotten china pieces, confirming the disposition of
barely remembered chairs and tables.

'It all smells very nice,' she conceded. 'Old Carter doesn't
let the room get musty, I must say that. Even when it is so
long since we did any entertaining.'

Sabina stood by the massive chimneypiece, a slight figure
grown thinner in recent months, a tautness in her stance,
her fingers nervously exploring the tumbler in her hand.
Aragon was radiant this evening. Her hair, smooth as
feathers, was caught up with crescent-tipped combs which
shone dully in the firelight.

After their promenade, Aragon flopped into a chair
while Sybil launched into a detailed description of the last
party in the house when her sight, though failing, had
been adequate. In the quiet remission from hostilities
Sabina judged it a perfect moment to offer her own
tribute.

'Aragon. I've been talking to Harry about a car for you.'

Aragon's eyes burned in the soft lighting of Sybil's
drawing-room.

'It's not a new car,' Sabina hastened to add. 'But if you
would enjoy driving a little runabout in Glasgow, Francis's
Renault is at Holland Park. You could pick it up this week
if you like or—' she paused—'perhaps it would be better if
I asked Tan to drive it up here. You'll be at Fernside for a
few days?' Placing her glass carefully on the mantelshelf,
Sabina slid a bunch of keys from her pocket and tried to rip
off Miss Mackenzie's orange plastic label. But Francis's
secretary had clearly won prizes for her knots. She gave up.
Aragon closed her fingers over the keys and glanced at her
grandmother. Sybil anxiously nodded, her sightless eyes
raking the air, critically aware that a gift is a double-edged
weapon and could easily provoke fresh antagonism.

Smiling, Aragon rose to her feet and touched Sabina's
arm, a small telling gesture which breathed relief into the
charged atmosphere.

Silence was broken by the noisy scatter of gravel in the

drive and with a whoop of delight Aragon ran out of the room to greet her friends.

They were a cheerful trio. Ushered into the overheated drawing-room, they refused to take off their coats, insisting time was running out. Two men and a redhead. Not a sign of fancy dress. In the mêlée of introductions and appraisal Sabina slid into the background, listening to the bantering exchanges provoked, she guessed, for Sybil's entertainment.

The old lady blossomed in company, became almost coquettish, one eyebrow lifted skittishly as the chatter flew from side to side like a shuttlecock.

'Tony's in his final year,' Aragon pointed out. 'He's rehearsing for the Christmas production. You must come up, Granny. It'll be stunning.'

Sybil demurred, laughing, her defences completely melted by their charm. Aragon's swift thrust went through almost on the nod.

'—a Guy Fawkes party, Granny. Such fun. In the garden. Jack Pierce said he'd see to the bonfire and so on. Safety and all that.'

'Here? When?'

'November 5th, of course, you old juggins. Do say yes, darling. It will be absolutely no bother, I promise. You could invite Rosie and the doctor and his wife. Your own chums. It's ages since you had a party here. We would do all the food on a barbecue, wouldn't we?' She appealed to her back-up. Four pairs of eyes were fuelled with enthusiasm.

Sabina quickly intervened, pointing out the stumbling-blocks, finding herself stuttering out familiar difficulties, scrabbling about for every reasonable excuse. She appealed to Sybil, fearful at plunging her short-lived popularity in reverse, the gesture of Francis's car keys seeming the abnegation of all her power.

'I don't see why not,' Sybil said. She quickly warmed to the idea and Carter, who entered just at the wrong moment, sheepishly agreed that she had in fact been sounded out that afternoon.

'And Mary's coming,' Aragon said with finality. 'She never gets any fun round here.'

The propulsion of Carter's despised niece into the fray struck even Sybil as below the belt but she let it pass, her imagination quickened by the glowing prospect of a party at Fernside, a real gesture of independence. Show them I'm not done for yet, she promised herself.

With dismay Sabina listened to a further ten minutes' discussion and with weary resignation counted the cost. Jack Pierce was sensible enough, a middle-aged Samson who would stand no nonsense. Drinks in the drawing-room with Sybil's friends able to view through the french windows. Bonfire on the flagstones at the centre of the lawn where the old birdbath used to be. She ticked off the possibilities in her mind and directed a wordless appeal to Betty Carter. The housekeeper gazed back and shrugged, her smile wistful, her acquiescence as feeble as her own in the face of Aragon's powers of persuasion.

When the door finally slammed behind the young people and the sounds of the car receded into the stormy darkness, Sabina moved behind the sofa from her defensive position and placed both hands on Sybil's frail shoulders.

'Well, old girl. We've done it now.'

Sybil's ringed fingers moved up to pat Sabina's hand.

'Don't worry, darling. It will be great fun. I do so *love* fireworks,' she said, her touch tremulous with anticipation of such a wild, wild scheme.

Next day Sabina parked the Porsche outside Geoffrey's Leeds laboratory with a feeling of exultation. Striking out with her briefcase bulging with reassembled data, she seemed oblivious of her surroundings and disappeared through the dirty glass doors without a backward glance. Abandoning £28000 worth of gleaming metalwork in a university town attracts lines of wide-eyed passers-by like the polarization of iron filings round a magnet.

Geoffrey eagerly led her through to his lab, ignoring the

only other scientist working in an apparently abandoned department.

'It's been closed down. Government cuts. The grants dried up,' he said by way of explanation. Handing her a white coat, he hurried her on, excited by the prospect of working together again at last.

'If we can sketch out a proposal, Geoffrey, I can arrange that facilities be available at Bracknell by the New Year. Once the data is verified you can put forward a solid case.'

His gaunt features were filmed with perspiration and he repeatedly wiped his spectacles, gazing at Sabina in an unfocused haze, half-expecting his dream to disintegrate.

They worked together under the harsh neon lighting, a partnership more passionate than any sexual liaison, their total absorption untouched by the darkness outside as the brief winter afternoon drew to a close.

A blast of cold air signalled invasion from the street. What seemed like a score of noisy students burst into the lab, shattering the earnest proximity of the professor and his student.

'Sabina!' Aragon's dramatic diction was unmistakable. 'What on earth?'

'We saw the Porsche outside,' screamed another, howling with delight.

'The Posh! The Posh!' Several voices chanted in unison.

Geoffrey stiffened, ashen with rage.

'We came on here,' Aragon fluted, 'to see Tony's brother, another boffin like you, Sabina. And when we saw the Porsche I just couldn't believe it!'

'Professor Tallent,' Sabina said curtly, 'is helping me with my thesis.' She turned to Geoffrey in mute appeal. 'Allow me to introduce my stepdaughter, Aragon Morland.' She drew him forward, clutching his rigid arm in desperation.

Geoffrey's icy glance froze their exhilaration, even Aragon was crushed. Quickly effecting introductions all round, Sabina shuffled papers together on the bench with an air of barely controlled panic.

'Is this your lab, sir?' one of the boys politely inquired.

Geoffrey shook his head and attempted to make an escape but the crowd seemed impenetrable.

From the corner of her eye, Sabina glimpsed a spark of wicked conjecture in Aragon's appraisal of the situation and found herself floundering in explanations, a seamless diatribe on scientific research which drew blank stares from Aragon's supporters and total amazement from Geoffrey. Her voice faltered and finally petered out.

In the temporary lull Aragon seized the initiative.

'It is so seldom the family meets my stepmother's friends. She's a dark horse, you know,' she said, throwing a meaningful glance over her shoulder. Geoffrey's anger had cooled to disdain and he began to repack stacks of graph paper into box files.

'My grandmother would never forgive me if we missed this opportunity to present you, Professor. She is so proud of Sabina, so grateful to anyone who gives her a leg up.' She choked back a giggle. 'We're having a party on the fifth at Fernside—I'm sure you know it. You will come,' she concluded, her unwinking eyes fixed on her stepmother. Geoffrey attempted to excuse himself but Sabina cut him short.

'Of course you must come,' she insisted. 'Bring Naomi.' And without giving him a chance to reply ushered the whole party outside.

The small group around the Porsche quickly dispersed and Aragon flamboyantly embraced Sabina before rejoining her friends.

'I'll be home in the morning. I've already phoned Granny,' she said. 'It's all arranged, Mother dearest,' this final shot delivered with painful clarity.

Geoffrey and Sabina stood at the kerbside and watched Aragon's noisy entourage disappear into the gloom.

'I shan't come, of course,' he said.

'Please, Geoffrey. Please come. If you don't she will exaggerate the whole incident and upset Harry's mother.

Aragon's dangerous. She's not a child. Bring Naomi and it'll pass off perfectly smoothly.'

She pressed her cold fingers to his lips blocking his protests. 'I don't want any trouble *now*. She's quite capable of concocting a drama out of this and putting Harry on his guard. He's been marvellous, Geoffrey, more than amenable to all our suggestions, but he's no fool. If Aragon alerts his suspicions before we've even got started our last chance is gone. Without fresh data nobody will ever take your work seriously, my dear. And without the use of Harry's computers it will take years.'

The man sagged under her urgent plea. Suddenly a wintry gust caught up his fine hair, blowing it into a silvery halo outlining his gaunt acceptance. He was caught in a shaft. He could only go on.

Opposite, across the street, a bleak Baptist chapel formed a dull silhouette in the mist, its only bright feature a colourful poster on the notice board advertising a forthcoming service. *Remember! Remember!* it admonished.

After the Porsche had gone, Geoffrey Tallent stood outside the lab hypnotized by the garish lettering. Remember? Remember what? Guy Fawkes? Armistice Day? There was so much. Forgetting. That was the thing. Forgetting would be better for everyone.

CHAPTER 16

Sybil's French clock was just chiming three as the telephone rang on the afternoon of the firework party. It was for Sabina: a man with a terse Yorkshire accent like gravel in a sieve. Evidently a local—the garage perhaps? Sybil hesitated to disturb her. Sabina hardly appeared downstairs these days, her bloodshot eyes raised in irritation when Carter arrived breathless and peevish to winkle her down for dinner.

Sybil sighed and, picking up the intercom, told the house-keeper to take her poor old feet to the turret room. 'Mr Arnott says it's important,' she said sharply, 'so don't mutter like that, Carter.' As she replaced the instrument on the coffee table an unbidden doubt floated to the surface of her mind: Was Aragon's party really such a good idea?

Sabina's appearance ten minutes later was a surprise, a certain grave rectitude stiffening her careful greeting. Sybil recognized by the same strange telepathy that alerted her senses to unseen obstacles that Sabina was unwell. She said, 'Sabina, my dear. How nice. Have some tea, it's just made.'

'A man's calling to see me, Sybil. Someone from London. A police inspector.'

'Oh heavens,' Sybil murmured.

Sabina sat down and patted the parchment fingers. 'Don't look aghast, darling.' She smiled. 'I'm not being run in. I think it must be about Francis.' She poured herself some tea, adding a slice of lemon, and crossed to the window.

'You haven't been speeding in that car of yours, I hope.'

'Nothing like that. I can only think it's something new since the inquest. He wouldn't come all this way unless it was important. Do you think the mews house might have been broken into, a burglary or some such thing? Everything gets referred to me these days. Nicholas is abroad again.'

'Australia, Rosie tells me. She saw him on television last month, she said. At least he's hit a gold streak this time.'

'I wonder if—' But the sentence hung in the air as two set of heavy footsteps echoed in the hall below. Both women sat still, straining to catch Mrs Carter's words as irritably she conducted the visitor upstairs.

Arnott was wearing a check suit, rather a loud pattern, his bushy brows and ruddy complexion suggesting a successful bookmaker paying a call. He smiled broadly, stomping across the pretty room hat in hand. Sybil was intrigued and after introductions they disposed themselves either side of the old lady. Sabina sat tight in her corner of the sofa, confused by the newly-minted inspector, a countrified version of the testy, almost seedy-looking policeman she vaguely remembered.

He refused tea and after a few moments Sybil graciously suggested Sabina took her visitor to the dining-room where they could settle their business.

'It is rather a delicate matter, ma'am,' he said, glancing from one to the other. Sabina looked as if she had been poured into a mould, a plaster maiden, all cheekbones, hollow-eyed.

Clearing her throat, she leaned towards Sybil. 'May we stay? I'm sure it's nothing serious.' She turned to Arnott. 'I have no secrets from Mrs Morland. Speak freely by all means.'

'If you're sure.' Arnott blew his nose and focused all his attention on the younger woman.

'It's this money that was supposed to be missing. £5000 in notes. It has come to my attention that perhaps it was never lost.' He paused, scanning the pale mask Sabina Morland presented.

'How do you mean?'

'You know a Mr Roger Mansell, of course.'

'Of course. Roger and I have been friends for years.'

'Mr Mansell was one of the last people to see Francis Swayne alive. They met at the Savoy, he said.'

'Yes. Roger mentioned it at the funeral. You see, Francis had agreed to attend a charity performance nearby and it was a beastly hot night. He slipped away to have a drink at the Savoy and missed most of the second act, I believe.'

'He certainly missed more than that! But the heat was not the reason he opted out. He met someone, presumably by arrangement, and gave her a package.' Arnott stared fixedly at Sabina. It was a toss-up really, Sabina Morland could easily deny all knowledge. But nothing ventured . . . Perspiration beaded her upper lip, the skin deathly pale.

Alarmed, Sybil intervened, sensing the tenacity underlying his quiet approach.

'I think my daughter-in-law has been overworking lately, Inspector. Have some fresh tea, dear.'

Sabina rallied, shaking her head. 'The estate made no insurance claim on the loss, Inspector. In fact, I am quite sure the solicitor has in no way pressed for further inquiries to be made.'

'Wasting police time is a very serious matter, Mrs Morland,' he persisted. 'But I grant you the fact that no member of the family so much as queried the whereabouts of such a large sum intrigued me. I interviewed Mr Mansell again recently and by the merest chance he was able to identify the mysterious woman your late brother took such a lot of trouble to meet. Bless me, I wouldn't be persuaded to miss half *Rigoletto* unless the young lady was a very special friend.'

'Don't play cat and mouse with me, Inspector. If you know who it was, why ask?'

'You owe the police an explanation, of course.' Arnott forced the pace, harrying his quarry. 'To close our files, you might say.'

'You've come a long way for that,' Sabina snapped, her temper rising, two high spots of colour flaring on the sculptured cheekbones. 'Sandy had every right to that money. Why Francis gave it to her is no business of yours.'

Arnott relaxed, the bait taken. 'In that case, Mrs Morland, it was a great pity the matter wasn't cleared up straight away. I flew to Guernsey to interview Mr Mansell. Public money is accountable, madam, at least to a Yorkshire lad like meself.'

'Do explain, Sabina dear, and the Inspector can dispose of the matter.' Sybil looked flustered, the nagging doubt compounded by Sabina's taciturnity.

'Oh, very well.' Sabina reached into her pocket for a pack of cigarettes and lit one, inhaling deeply.

'My sister-in-law is a passionate woman. I don't care for her particularly and neither did Francis, but she is a wonderful wife. Nicholas drinks. He also has other failings

I don't wish to discuss. In a nutshell, he's a God-awful actor and a hopeless father to the boys. Things got into a parlous state and my husband refused to help. Sandra Sullivan's name often features in the press in connection with her Communist sympathies and Harry shared Francis's reluctance to throw good money after bad.'

Arnott looked away, and through the window studied the trees clawing at the grey skies, his Mr Punch profile jagged as an outcrop of rock against Sybil's dainty wallpaper.

'But Sandy was caught in a trap finally. Francis snatched his chance and decided to trade on it. I knew nothing of all this at the time but the entire transaction was explained to me by our family solicitor after the funeral. In return for Francis's intervention with creditors Sandy and Nicholas signed an agreement to allow Francis free rein to direct the boys' education. Only after this power was transferred to Francis, £5000 would be exchanged to sweeten a very bitter pill. In cash to circumvent Sandy's bank manager. The educational trust is legally watertight and for someone of Sandy's political persuasion it will probably rankle for a very long time. Frankly, I believe Nicky's privately relieved that the responsibility has been taken off his hands and they are both, of course, delighted that Francis's money was transferred in time to save their theatrical venture—Sandy must have got a lot of satisfaction there, I fancy. For the present at any rate,' she added with a wry grimace.

Sabina stubbed out her cigarette and Arnott brought his penetrating gaze back into play. The granite physiognomy cracked, the smile sweet as he rounded off the interview with the benevolent air of a dentist congratulating a nervous patient.

'There, Mrs Morland. Not so painful after all, was it?'

As if to spare Arnott Sabina's sarcastic retort Aragon burst in, her entry hampered by a large bundle of clothing bulging between herself and Mary Carter. The two girls almost fell into the room with the burden. Aragon's enthusiasm was incandescent.

'Whoops! Sorry, Granny. Didn't know you had a visitor.' The plump face of her collaborator, Mary Carter, shone with shy delight.

Sabina had risen and would have made a bolt for it had the way not been unequivocally blocked.

Sybil's head bobbed from one voice to the other. She quickly cut in to save further awkwardness.

'Mr Arnott had just concluded, I think?' She touched the teapot on the tray in front of her. 'Would you like some fresh tea, Mr Arnott? This is quite cold. I'll ask Aragon to make it.'

'Aragon! What on earth have you got there?'

Sabina's tone was brittle, unamused. Mary Carter's smile faded and she dropped her end of the bundle. It fell on to the carpet with a dull thud, a wide brimmed hat rolling under a chair.

'Oh, Mary!' Aragon moaned. 'Watch it!' She proudly held the burden upright. 'It's our guy,' she said. 'You should see it, Granny. It's absolutely fantastic.'

She supported the effigy under the arms, an adult-sized figure in a short cape, uncannily lifelike, its paper mask tilted under an auburn wig. Mary retrieved the hat and stuck a sheaf of pheasant's feathers in the hatband before jamming it back on.

'Aren't you a bit old for this sort of thing?'

'Don't be stuffy, Sab. How can we have a bonfire without a guy?'

'It's ever so lifelike, Mrs Morland,' Mary appealed to Sybil. 'That lace blouse you said we could have looks t'riffic. Froths out in front just right.'

'It's the hair tops it off,' Arnott chimed in. Having confirmed Mansell's conjecture, he became expansive, entering into the spirit of the occasion.

'We tried to make it look right,' Aragon explained. 'We copied a picture of Guy Fawkes. We had trouble sticking bits on the mask to make the beard so in the end we painted it on.'

Encouraged, Mary chipped in. 'Then my mum gave us this hairpiece she used to wear in the 'sixties.'

'Can you *believe* it!' Aragon shrieked. 'All bouffant, a real beehive.'

'We shaped it round to look more historical. Aragon found her dad's old scout hat in the attic and that made all the difference.'

'As it will go up in smoke,' Sabina pointed out, 'historical accuracy seems hardly necessary.'

'Don't be such a wet blanket, Sabina.' Sybil smiled, relieved that Sabina was outnumbered. 'I'm sure Mr Arnott is all for a bit of fun at this very dull end of the year.'

'By 'eck, you've put your finger on it there, Mrs Morland. It's a pity to let these old traditions die.'

'Then,' Sybil agreed, 'we can only congratulate you girls.' Anxious to smooth over a difficult patch, she impulsively invited Arnott to join the party.

'Oh, do come,' she pressed him. 'We need an able-bodied man to give Pierce some moral support. Keep these minxes—' she affectionately squeezed Mary's plump arm —'in order.' Mary giggled.

'Sabina's friend is coming,' Aragon put in maliciously. 'Her professor who's been giving her private lessons. He said he—'

'I'm not sure he can come,' Sabina interjected. 'Professor Tallent's not very sociable. I really think—'

Arnott stood up, cutting her short. 'I would be delighted,' he said, addressing himself to Sybil.

'About seven,' she replied. 'Wrap up warmly. Aragon's friends are trying to get us outside for the fireworks. Not all of us will be dancing round the bonfire,' she assured him, 'But my grand-daughtrer has an uncanny knack of getting her own way.'

'You can say that again,' Sabina muttered.

Arnott helped the girls convey their lifelike dummy outside the house and obligingly tied it to an old bentwood chair before hoisting the whole contraption to the top of an enormous pile of brushwood that the gardener had stacked in the centre of the lawn.'

It was pitch dark. As his car headlights pierced the foggy country lanes Arnott's grim satisfaction glowed with the faint possibility of meeting the fraudulent professor Roger Mansell had described so vividly. Booking his room at the Feathers for a second night, he ordered a pint of Guinness and shambled through to the empty snug to check back through his notes.

Sybil's drinks party was in full swing when Arnott returned that evening, the drive occupied by cars strung almost to the gate. The Porsche was tucked away on its own, sleek as a crouching beast under the trees.

It was misty and very cold, squally gusts of rain stinging his ears as he tramped up the steps to ring the bell. A young man flung open the door, casually introducing himself, his loud confident tone marking him out as one of Aragon's friends from drama school. He took Arnott's coat, explaining that Mrs Morland's party was in the drawing-room and politely conducted the older man towards an open door before dashing off upstairs, two at a time, to join a separate, noisier party crowded round a jumbo-size boogie box on the landing outside Sybil's boudoir and sorting tapes.

Arnott ambled into the drawing-room, its ample Victorian proportions already clouded with smoke, several chattering groups of middle-aged and frankly elderly people in animated conversation. Seeing him enter, Sabina detached herself from Sybil's coterie and drew him to a side table set out with cup-shaped glasses into which Mrs Carter was ladling hot punch. The housekeeper looked flushed and rather pleased with herself, a delicious spicy aroma rising from the punch bowl in which pieces of fruit floated in a seemingly innocent brew. Sabina smiled.

'Glad you came, Inspector,' she said. 'I'm afraid I was rather rude this afternoon. I've been a bit shrewish lately, my apologies. Getting back to serious study after a long gap has been a shock to my system. No excuse, I'm afraid, but Sybil was right. I've been burning the midnight oil.'

'Let's forget the "Inspector", shall we? I'm off duty now. And congratulations. Mr Mansell was full of praise for your research. He will be delighted to hear you've decided to pick up your scientific work again.'

She looked more relaxed, relieved in all probability that Sandra Sullivan's pay-off was out in the open, a family skeleton that was not as interesting to outsiders as the solicitor's obsessive desire for discretion had made it seem. Arnott wasn't such a bad old stick, she decided, maybe London made everyone more aggressive.

'I hope you didn't come all this way just to write off the missing £5000?'

'No, Mrs Morland. To be honest, I've been combining business with pleasure, you might say. I'm thinking of buying a little place up here, near Whitby maybe. I retire this year and I've no one to consider but myself these days.' He paused. 'My wife died.'

'I am so sorry.'

'It's taken a long time to sink in. But she was a southern lass, liked being near her own kin so I've only just got used to the idea I might come back to my roots, like. Peg didn't care for Yorkshire.' Arnott surprised himself: speaking of Peg in such a matter of fact way to this young woman, not a sympathetic sort by a long chalk, not really. Maybe his rough edges were mossing over at last.

Sabina refilled Arnott's glass and after a few minutes introduced him to a grey-haired man, the village doctor, Colin Simcock, and Sheila, his dumpy wife. Arnott, red-faced and wearing his check suit, blended with the country set surprisingly well, his bluff good humour fitting neatly into Sybil's motley crowd, composed for the most part of neighbours retired like himself, an eager audience to the capers of Aragon's accomplices.

Sybil's friends drifted round the smoky room, exchanging local gossip, cheerfully buttonholing the doctor with impromptu consultations about niggling aches and pains, the minor inconveniences of 'getting on'.

Arnott found himself in a trio pressed against the french windows. Aragon and her rackety crowd had moved outside and were cavorting round the barbecue, their leaping silhouettes forming a lively ballet against the glowing charcoal grill.

A man in a ragged pullover and peaked cap towered over the coals, feeding the flames and fending off interference with calm indifference. It occurred to Arnott this must be the gardener whom Sybil had suggested he back up, though it seemed unlikely that Jack Pierce would need support, moral or otherwise, in dealing with the young rascals.

His fellow guests were talking about their gardens and, dragging his attention from the fire dance, Arnott tried to pick up the conversation in mid-flow. He decided he hadn't missed much and found his gaze wandering again, distracted by a demoniacal yowling outside the french windows. It was a Siamese cat crouched as if to spring, magnificent eyes burning in the dark.

'Oh, you poor darling,' exclaimed the doctor's wife. She called across the room to Sabina. 'My dear, Sybil's cat's outside. Shouldn't we bring it in? It's demented with fear.'

'Shouldn't be loose once the fireworks start,' rasped the doctor, releasing the door-catch just as Sabina reached them. The door swung outwards, admitting an icy blast of smoky air and a cat in a great hurry. Scooping it up, she said, 'Tai-Tai. How on earth did you get out?'

The delicate tipped ears flattened as the cat struggled in Sabina's grasp, sinews flexing under the pale fur with the ferocity of a trapped lynx. The amazing irises intensified under the lights of the drawing-room as if manipulated by a dimmer switch, and the cat emitted an unearthly growl.

Sabina laughed. 'Excuse me,' she said, elbowing through, hugging the wild thing to her coral sweater. Arnott hurried forward to open the door into the hall, a perceptible sigh running through the room as she departed like a crowd witnessing a near-disaster.

Sybil touched Arnott's arm, a grave Dr Simcock at her shoulder.

'Mr Arnott, I am so delighted you've come. You have met Dr and Mrs Simcock, I gather. You must help Mr Arnott to find a little cottage near here, Colin. He's looking for a small place to retire.' She inclined her head, smiling wickedly, and Arnott guessed a manoeuvre to elude the doctor's attention. He was not to be so easily deflected.

'Yes, indeed. We've already met.' He nodded to Arnott in a man to man gesture of solidarity and took a firm hold of Sybil's elbow. 'As I was saying, my dear. That Siamese is a killer. It's already tipped you over the terrace. Sabina must take it back to London before it does more damage.'

Sybil tut-tutted, scorning his grim prognosis and called Betty Carter to replenish the glasses. 'Tai-Tai's a sweetie, Colin. She's just flustered with all the excitement. Sabina shut her in the laundry room for the evening but she's an expert escaper.'

'The cat used to belong to Sabina's brother,' Mrs Simcock whispered to Arnott, 'the one who hanged himself.' Vigorously shaking her head, she drew him to one side and with relish related the details of Francis Swayne's bizarre suicide and Sybil's subsequent adoption of his pet Siamese. Arnott recalled the first occasion he had seen the cat, also through a glazed door and also yowling it seemed directly at him. This time unfettered by the red harness thing. It was a pity to spoil Mrs Simcock's story and Arnott stood stolidly by as the account of the death at Sherbourne Mews was dramatically embellished.

Sabina returned with a plate of hot sausage rolls and cheerfully circulated, Sybil's guests already re-animated to loud conversation now that their brush with the wild cat had passed.

At that moment a late arrival slid into the room, unobserved except by Arnott and Sabina, whose face drained as if she witnessed a spectre at the feast. His dark suit was pressed though far from new, the points of the shirt collar had driven small holes through the fabric but the club tie, composed of strident orange and yellow, struck a defiant note, a flag of convenience hoisted against a hostile world. His face was narrow and very pale, the high-bridged nose forming a firm line from the forehead, the head poised proudly, presenting a classic profile. A man apart in any company but insinuated into the 'country folk', as they liked to call themselves, the stranger clung like a shadow to the periphery of Sybil's jolly party.

Sybil and the doctor still hovered in the doorway, their prattle now lighter, manipulated by Sybil's sleight of hand, back on the safe conversational rails of peat-based compost.

Sabina abruptly shoved the plate of food on a side table and hastened to the new guest. Arnott abandoned all semblance of polite attention to Sheila Simcock and frankly surveyed the stranger, his presence almost effete in that robust gathering. It could only be the professor. Well, well, well. Arnott moved in fast.

'—how could you?' Sabina was speaking in an undertone, almost hissing, the words escaping from her throat in strangled bursts. 'I'll get you some coffee,' she said, reaching for his arm.

'No!'

He roughly shook her off and stared round the room, the cobalt eyes frankly curious. 'Leave me alone.' His words were thick, slightly slurred, a glimmer of moisture at the corner of his mouth forming itself into a sparkling drop like a tear.

He was very drunk. Coldly, joylessly inebriated like someone who had deliberately distanced himself from despair.

Sybil stood nearby, sharply turning her head as the man spoke. Standing stiffly to attention, he took her hand and raised it to his lips, a gesture of arrogance and simplicity, utterly disarming. Sabina shrugged, introducing him to her mother-in-law, to the Simcocks and finally to Arnott. They bunched in the doorway, a tightly knit circle hanging on the charming phrases of the newcomer.

His words tumbled out. An irrepressible flow of anecdote and commentary, its carefully modulated phrasing as hypnotic as a dramatic performance, a man little used to conversational give and take one would imagine, a speaker well versed in lecturing, finely tuned to audience reaction.

Clever bugger he may be, Arnott happily concluded, but the bloke's pissed.

At the first appreciable pause in Geoffrey Tallent's narrative Sybil's fluting tones broke in, her amusement effervescent.

'Did you bring any magazines this time, Professor Tallent? A tract or two perhaps?' The extraordinary eyes stared at her, unwinking, as if to penetrate the sightless pupils trained on him.

'We've met before,' she announced, waving a languorous hand towards the spellbinder. 'The professor is a "fisher of men" in his spare time. An evangelist, Sheila,' she elaborated. 'He thought I wouldn't guess. Isn't it fortunate Tai-Tai's already been taken from the room? You see, Sheila, this charming young man rescued me after I toppled over the terrace and, like the Good Samaritan, undertakes his good works by stealth.' She turned towards Geoffrey Tallent who, in his inebriated state, was totally unaffected by her sardonic recognition.

'Unmasked!' He laughed, throwing up his hands in comic submission.

'Good God, Sybil, you're right!' shouted Simcock. 'I know him now. The fellow who drove you to the hospital after you broke your collar-bone. Fancy you remembering his voice straight off like that. I'd completely forgotten,' he explained to Arnott, 'I would never have recognized the man—and I've got my sight.'

The doctor gave Arnott an account of Sybil's arrival at the cottage hospital in the car of the mysterious bible-thumper who discreetly withdrew before anyone could thank him.

Geoffrey Tallent's laughter suddenly broke into a choking spasm, his control exhausted in a paroxysm of hiccoughing just as a roar from the crowd in the garden signalled the lighting of the bonfire.

Aragon's friends burst through the french windows, scattering the adult party, Mary Carter appearing simultaneously from the hall with a bundle of coats and boots. The laughing group herded the older guests into overcoats, bullying them to come outside.

In the confusion Sabina dragged Geoffrey Tallent into the hallway, whispering urgently in his ear as she pulled him upstairs. Arnott watched her whisk him into Sybil's deserted sitting-room, closing the door behind them. Arnott followed, passing the door on his way to the bathroom. After a few minutes he emerged on to the empty landing and surreptitiously tried the handle of the door. It was locked. Inside, voices raised in bitter dispute were clearly audible.

Lighting a cigarette, Arnott wandered along the wide landing to stand at a Venetian window at the end. Below, in the garden, the scene was all flames and black darting figures vanishing and reappearing in the smoke. The bonfire was slowly catching, a ring of fire illuminating the flushed, excited faces, the pyramid of damp wood surmounted by the outline of a figure tied to a chair. A scene which could have been drawn directly from Goya.

CHAPTER 17

Sabina leaned against the door, gasping with the effort of propelling Geoffrey upstairs away from the party. Sure-footed, he made straight for Sybil's drinks tray in the dark, Mrs Carter's punch seemingly working downwards from his brain. Pouring a large whisky, he stood in the bay window gazing down on the hellish scene below.

Aragon had ringed the lawn with garden flares and the guests crowded within the magic circle round the bonfire watching the first rockets explode above the trees in maroon and gold stars. Smoke caught up in the squally rain swirled overhead, occasionally belching up from the fire as Jack Pierce fed the flames.

'You found the drinks easily, I see,' she said with asperity. 'But, of course, you've been in this room before.'

'Mm. Sherry for the injured party,' Geoffrey replied drily. 'Your mother-in-law keeps no brandy even for medicinal purposes. Pity.'

'Why did you come straight up here when Sybil fell? There's a phone in the hall.'

'The front door was closed, as a matter of fact. I slipped in through the french windows at the back and ran up here on a hunch. I was brought up in a house just like this. Victorian nouveau gothick. Identical lay-out. I knew this room would have the best view. My revered parents— adoptive naturally!—' he added bitterly—'also used this room as their private sitting-room. It was obvious I would find the liquor up here and medically speaking the shock of the old lady's accident was more injurious than the broken collar-bone.'

'How dare you speak of her like that!'

He laughed. 'Old ladies of her calibre are indestructible.' Swallowing the whisky, he refilled his glass, his clumsy movements spinning a wine glass from the table to splinter against the wall. The alcohol had claimed more territory now, the legs splayed to counter his fuddled brain. He stared out, mesmerized by the lively scene.

The bonfire was burning well, sparks exploding in the darkness as Jack shored up the glowing embers at the base with more rotten wood.

'But why did you come that afternoon? I can't imagine what you were doing here. Religion hasn't got you at long last after all? I can't believe that!'

Sabina moved beside him in the alcove, kicking aside the broken glass.

Geoffrey twisted to stare at her, the extraordinary eyes reduced to black holes reflecting like dark mirrors the cascading coloured lights outside.

'Religion?' He giggled, an ugly falsetto. 'Oh, you mean that *Watchtower* rubbish?' and slurped more whisky, splashing it on to the garish tie. 'I came to see you, my darling. You didn't answer my letter,' he whined, the lips loose and moist, fleshy with self-pity.

'I didn't receive it for weeks. I was abroad,' Sabina retorted. This was getting beyond a joke! 'Anyway, what gave you the idea I would be here?'

Sensing her contempt, Geoffrey stiffened, instantly aggressive. 'That clever bastard Morland.' He slowly enunciated each syllable with growing rancour. 'Your rich husband is easy to pinpoint. Quotes this place as his "family home" in all those arse-licking business supplements. It's no secret, my lovely Sabine woman. Fernside is printed in the directories and even a stupid alien like me knows that anyone who is anybody retires to the country after the "glorious twelfth".'

'Geoffrey, what claptrap! You're totally out of date. Harry's not landed gentry. He works harder than anyone I know. You still haven't explained why you pretended to be an evangelist, hoodwinking a poor blind old woman with all that after-life nonsense.'

'And I was given to understand that a sense of humour was the first step in acquiring acceptability in this baffling country.' His tone was icily sardonic. 'That "poor blind old woman", as you sentimentally phrase it, was trying to hoodwink me from the start and probably appreciates a jape more than you, my darling. Your ability to see the joke has always been a trifle thin.' Geoffrey sipped his whisky, frowning, as if trying to pick up the thread.

'As I was saying. When I found you were not at home I thought I'd make a quick retreat. Bible-punchers get the boot quicker than most and are swiftly forgotten. I happened to have been cornered myself by a so-called city missionary in Leeds that very week and bought his magazine or pamphlet or whatever just to get shot of the man. I merely passed it on to your mother-in-law. It wasn't my fault she fell off the terrace, you know. The cat got under her feet.'

'Oh, shut up about the cat!'

Sabina tried to take away his tumbler but his reactions were instinctive if somewhat wobbly. He swung his arm awkwardly, stepping sideways in an effort to evade her and crashed into the paraphernalia beside Sybil's chair.

'Geoffrey! For God's sake! Don't break anything else.'

Taking a deep breath, she tried another tack and coaxed him back to the window. 'My dear, don't let's quarrel.' He allowed her to take his glass and to her consternation began to weep.

'Please, oh please don't cry, Geoffrey. Things are going to get better, darling. We're on track again.'

Furiously shaking off her sympathy, he jerked away and started shouting at her—or perhaps at the world in general —anger displacing his grief with alarming rapidity.

'Only if Morland deigns to allow me to use his computer plant as well as his wife.'

Sabina recoiled, totally confused, his pent-up recriminations curdling into a violent diatribe, a foul recapitulation of their visits to the hotel in Knaresborough, a sadistic description of her 'entrapment' and finally a sneering attack on money-grubbing capitalists like Morland who got rich on the research of poor academics like himself.

Producing a hip flask, he swallowed the contents. Then, attempting to push past her in the darkness, he stumbled on the broken glass and cannoned into her, catching his feet in the trailing curtain. For a long moment they lurched in the alcove, Sabina clinging on, terrified he might actually crash through the glass on to the terrace below.

Numb with the ferocity of his disillusion, she steadied him against the embrasure, shrinking from his foul breath as if from a blow. He swayed against the side wall, his pallid features spasmodically illuminated by the green and red firework display. Dully the sound of exploding rockets penetrated the room in a nightmarish cacophony like bizarre applause to his bitter accusations. Geoffrey gazed down at the scene, suddenly straightened and took a step forward. He clutched the window-frame for support, utterly absorbed, his eyes no longer vague, seemingly mesmerized by the ascending flames.

A roar broke out from the crowd below. The bonfire was now a tower of flame, Aragon's guy enthroned in a pall of smoke. The stuffed figure roped to the chair seemed to writhe in the fire and, as if plucked by demon fingers, the wide-brimmed scout hat blew away in a shower of sparks.

The chair slowly toppled, the rope burning like fuse wire round the legs of the effigy. For an instant, released from its bonds, the guy appeared to rise above the inferno, its mask tilted up towards them, the wig rakishly askew. Then a strong gust whipped the flames six feet into the sky, engulfing the seated figure, its hair finally igniting.

Geoffrey screamed.

'Naomi! Don't, Naomi!'

Leaping forward, he flung open the long window as if he would jump out, Sabina wrestling with him with strength she never knew she possessed, clinging on as he wildly beat against the lintel.

The fire suddenly collapsed in on itself, the figure entirely absorbed. Geoffrey swung about, his face livid, pinning Sabina against the wall. '*You* killed her, all of you!' Instantly the strength drained from him, and whimpering, he fell on the floor dragging her down with him.

A cheer went up from the garden signalling the final extinction of Guy Fawkes. Scrabbling to extract herself, Sabina scrambled to her feet, vaguely aware that a persistent banging like a drum beat accompanied the shouting outside. Dazed, she reached across the crouching figure at her feet to shut the window and as the noise from the garden was excluded she realized that the banging came not from outside but from the locked door to the landing. Not only that, someone was rattling the handle demanding to be let in. Dear God, what next?

Geoffrey pulled himself up, hanging on to Sybil's curtains like a drowning man. She crossed the room and put her ear to the door. 'Who is it?' she croaked, her voice seemingly fled in the course of Geoffrey's tirade.

'Police. Open up!'

Geoffrey Tallent passed out, crashed on to the floor among the broken glass, still clutching the folds of velvet.

Sabina wearily opened the door.

Arnott stood there, filling the rectangle of light with his bulky person. She pulled him inside. Shutting the door, she put her finger to her lips.

'I 'eard him carrying on,' whispered Arnott. 'I've been on the landing the whole time. Fighting drunk, was he?'

Sabina slipped back to the alcove and closed the curtains before putting on the light. She beckoned Arnott.

'Quick. Help me get him into the spare room before they come back into the house.' Already sounds of tramping feet and excited voices below indicated the end of the party. A nightcap or two, hot coffee perhaps, and the guests would be off home. 'There's no way of getting him out in this state.'

Arnott nodded. While she checked the landing he grasped the unconscious professor and hauled him to his feet. Coming to, he feebly tried to push him away. Sabina grabbed one arm and together she and Arnott staggered into the corridor and along to the guest bedroom at the end. They pushed Geoffrey on to the bed, laughing with relief, and Sabina darted to close the door just as Aragon and her crowd appeared at the top of the stairs and surged into Sybil's sitting-room. Sabina nodded towards them.

'I expect they're borrowing Sybil's tape-machine for bopping,' she muttered.

Arnott looked puzzled but energetically agreed. 'We only just made it, then.'

Like bumbling actors in a French farce they struggled to remove Geoffrey's suit and loosen the ghastly tie. Arnott was staring closely at the sleeping figure laid out in his shirt and underpants, his legs stiff as a corpse. He pointed to the puckered scar on Geoffrey's thigh, an uneven scribble on the white flesh. He grinned wolfishly, still tickled at the idea of this drunken sot posing as a Jehovah's Witness. A real card. 'What's that? he said. 'Wounded in the Holy Crusade, was he?'

'Oh, that.' She shrugged, smoothing out Geoffrey's trousers before laying them across a chair. 'Said he got it in a climbing accident but he's an automatic liar.' She smiled indulgently. 'Looks more like a pub brawl to me.'

Arnott pressed Sabina to elaborate.

'He told me he got caught up in some tackle and bled like a pig. Funny thing was, he mentioned having to get it stitched up in Chelsea of all places. Joked about getting AIDS from all the punks in the out-patients' clinic.'

Arnott looked startled. 'London, you mean? He said he was in a climbing accident in the middle of London?'

'Ridiculous. It didn't strike me at the time. We were laughing about the AIDS scare, the panic when anyone has to have a blood test or injection these days. No joke really, whistling in the dark, I dare say. But the nearest casualty department was in that hospital in Fulham Road, it was in the news when I first arrived from Hong Kong—they'd opened a small ward for AIDS patients.'

'St Laurence's. Does more than its share. It was in my manor. You should see the funny crowd gets in there! Punks, tramps, winos. Beatings up. Knife fights. Overdoses. The lot. I'd love to have seen your toffee-nosed professor mixed up with that crew!'

Sabina lined up Geoffrey's shoes neatly by the bed, turning a blind eye to the holes in the matted woolly socks,

Arnott gently covering the snoring academic with the pretty pink counterpane.

'He was boozed before he got here.' He draped Geoffrey's jacket over a chair and, as an afterthought, felt inside the pockets. He held up a bunch of keys. 'Shall I take care of these?'

'Car keys?'

'He might try to drive off if he comes round. He won't be sober till morning.'

Sabina regarded her unlikely conspirator and tried to refocus the image to that of a detective-inspector.

'I suppose so,' she agreed.

'I'll bring back the keys first thing in the morning before he's up and about. Avoid more bloody dramatics tonight. The traffic cops are on the look-out for drunk drivers after the pubs close, he'd be sure to be picked up. Leeds was it, you said. Where he lives?'

As she was about to reply running footsteps sounded on the landing. Sabina doused the bedside light. In silence they waited for the danger to pass. Arnott suggested it was time he made himself scarce.

'I don't want to be caught up here after everyone else's gone,' he said.

Reassuring themselves that Tallent was truly out for the count, they tiptoed out and descended the stairs to mingle with the departing guests. Shaking hands all round, Arnott could have passed as the life and soul of the party but nobody seemed to have missed him. Sabina mumbled her apologies for the professor's early departure. With luck, she thought, I'll get him out after breakfast. Aragon was catching an early train from Harrogate: it should all fit together nicely.

Sybil was blissful, tired but radiant with the success of her first party in years. 'A lovely do, Sabina,' she said, linking arms affectionately as they trailed upstairs. 'Thank you for being here. Wouldn't Harry have been astonished?'

Sabina nodded fervently. Oh yes. Yes indeed, mother-in-law, Harry Morland's astonishment would have been something all right. She decided to spend the night in the guest-room and keep vigil by Geoffrey's bed. What a ghost-like figure he would present if he came stumbling down in the middle of the night. Or worse, was sick: choked to death on his own vomit! One read of such things . . .

Sabina shuddered at the prospect and slipped into the darkened room, the air stale from long disuse. Opening the window, she leaned out surveying the empty garden, the bonfire reduced to glowing embers, the smell of spent rockets acrid in the November mist.

Why had Geoffrey been so terrified by the fireworks? And why did he call out to his wife like that? And accuse herself of murder? What had Naomi Tallent to do with anything? Had ever counted for anything, come to that . . . She shrugged, utterly mystified, and closed the window. Geoffrey sprawled on the bed, snoring loudly, his face flaccid, white as a mask.

Arnott drove away, waving cheerfully to the doctor and his wife as they parted at the gates. Steering the Vauxhall away from the village, he drove to a quiet lay-by, turned off the ignition and sat in the country silence slowly acknowledging the sounds of an owl and rustlings in the hedgerow. He dozed until the small hours, occasionally checking his watch, and then started off, turning the wheel to head back to Fernside.

He shut off the engine two hundred yards from the house and coasted downhill, through the iron gates and on to the drive. The house was almost invisible in the rain, the windows blank. Creeping along the grass verge, huddled in his sheepskin coat, Arnott seemed a queer tramp of a man, his shambling gait unfamiliar with the utter blackness of a rural backwater, sliding on the slimy vegetation.

But he found his objective quite easily and fitted the key into the door on the driver's side. It swung open without a sound, the interior exuding the faint luxury of cigar, both front seats sporting garish stretch covers in a busy floral pattern, all very prim and neat.

As he shone his torch around the professor's car a small sticker on the dashboard sprang into focus. Arnott snorted. PLEASE REFRAIN FROM SMOKING it read. He bundled inside and closed the door. It was a bloody freezing night for this sort of caper.

After a restless hour trying to sleep in the chair Sabina stretched her cramped limbs and peered at her watch. The room was icy. In desperation she moved to the bed and lay on the rosy counterpane, warming herself beside the sleeping figure. Without waking, he drew her to him and she fell into a dreamless slumber, totally exhausted.

At three o'clock a vixen screamed in the woods. They woke with a start. The appalling sound froze the blood and they clung together in the darkness listening to the vixen calling again and again.

Geoffrey began to speak, slowly and entirely lucidly, the alcohol as cold in his veins as the ashes of the bonfire. He answered all her questions. Yes, it was true. Naomi was dead. He had lied. Naomi had died months before, in late spring, when he knew that his contract was not to be renewed. Then the letter from Maryland. Injustices rankled with her. She brooded over the newspapers, politics, everything . . .

'It must have been the last straw,' he whispered. 'Always sensitive despite her funny ways. She got alopecia, you know, after the university row, after we had to leave.

'What's that?'

'Her hair started to fall out. A little patch at first and then in clumps. It distressed her a good deal.'

'It would,' Sabina murmured, her eyes wide in the dark.

'We moved about a lot, after jobs, and she kept up a brave front with her father. Pedantic little man, narrow-minded. Irish physicist of very poor standing but proud, very proud, and poor Naomi valued his silly opinions.'

'I am so sorry.'

'Not your fault, my love. In fact, the thought of your bright loveliness kept me sane all those years. I had something, you see, my secret treasure. Naomi had nothing. I was immune right up to the end.'

'The end?'

'We had moved into the cottage I told you about. A lodge, really. On the edge of the estate belonging to the Foundation. A lonely little hovel, not what Naomi was used to. After she began to lose her hair she hid herself away, became morbid, seemed even to welcome the obscurity of our little hidey-hole. She thought everyone was whispering behind her back. Probably were,' he added. 'But not for the reasons she imagined. My "disgrace" was of no interest whatsoever, not even a ripple on the still waters of Academe. We must have appeared an odd couple nevertheless . . .'

He paused, assembling the facts like notes for a lecture, clearing his throat, the stilted formal delivery inexpressibly touching.

'The morning the letter from Maryland arrived was bright, the first really warm day. I passed the letter over, she read it and we avoided each other the whole morning. We didn't talk about it. We both realized, you see, we each knew it was the last chance to pick up the old life. Naomi had always lived in academic communities. All her life. In Ireland—a splendid establishment—she acted as hostess for the Rector before we married. Out of the frying pan into the fire.'

He chuckled and in the darkness Sabina imagined his funny twisted smile, his delight in English clichés, a curious literary kleptomania which gave him secret pleasures she barely understood.

Geoffrey's voice ran on, unhurried, without passion. He might have been recalling for her dwindling attention an anecdote of no importance.

'I left Naomi forking about in the garden, planting vege-
tables of some sort, she said—marrows, I think. I went over
to the lab just to get away from the cottage. And yet, when
the police came to fetch me I almost guessed. You see, I
knew Naomi so well, her pain broke my heart. She set fire
to herself, you see.'

Sabina gasped, flinching against his embrace. Relentlessly he continued.

'She sat in the garden shed, lit a candle and poured petrol
over her head. They found the brass candlestick later. She
must have held it in her lap as she sat in that filthy hut.
Maryland was our last chance, it seems.'

'But it wasn't, Geoffrey. It wasn't! How could you let her
think that? Why didn't you tell me all this before? Why
didn't you tell me Naomi was dead?'

He turned away, nerveless, blank, not daring to witness
the mirage in his wilderness.

'Tomorrow, Geoffrey. Listen to me!' She laid her hand
against his cheek and forced him to face her. 'We'll drive to
London and I'll take you to see Harry's unit. I'll prove it
to you, Geoffrey.'

'But you don't love me.'

'Love? But the work, Geoffrey, the research . . .' She
faltered. And then briskly, 'In the morning everything will
be new. Trust me.'

CHAPTER 18

Next morning the rain had cleared but Arnott at the
Feathers, jammed in the cubbyhole which masqueraded as
a call-box, was oblivious of opal skies. Conjuring with coins
in a place no bigger than a bloody coffin was bad enough,
but treading the tightrope of investigation in the invidious
role of inspector was not his style at all.

Arnott's temper finally exploded when he was laconically

advised to call back after nine and speak to the Chief Clerk. 'Crime's like first aid, mate. It don't keep union hours. I'm not sitting at me desk in Baker Street like Sherlock bloody Holmes.'

He slammed his fist into the varnished partition and then, slowly grinding out each syllable through gritted teeth, said: 'Right, lad. I'll ring back in 'alf an hour. But if this Chief Clerk of yours is not out of bed your baby blue eyes'll be sticking out like chapel 'atpins when you 'ear what I've got to say to the Secretary. Mr Bayliss knows me of old. Say Inspector Arnott called.'

He banged down the receiver. After consulting a pocket diary, he prised himself out of the kiosk and ambled over to the landlord checking the till in the public bar and acquired more change. After a few pleasantries he lit a cigarette and eased his bulk back inside the call-box. It was time he got some help. Judy Pullen had got him into all this. She'd better back him up now he was right out of his depth. But Arnott was out of luck; Judy was away on a job and, despite a disinclination to leave a message with any member of the Fraud Squad, all of whom he personally considered slimy buggers, he saw no alternative and asked that she rang him at the Feathers. Arnott resigned himself to wade in on his own.

He made one more call. After a brief conversation he spoke up firmly, keeping his tone absolutely level.

'Mrs Morland, there have been some alarming developments you must hear about. Stay put. I'll be late getting over to you at Fernside but I'll bring back the keys, so keep the professor amused for a while. And don't mention my police work.'

Sabina stiffened, her mind flitting through various delaying tactics which might satisfy Geoffrey. After raiding Harry's dressing-room for shaving tackle and a clean shirt, Sabina congratulated herself on the spruce if somewhat subdued figure left to wait in the guest-room when Mrs Carter called her to the phone. To give the housekeeper due credit, she not so much as raised an eyebrow at finding a strange man in the house.

Drifting into the dining-room, Sabina was surprised to see Aragon seated next to her grandmother tucking into bacon and eggs. Sybil beamed. Presiding at the head of the table, she looked her usual self: hair fluffy and white as angora, a marcasite brooch gleaming dully at the collar of her Vyella blouse, the blue gaze sightless but tilted at just the right angle towards Sabina's step on the parquet.

'Was that Harry, dear?'

'Not Daddy!' Aragon wailed. 'I wanted to speak to him. Granny *said* he'd call this morning.' She threw down her knife. 'You are the absolute end, Sabina.'

Sabina slid into her place and calmly poured coffee.

'Aragon!' Sybil remonstrated, 'apologize now! I won't have you speak to your stepmother like that.'

Aragon speared a tomato with malice aforethought.

'It's quite all right, Sybil,' Sabina said. 'Actually, it wasn't Harry.'

'But he *is* flying in today. Granny said so.'

'I'm sure he'll ring you in Glasgow if he can't telephone here before your taxi arrives.' Sabina looked anxiously across the table. 'You did order a car from the village, I hope?'

Without haste Aragon chewed a mouthful before nodding. 'Just because you've started playing about with your test-tubes again, Sabina, it doesn't mean the rest of the family are brainless.'

Tapping the girl's wrists with mock severity, Sybil smoothly interceded. 'Don't be tiresome, Aragon. You were sweet as honey yesterday, I can't think what gets into you. You're as changeable as the weather.' She paused, mentally smoothing the girl's feathers. 'We shall miss all the excitement when you've gone, darling. Wasn't the party lovely? A pity your friends didn't stay overnight. You could all have gone back together.'

Aragon savagely placed her thrust. 'Sabina's friend was too drunk to drive home, I hear.'

Sabina flinched and the coffee, almost to her lips, spilled on the starched tablecloth.

The old lady's head bobbed up sharply and she half-imagined Aragon's words barbed with Lola's asperity.

'Aragon's very perceptive,' Sabina confessed. 'I was about to ask you, Sybil, if the professor might join us? I hardly liked to mention he was staying in front of everyone last night. He's obviously not used to drink. Mrs Carter's punch proved to be something of a secret weapon,' she added with mingled affability and embarrassment.

Aragon smiled at her plate and reached for more toast.

Somewhat surprised but with commendable *sang-froid*, Sybil effusively agreed with the suggestion and as the younger woman rose to invite their unexpected house guest down to breakfast the doorbell pealed.

'Oh dear. Carter's so busy this morning. I wonder if you would mind, Aragon darling? Just see who's at the door, will you? It's too early for your taxi, isn't it?'

'Miles too early, I'm getting the later train.' She bounced up, cheerful again having scored a palpable hit. 'I'll go and fetch our hungover professor, Gran, and Sabby can play housemaid.'

Before anyone could argue Aragon had slipped from the room, anticipating mischief. The doorbell rang again, insistently and long.

It was Arnott, looking considerably more formal than previously, his white shirt and dark suit almost funereal after the bookmater's check number. Sabina and he stood in the dark hall and had just begun their hurried conference as the telephone shrilled at her elbow.

'Put the keys on the hall table with mine, Mr Arnott. On that little brass tray. I always leave my keys there and can discreetly hand Geoffrey's back as he leaves. Aragon is in a very funny mood this morning, I wouldn't like to embarrass

Geoffrey any further by making it obvious we had confiscated his car keys.'

She reached out to answer the phone as the housekeeper, extremely flustered, appeared from the kitchen brushing wet hands across her overall.

'It's all right, Mrs Carter. I'll take it. Just show Mr Arnott into the dining-room, would you, please? And fresh coffee would be wonderful.'

'We'll talk later,' Arnott grunted, tapping his Mr Punch nose in a conspiratorial gesture which was the only thing in this most ghastly of all mornings to bring a fugitive smile to Sabina's lips.

'Hello. Yes, put me through. Mrs Harry Morland speaking.' She toyed with the keys, nervously tapping them against the brass salver, waiting to be connected. 'Yes, I'll hold. Yes, of course, mmmm . . .'

Arnott's broad outline receded into the dining-room followed by squeals of laughter from Aragon heralding her reappearance at Sybil's levee, presumably with the hapless Geoffrey in tow.

Sybil extended ringed fingers to Arnott as his shoes squeaked across the gleaming floor. 'How nice to have friends to breakfast. It's the best time of the day, of course. I hear from my son that breakfast meetings with business colleagues are in vogue now, especially in New York. He has an office there, you know. All this travel has ruined his digestion, poor man.'

Aragon stood behind her grandmother's chair dressed for the journey, a bulging macramé bag slung across her shoulders, her attention darting from Arnott to Geoffrey, amused at their discomfiture.

'You didn't stay the night, too, by any chance, Mr Arnott?' she sweetly inquired. 'Sabina is so hospitable, isn't she, Granny?'

'Don't be provocative, Aragon. It was extremely sensible of the professor not to drive last night, the roads were lethal. Black ice, Jack Pierce tells me.'

'I came to thank you, Mrs Morland,' Arnott said, 'before I go back to London.'

'So soon? Oh dear, everyone's leaving at once. I thought you were househunting.'

'Some unfinished business, I'm afraid.'

'Aragon is travelling back to Glasgow this morning.'

'Are you at the University?' Geoffrey sipped his coffee and launched himself down the smooth slipway of social intercourse. He looked very pale but fully at ease seated at Sybil's dining table, his æsthetic features courtly as those of the knight in armour pictured over the fireplace.

'No.' Aragon's appraisal of Sabina's guru was less kind.

Mrs Carter entered, placing a fresh pot of coffee at Sybil's hand. Arnott accepted a cup and tried to adjust to the high-backed discipline of his gothic-style dining chair. 'You're a cricketing man, I see.' He pointed at Geoffrey's noxious tie. 'MCC. Very exclusive. I'm a Yorkshire supporter myself.'

Geoffrey smoothed the yellow and orange stripes, conscious of the new whisky stains, and slipped in a smooth analysis of the winter tour. Aragon grew bored and glanced at her watch.

The door suddenly opened and Sabina entered, beckoning in an irritable, plucking gesture. 'Aragon! Your father's on the telephone. Be quick. The taxi's due.'

The girl fled, Sabina flopping into the seat next to Sybil, gratefully accepting fresh coffee. Outside in the garden Jack Pierce was dismantling the bonfire, trundling away ashes in a wheelbarrow. The four unlikely breakfast companions did their best to pass the time, each uneasily aware that only Aragon's departure could release them.

She burst in, exploding into the gothic gloom like forked lightning. Both men scrambled to their feet. White with anger, Aragon stood in the doorway gripping the brass handle, her words shrill.

'Sabina, you cow! You cheating, sly bitch! *You* put Daddy up to it, didn't you?'

The old woman shuffled in her efforts to rise and then flopped back, the strain too great, words failing her.

'Don't pretend you know nothing about it, Sabina!' Aragon crossed the room, confronting her stepmother with the full impact of her rage. Arnott and Geoffrey stood motionless, glazed by the child'a appalling bitterness, Sabina, strangely enough, staring back at Aragon almost with indifference.

She countered smoothly, 'Cut out the drama, Aragon. You're not at Glasgow now.'

'What do you mean, Aragon?' Sybil croaked, finding her voice at last. 'What did Harry say to upset you like this?'

Tears welled up in the girl's eyes, her fury undiminished. 'Sabina put him up to it. It's just her sort of creepy manœuvre.'

'You are quite wrong.' Sabina remained calm and, turning to Sybil, covered the old lady's trembling hand with her own cool one. 'Harry made a deal. He offered Rick a commission,' she explained. 'An entire mural in the new building.'

'Sounds just the job to me,' Arnott put in, struggling to find a raft in the damburst. Aragon turned on him, tears brushed aside.

'In New York, you stupid man! Rick's been paid off. To go to New York, providing he breaks all contact with me, of course! To paint some stupid wall in Daddy's stupid building. Bribed by my father's fat wallet, prompted by his bloody wife who's the last person to throw stones. I could tell you about—'

'Aragon!' Sybil's shrill remonstrance barely rippled the surface of the cataract.

'I *am* going to see Rick. Now! Before he goes on Wednesday.' Aragon swung about just as the housekeeper re-entered.

'The taxi's here.'

'Sod the taxi!'

Mrs Carter fled.

Aragon advanced to the table and threw down a set of car keys amid the butter and marmalade, Miss Mackenzie's indestructible label a focus to four pairs of eyes as if the orange plastic keyring tag could decode the mystery.

'You can keep your poofy brother's car, Sabina. I don't want anything from your disgusting family.' Drawing a tape-casette from the string haversack, she thrust it forwards from the hip as if it were a revolver. 'This,' she quietly promised, 'will show Daddy exactly what sort of double-dealer you really are, Sabina. Don't look at me like that, Mother dearest. I didn't bug your private conversation. You and your academic drunk must have accidentally started up Granny's machine last night when you were sparring in her room. I thought the tape was my audition piece and played it to Caroline and Roddy last night after the party. Did we have a laugh! You should hear it, Gran. Sabina and her very own "undesirable friend", as you call it. Also married, of course. And she dares to criticize Rick for being bribed. That so-called scientist over there would sell his soul for the use of Daddy's computers. Don't talk to me about pure research! Once my father hears this, paying Rick to go away will seem like pin money. This man—' she pointed a trembling finger at Geoffrey—'won't even get through the gates at Bracknell once Daddy knows the real score. The professor's assessment of businessmen in his own vulgar words. Wow!'

Thrusting the cassette back in her bag, she ran out, leaving the quartet in the dining-room momentarily stunned.

Sabina flew round the table and caught Sybil as she tottered, almost falling. Geoffrey rushed out, his face ashen.

Holding Sybil in her arms, Sabina appealed to Arnott who was about to bolt, presumably in pursuit of the hysterical girl. He supported Sybil while Sabina poured water into a tumbler, holding it to the old lady's lips. Mrs Carter ran in aghast at the row clearly audible from the kitchen.

'Quick! Help me get her upstairs, Mrs Carter. The shock . . .' Sabina gasped.

Arnott grabbed Sabina's arm. 'Can't you leave her?' and then, spinning round on the housekeeper, 'Don't just stand there, woman, help the old lady upstairs.' He pulled Sabina away. 'We must get them back.'

Impatiently shaking him off she turned on Arnott. 'Aragon can fend for herself. I can't leave Sybil.'

The two women shuffled into the hall, Sybil between them, Arnott impatiently in the rear. The unmistakable growl of the Porsche engine revved on the drive and through the open front door they watched with horror the sports car accelerate towards the gates.

Sybil rallied, clutching Sabina's arm. 'That was your car! She'll kill herself. Go after her. I'll be all right.'

Arnott jerked Sabina aside. 'She's right. Don't waste time. Where's Tallent?'

As if on cue a second swirl of gravel answered his question. 'By 'eck,' he murmured, 'he's gone after her.'

'He wants the tape.' Sabina looked wildly at the receding exhaust fumes. 'It's dynamite, Mr Arnott. We said a lot of things . . . Harry won't lift a finger to help Geoffrey if Aragon gives him that tape. It's his last chance. He'll murder Aragon if she spoils it for him now!'

Arnott was starting his clapped-out Vauxhall even before Sabina had slammed the passenger door.

'Can she drive that rocket of yours?'

'I suppose so. She *has* driven it but it's not a car to tackle when one's in a temper. Harry thinks she's a natural—he taught her to drive at his factory. We'll never catch her.'

'Well, if *we* don't Tallent doesn't stand a hope in that Renault 5.'

'She can't get far anyway. There's hardly any petrol. I was going to fill up this morning. Hey, turn right here,' she directed. The Vauxhall gained speed, skidding on the icy tarmac.

'Which way's she likely to go?'

'Try the back lanes. It's a quick route to join the motor-way, the usual way we set off to London, she's gone that way dozens of times. In her state of temper she won't stop to think up anything new. But slow down, Mr Arnott, it's twisty and narrow till we get to Ashton.'

'Tell me about this Rick character that started her off.' Arnott peered ahead, the tree-lined road still frosty, un-touched by the weak November sunshine. 'No,' he added. 'Don't bother, lass. I reckon that story's as old as the hills. Heard it all before.'

A mile further on they crested a rise and spotted a black streak far below on a loop of country road.

'That's it, by 'eck!' Arnott crowed, crouching over the wheel.

'We'll never do it.'

'She's not used to a car like that. Bound to take it careful. Don't fuss, woman. That girl shouts the odds an' all but underneath she's a right canny little bugger. Jealous. Bound to be. Wants to get 'er own back, that's all.'

'Good God. Look down there! That white car. That's Geoffrey. Hurry, Mr Arnott. Geoffrey mustn't reach her first.'

Arnott's mouth hardened and he pressed forward, now thoroughly alarmed. The freezing fog made driving difficult, drifting in patches like landlocked clouds.

The sound when it came was sickeningly familiar. The crash and splinter of buckled metal froze their blood. A tongue of flame shot briefly skywards, the pall of smoke sifting through the bare branches presenting a scene almost predictable in its terrible implications.

With all sense thrown aside Arnott flung the Vauxhall down the twisting lane to reach the scene of the accident.

As they took the last turn the fog clouded their view. Arnott blinked and slammed on the brakes. Sabina leapt out and he stumbled after.

The Porsche had grazed a drystone wall, the girl's head bent over the wheel. Beyond the Porsche a huge gash in the stonework was jammed with the twisted remains of the Renault, the driver's door half hanging from its hinges like a loose tooth. Sabina reached into the Porsche, aching with relief as Aragon's head lifted, dark eyes luminous with fear.

'Are you all right?' Sabina fumbled with the seat-belt, tearing the girl's hands from the steering-wheel, watching closely as she clambered out, stiff, profoundly shocked but apparently unscathed. They clung together in the misty lane, the only sound the cawing of a rook, every inch of Aragon's body trembling like an aspen.

Arnott called from the wreckage, his florid face appearing above the drystone wall like a farcical copy of the huge winter sun rising over the fields.

'Get over here quick,' he called. 'Hold his 'ead . . .'

Sabina pulled Aragon away from the Porsche and gently led her under a clump of scrubby hazel saplings, screened from the sight of the crash. She crouched there, shivering, like a nymph in a thicket. Sabina hurried to help Arnott, clambering over the scattered stones to reach the car door.

'He's still alive but we've got to get him out quick. His leg . . .' he muttered. Miraculously, Geoffrey opened his eyes and gazed about him at the shambles. Arnott scrutinized the professor with the swift appraisal of an experienced veteran of many such accidents, gently running gnarled hands over Geoffrey's legs and chest, checking his pulse, examining the intense blue eyes. He twisted sideways to reassure her. 'It's only his leg and the fire's out. But the boot's jammed. I don't know what he's got stashed away in there. We can't take any chances, we'll have to get him out in case there's an explosion.' Sabina was totally baffled by Arnott but it was no time to argue.

'Help me get him on the grass,' he said. 'Then see if the Porsche is moveable. Looked OK to me. If the Porsche starts, make off with the girl, keep her right out of it. I'll square it at this end when the police get here but don't let anyone know she was driving.' He drew Sabina aside, keeping one eye on the casualty. 'I'll drive to that village down there and say I was overtaken on the bend—almost true!—and the Renault must have slid off the road and hit the wall. Tell them back at the house that you caught up with the kid when the car ran out of petrol and I've buzzed off on my own. Got it? Nobody knows nothing about this character in the Renault, he's blacked out and likely to be confused when he comes round. My guess is he tried to force the girl into the verge to make her stop. She seems to have kept control, you've got to hand it to her there. The Porsche looks hardly scratched to me.'

Sabina nodded, barely understanding the complicity of this extraordinary policeman. He glanced at the professor and back at Sabina and together they pulled Geoffrey smoothly from the car.

As he was freed the loose seat cover dragged off and Arnott stopped short, still supporting their burden, staring at the brown stain on the driver's seat suddenly revealed.

'Blood,' he muttered.

Sabina impatiently glanced inside, Geoffrey a dead weight in her arms. 'For God's sake, Mr Arnott! That's old blood. He's not bleeding now, very little anyway.' Sabina glared at Arnott who seemed to be deflected by anything remotely interesting. 'Do come on!' she urged. 'If I'm to get Aragon away from here before anyone comes we can't start investigating old upholstery marks. Geoffrey's obviously been in an accident before.'

They placed him on the springy turf in the shelter of the wall well away from the mangled wreckage. He groaned as they laid him down but blissfully slipped back into unconsciousness as Sabina turned back to Aragon.

They pushed her into the back seat of the Porsche where she curled up like a frightened hedgehog. Sabina tried the ignition, reversing the car into the lane, her trembling hands slowly gaining composure as she mastered the powerful engine and negotiated the wreck.

She wound down the window and peered at Arnott, solid

as the rolling landscape around them. 'Why are you helping us like this?'

'I'll tell you later. Just cut off home as quick as you can, don't stop and don't get involved in explanations. You saw nothing. The girl's shocked, had enough trouble for a bit. Just leave it to me. If they find out this little lady of yours was driving the Porsche the fat'll really be in the fire. If I was you I'd pack her off to school with her mates right away.'

He abruptly stopped her driving off just as she was pulling away. 'Hang about! Pass me that tape, I'll keep it safe. Can't be too careful.'

Sabina scrabbled in Aragon's bag and passed over the offending cassette with a rueful smile. 'Thanks,' she said.

'I don't want to rub it in, love, but all this could have been avoided if you hadn't given the hot-headed professor his keys back.'

The engine stalled. Sabina stared, open-mouthed.

'But I didn't, Mr Arnott. Believe me, I swear I didn't even mention the keys to Geoffrey. There wasn't time with Aragon screaming at everyone.' She hesitated and then went on, 'Now I think back, I saw those keys still on the hall table where I left them. As you and I rushed out I remember noticing his keys and thinking Aragon must have snatched up mine as she went. I always leave them handy by the telephone, she knows that.' Sabina laughed. 'Appropriating Geoffrey's keys until he was sober was a waste of time, then. He obviously carries spares. You got dragged back to Fernside this morning on a fool's errand, I'm afraid. Sorry.'

'But Tallent's keys were with yours.'

'Yes. But Aragon didn't scoop them up with the others, I'm almost certain they're still at the house.' She tipped the contents of the macramé bag on to the passenger seat. There were no keys.

'Don't bugger about with all that now!' Arnott impatiently banged on the side of the car as if he were slapping a racehorse. 'Get away from here. I'll contact you at the house tomorrow when everything's calmed down. When you get home, check the brass tray thing. If Tallent's car keys are there put them in an envelope and lock it up somewhere safe. Don't discuss any of this even with the old lady. It'll all be sorted out, you'll see. You're safe now. Just put the fear of God into that stepdaughter of yours that if she so much as whispers any of this you'll turn her in on the driving charge.'

Arnott stepped back off the road and Sabina started up the engine for the second time. When the Porsche had gone Arnott went back to the injured man lying on the grass like a crusader on a tomb. He bent down to feel his pulse and Geoffrey's eyelids fluttered, opening briefly with an expression of fear and incomprehension.

As Arnott straightened, the roar of a motor-cycle broke the silence, swiftly emerging round the bend. Arnott waited for the rider to slow down. A young farm labourer by the look of things.

'Christ!' he said, skidding to a halt. 'What's up?'

'A bit of a bang. The car's a write-off.' Arnott jerked his head towards the man on the grass. 'He's hurt his leg, smashed his knee, I think, but nothing fatal. Get an ambulance quick as you can, lad. I'll stay here and keep an eye on the poor bugger.'

'Aidenswell's not more'n a mile down the 'ill.' The boy looked sickly under his crash helmet but Arnott's gruff instructions seemed to allay his shock. After a brief exchange Arnott waved him on and the motorbike burst into full throttle, swerving off at speed.

He went back to the victim, gently turning him on his side and then, after a few moments, Arnott climbed back over the rubble to look inside the car.

Still attached to the keys hanging from the ignition was Miss Mackenzie's tag last seen flung down on Sybil's damask breakfast cloth. A satisfied breath whistled through gritted teeth like the hiss of a punctured tyre as Arnott reached across the dashboard to claim his prize.

Pocketing the keys, he made his way back over the wall, turning to stare out across the shrouded valley towards the village where a church spire pierced the November mist like an admonition from Heaven: Thou Shalt Not Bear False Witness.

'Don't wag your finger at me, sir. I'm retired.' Arnott laughed.

CHAPTER 19

It was there all right. Arnott grimly acknowledged that however often he circled the course the next fence was unavoidable. Like a weary old nag he judged the obstacle from all angles, seeking a gap in the professor's alibi.

He had grown to appreciate the man. Not like him exactly, but for two so utterly diverse their bondage was something Arnott could understand. Both ridden by the dead? Detective-Inspector Arnott would have barged through without so much as a blink. But Ralph Arnott didn't have to bring the poor devil down. But then he would be back where he'd started: a messy end to a working life and no peace anywhere. He'd promised himself he would finish in style, no loose ends.

And here he was hunched on a plastic seat in the tiled waiting-room of some piddling little hospital guessing the odds. He'd phoned the Feathers from Casualty and left a message for Judy with the publican in the faint hope she would ring through. Fat chance!

Knowing was one thing. Doing was something else.

Arnott had taken up this case again for pride's sake and slithered in via the tradesmen's entrance. Typical. If he had got everything laid out nice and neat before crashing into retirement this newfangled introspection would never have kept him awake at nights. The funny thing was, Arnott reluctantly conceded, the bloke who'd started on this bloody outing had begun to notice the scenery on the way round. All the sharp angles he had promised himself when Judy Pullen first offered him another crack at it had blunted. Attainable all right but so what?

Everyone, including Judy's boyfriend Erskine, had lost interest. Arnott gloomily shuffled his options. He'd been clamped in the stuffy waiting-room for an hour, forbidden to smoke, his mind fuzzy after a sleepless night churning the facts over and over.

Gradually, it had dawned on Arnott that he, the rough policeman, and Geoffrey Tallent, the brilliant scientist, were in the same box. All that about his wife setting fire to herself, the smashed-up career, two widowers with infinite regret their mutual goaler. Fucking marvellous!

He sighed, twisting his wrist to check the time. The only appeasement by the NHS was sparing the survivors in this limboland the painful measurement of time. No wall clock. At ten-thirty he was the only visitor. In his crumpled tweeds, clutching a bag of grapes, his sagging features settling into loose folds about his chin, Ralph Arnott seemed an unlikely 'friend'. The ward sister was much too busy to trouble herself with conjecture but hastily agreed to allow him through after the doctor's rounds. Twenty-four hours after the accident, yes, she admitted, the injury was painful and recuperation would be slow but the concussion had been mild and traffic accidents were common. Yes, Professor Tallent had been lucky and no, the police would probably not get around to statements till later in the day, there was such a thing as consideration for medical opinion even in Yorkshire. But Arnott would be given priority to visit his friend now his condition was stable. 'The Health Service is not without compassion even out of visiting hours,' she finally admonished before abandoning him to the dreadful waiting-room.

By the time a coloured nurse put her frizzy head round the waiting-room door and beckoned him, Arnott was almost submerged in a morass of recrimination, compounded by lack of sleep. He lumbered up, following her out, her black stockings provocative beneath the starched apron.

By the blessing of Providence Geoffrey Tallent was in a side ward, presumably his temporary unconsciousness conferring some concession. Arnott eased into the tiny room, its sterility almost refreshing after the airless waiting-room. Geoffrey lay back, his grey hair like ashes against the crisply laundered pillows, bedclothes tented over his smashed knee.

Arnott pulled up a chair and dropped the bag of fruit on the locker. Geoffrey eyed him with dismal recognition, blue eyes naked as only those habitually protected by spectacles are.

'Why are you here?'

'My name's Arnott. Ralph Arnott.'

'The man who reported the crash.'

'That's the ticket.'

'Funny you being there,' Geoffrey said, bewilderment ruffling the blue defenceless gaze like a breeze across a lake. There was something else, a word on the tip of his tongue, just out of reach.

Arnott searched his pocket.

'I brought these,' he said, producing a pair of glasses crudely cobbled at the bridge with sticking plaster. 'I found them in the footwell under the dashboard of the car after the ambulance had left. Best I could do, the sticky tape, but better than nothing.'

He handed them over and Geoffrey sat up, carefully donning the broken spectacles, a fugitive smile snatching at one corner of his mouth.

'That was good of you. I'm lost, as you see.'

His hands opened in a gesture of defeat, the elegant fingers with their almond-shaped nails as sterile as the fold of sheet on which they lay. A bruise on his temple was beginning to darken like a mildewed stain.

From another of the numerous pockets in the tweed suit Arnott plucked a second trophy. A short length of red terylene tape, half an inch wide with a neat metal clip at one end. 'I found this too, under the seat. It had worked its way under the rubber matting. Your nice loose covers dragged out as well, them on the front seats. Very cosy-looking. My wife used to go in for stretchy things like that on the chairs. Never appealed to me to be honest, covering up old stains under flowery covers.' His tone was even but the two men eyed each other cautiously like cockerels in a pit.

The door burst open, the ward sister's brusque acquiescence now bristling, a milky fluid slopping wildly in a small glass on a tray in her hand. Casting a withering glance at Arnott, she stood by while Geoffrey swallowed his medication and then held open the door for Arnott to follow. 'A word with you,' she said.

Arnott shambled out, his temper rising, prepared for combat. Closing the door, she faced him, grim lines settling either side of her pert little mouth. She was pretty despite the starched trappings of her rank, quite young in fact. But wasn't that what was said about policemen? Arnott sighed. He must be getting old.

'I've just had an instruction,' she said tartly. 'Matron informs me an Inspector Erskine of Special Branch has cleared your attendance here. We are to allow special facilities it seems for some sort of undercover investigation.' Her cold gaze flickered with disbelief over the scruffy suit. 'Most secret he said, even from the local police, something to do with the professor's scientific experiments.'

Arnott's bushy eyebrows rose in gratifying arcs like furry caterpillars on a cabbage leaf. God bless you, Judy Pullen.

'Professor Tallent is still in shock. We normally get documentation for this sort of intrusion. You may have one hour.'

Arnott remained silent and after an angry pause the ward sister turned on her heel and transferred her irritability to a luckless orderly who chose the wrong moment to trundle past with a tea-trolley.

Arnott re-entered the side ward and resumed his place at the bedside. Geoffrey stared at him afresh, taking in the old-fashioned tweeds. Recognition dawned. He remembered now. This silly old buffer was a friend of the Morlands. He'd been at the party and witnessed the appalling fracas at the breakfast table. His mind cleared now that he could place the man.

Arnott swung the red webbing from his craggy fist like a pendulum. Geoffrey stared at it and then at Arnott, faintly puzzled.

'You recognize it, Professor?'

'I've seen it in the car. It's not mine. Presumably one of my students left it behind. It's from a handbag, I imagine. I sometimes give students a lift into town. The Foundation is rather off the beaten track,' he added smoothly. Salvaging his spectacles was one thing, scavenging this bit of strap seemed entirely pointless. Another eccentric Englishman, Geoffrey concluded, smiling quietly to himself.

Arnott stretched the terylene tautly between his hands, testing the man's response with the appraisal of a professional inquisitor. It evidently meant nothing. He sighed. A punch below the belt was called for.

'Tell me about your wife.'

Geoffrey started violently and then leaned back, closing his eyes, waiting for the pain in his knee to roll back like a wave on the shingle.

Arnott sat out the silence, the little room wrapped around by the distant clatter from the sluice along the corridor. It was all too familiar: the smell, the artificial jollity of the nurses, rain pattering against the glass.

'All right,' he sighed. 'I'll tell you about mine.'

Arnott's voice rumbled in the bare room, bouncing off the white walls in staccato bursts.

'Peg was a pretty thing. Caught me good and proper on a thirty-six-hour pass, me and some of me mates come down from Catterick to see the bright lights. Lively lads, none of us more than twenty-odd . . .' he murmured. 'But Peg got homesick, fed up with Army life. So I joined the police and we set up near her mother, south of the river.'

Geoffrey closed his eyes, Arnott's voice chugging back and forth like a goods train in a siding.

'It worked out all right. But no kids. She was very good about it. Peg wasn't one of them moaning minnies. Three years ago she got ill. It struck me as a bloody rotten turn-up for a decent woman to be snared like that at the finish, just when we'd begun to take things easy. She asked so little, you see, deserved a better 'and than she got.'

'Don't we all,' muttered Geoffrey. 'Is she recovered now?' he added politely.

'Dead. Cancer. Dragged out with this and that treatment. We never admitted she was getting no better. All she ever nagged me about was keeping t' bloody 'ouse dusted.'

'My wife was never much of a housewife,' Geoffrey said. 'Servants were cheap in Ireland. She never really got the hang of it. No children for us either, but I don't think Naomi missed them. We never spoke of it, it would have seemed unkind. That sounds strange, I know, but that was how we were. The University was her life. All that tradition, it was a religion to her. She fussed with my students, entertained the faculty, bossed the other wives a good deal, I imagine. My work was immaterial to her in some ways, an incidental, you might say.'

'This was when you were in the North?'

'Did Sabina tell you about it? Things were never the same after. She was Anglo-Irish, dogmatic, very much concerned with honour, integrity and scholarship. Poor Naomi. Bred in her, naturally. That was why her mind was shattered by my own little mishap.'

'The accusations?'

'The validity of my research questioned. Nasty rumours of deceit and plagiarism. Heresy! Naomi found that as awesome a conjecture as refuting her own femininity, the very fabric of her life dishonoured. It was inconceivable to her.'

'But charges were never brought.'

'The whisperings alone were enough to destroy us. Her hair fell out.' Geoffrey turned sharply, filled with impotent rage. 'Sounds comic, doesn't it? Go on, laugh! A bald woman. A very minor affliction, you are thinking. In comparison with your own wife's agony. A little hair loss . . . But it shrivelled her entire being, the shame of my corruption literally brought down on her head. It was all too much. She wore a wig.'

Arnott's breath exhaled like a puff of feathers. Suddenly it all seemed to settle into place. 'I guessed it must be that,' he said softly.

Geoffrey's attention was abstracted and he shrugged off his listener with dazed irritability.

'We had to leave, of course. Her father got to hear of it. Splashed all over the educational press, thanks to Swayne's intervention. He was Sabina's brother, you know. Later it was hushed up, the university was seriously embarrassed by the publicity. After a year or two I would have been able to slip back, retrieve my reputation. Academic fraud is commonplace, a vexing minor problem in research. Those outside think demarcation lines are clear but it is not so. As head of a team it is impossible to do all the work oneself. A certain amount must be taken on trust and who does what is by no means obvious.'

'But there were irregularities?'

Geoffrey shrugged, glossing over Arnott's interruption and continued. 'After a year or two in the wilderness I could have slipped back, but Naomi who had been such an asset when times were good was unhinged by the academic witch-hunt, the slur concocted she considered by the gross interference of Sabina's brother.'

'Your wife knew nothing of your feelings for your research student?'

'Sabina? Naomi discounted that sort of gossip. It was

inconceivable to her, and to be frank it was a passing obsession on my part at the time. It seemed to ripen later, like fruit laid aside in the dark.'

'Tell me about Francis Swayne.'

Geoffrey launched into his assessment with the aplomb of a professional analyst, almost unaware of Arnott and dismissive of his validity as an interlocutor.

'Francis Swayne was a windbag. For prurient reasons he attempted to destroy my research project, my entire academic career. As if his sister's virginity was central in all this.' The patent absurdity of Swayne's complaint brought a grim smile to the chiselled features. 'The formal grievance procedures were never implemented by the faculty and our invidious position grievously affected Naomi. With the passing of time, her despair took on manic proportions and I seriously considered requesting her people to allow her to return to Ireland for a year or two. And just as matters were beginning to fade, Francis Swayne was in the news again.'

'His defence of O'Laughlin, you mean?'

'A terrorist. A blatant murderer released on some trifling legal whimsicality invented by the same man who had destroyed my work. The sheer injustice of it exploded in Naomi's brain, the final blow. The judicial cabal that flung us into shame and disgrace dispensed mercy to a killer. By default! No one claimed O'Laughlin was innocent, not even Swayne. But they let him off because his barrister performed a legalistic sleight of hand. It was too much to bear.'

Geoffrey Tallent's cheeks were filmed with perspiration, the broad high forehead glistening under the neon lighting, the day already dark at the window, threatening a deluge. 'Why should Swayne juggle with justice like that? Was no one to redress the balance? I thought the boat was his.'

'What boat?' Arnott persisted.

'That yacht. He won a race off Fastnet. I saw it in some yachting magazine in the dentist's waiting-room. Pictured with Mansell, the two of them. Champagne. I'd forgotten about Mansell. He hadn't suffered,' he added bitterly.

'But *Seraphina* was Roger Mansell's boat.'

'I know that *now*,' he countered, 'but at the time I had no idea Mansell had money. He was just another penniless research assistant of mine before Swayne indicted me.' Geoffrey's contempt was universal, embracing Arnott, Swayne, Roger Mansell and the academic world at large.

'You caused the arson?'

Geoffrey ignored this last remark and drifted off into private reverie, wide awake but lost in sour recrimination which seemed almost palpable in the confined hospital room.

Arnott said: 'Tell me about going to the mews.'

'Why?'

'Because I have the tape.'

Arnott jerked Geoffrey's attention back to the present, jabbing at the plastic cassette on the bed, just out of reach. 'It's your last chance, Professor. A straight exchange. Mrs Morland will give you the tape and recommend your project to her husband but you must tell me how it happened.' He paused, Geoffrey eyeing him with sly calculation. Then Arnott thrust home his advantage.

'I have proof.' He dangled the red terylene webbing between his hands. 'You didn't recognize this. It's the cat's lead.'

'What cat?'

'Swayne's Siamese wore a harness and lead like a lapdog. The strap was in Swayne's car. That's why the cap leapt into yours and toppled the old lady when you were trying to pass yourself off as a Jehovah's Witness.'

Geoffrey shook his head, the significance of a Siamese cat quite lost.

'And the car.' Arnott's breath laboured as he leaned across the bed, his palms sweaty with the stress of this final throw of the dice. 'I only have to get the police to check the engine number. Did Swayne stain the driver's seat?'

'Why doesn't Sabina come here herself if she wants to bargain?'

'She can't. Morland's back. He arrived at Fernside this

morning. She had to get the girl away to Glasgow first thing before he got home: Aragon got a nasty fright. It'll be a long time before that little madam goes joyriding again.' He paused long enough for this to sink in and then inserted the second barb. 'We could always call her back, of course. To tell the police about you forcing her off the road.' The seconds ticked away in silence until Arnott gave the line a firm flick. 'Mrs Morland can't get away this morning. She sent me. Before the local police get a statement from you. You don't mention the Porsche or the girl or the tape. You skidded on the ice and hit the wall. I happened to come along on my way back to London, someone you met at a party, a mere acquaintance. Get it, Professor? It's now or never, Tallent. Either come clean about her brother and she promotes your work to Morland and gets you the back-up you need. Or finish yourself off for good an' all. She's not so fond of that stepdaughter of hers as to shield her from prosecution if you won't play ball.'

Geoffrey's calculations were falling slowly, in rotation, like a row of dominoes.

'Who are you?' he rasped.

'Detective-Inspector Arnott, CID. I investigated the death of Francis Swayne and made a right balls of it. I'm trying to put that right. For my own satisfaction. Not for official consumption. Mind you, a coroner's verdict can always be set aside and you'd have a lot of explaining to do if it went beyond these four walls.'

'Are you bribing me? Or her?' Hope flared like a light at the end of the tunnel in Geoffrey's mind and he regarded Arnott with shrewd reappraisal. A bent policeman—wasn't that what they called it?—might just save the day.

'Tell me about going to the mews.' Arnott's tone was relentless, his massive presence in the tiny room seeming to expand like a genie from a bottle.

Geoffrey shuffled his options and decided there was nothing more to lose. A moment's quietness, then the curiously clipped accent rumbled on.

'After the fiasco of the boat fire, I started to watch Swayne all hours. I wasn't going to let him get away with it a second time. A colleague, contracted to the Mayo for a year, allows me to use his house in Fulham and after Naomi's death I spent most of my time in London. The mawkish sympathies of the people at the Foundation were insupportable and it was a welcome escape from the cottage.'

Geoffrey hesitated, gently exploring the bruise at his temple, the slim fingers waxy, trembling slightly as they slid along his hollow cheek.

'Swayne was a man circumscribed by routine. I sat in the public house opposite his home charting his comings and goings, checking his movements. It took my mind off Naomi, imagining her torment, shifting the blame. It was very simple. Every Friday evening he drove off for the weekend, locking the house with obsessive care. During the week his movements were more erratic, he seemed to work at home from time to time and the black woman was much in evidence. The cleaner,' he elaborated. 'She spoke to me once but . . .'

Arnott nodded, anxious not to disturb the flow. 'Go on!'

Geoffrey shook his head as if to clear his thoughts and after reflection, continued.

'I had no reason for this surveillance initially. Merely a desire to know this stranger who had casually orchestrated my destruction. Then, over the days and weeks, a plan formed in my mind. I wanted to obliterate something *he* valued. To make him suffer some fraction of the annihilation he had brought on us. The boat was a special joy to him and it was only later I discovered it belonged to Mansell. Too late. The house was the obvious target. I wanted to set fire to it, a tribute to Naomi, I suppose. I had no wish to injure the man personally, you understand, I'm not mad. But it was important he was made to pay. A reckoning.'

'Making bombs,' Arnott sneered. 'Where d'you pick up that little game?'

Geoffrey burst into laughter. 'You haven't a clue, have you, Arnott? You think I'm some tuppenny-ha'penny crank. To anyone involved as I was with the construction of a radio-frequency superconduction quantum interference device, putting up a simple timing mechanism to detonate a small charge is like setting a mousetrap!'

Arnott knew when it was time to back off and attempted to arrange his features in an expression of contrition.

'It was a hot night. I wore a tracksuit and coiled a climbing rope under my sweatshirt and jogged over to the mews after dark. It was a simple matter to reach the top of the high wall from the mews archway but a party was in noisy progress in one of the big houses at the back, people spilling into the garden, drinking and jigging about. I was loath to abandon my plan and decided to brazen it out. I simply crawled along the wall in full view, in fact made quite a fool of myself, acting drunk, waving to the girls.' Geoffrey smiled.

'And none of these partygoers remarked on it?'

He sniggered. 'Once these young people are partying no sort of bizarre behaviour is remarkable. You obviously have never observed the British student at play, Arnott!'

The air of superiority was irksome but Arnott had to admit the man had guts, carrying off a stunt like that.

'Once over into the garden it was a brief matter to throw the rope up to the parapet. I had a grappling hook and have kept myself fit potholing in Derbyshire for years, you understand. The back of Swayne's house is screened by a tree and anyone crouching over the skylight would be invisible. Inside the bathroom I hauled up the rope and wrapped it round my waist again. I intended to let myself out through the front door, of course.'

'The house was empty?'

'For the whole weekend, I thought. I took my time inside, poked about the bedroom in the attic, checked the layout downstairs, made sure the coast was clear. It was almost a pleasure handling that man's fancy baubles, the sort of trash

poor Naomi would have drooled over. Imagine his distress
when it went up in flames!'

'What about the pub? Busy Fridays, I would have
thought. A hot night, people drinking outside in the mews,
anyone might have seen you.'

'All closed up. Gone home hours before, no problem
there. I set the explosive device in the kitchen, a small
enough charge to fire the house without killing the neighbours. An apparent reprisal from disaffected Irishmen when
the news broke. Swayne was a marked man in Ulster, you
know. Then I went back upstairs to check I hadn't left any
evidence before I cleared out.'

'I hand it to you there. Not so much as a whisper and my
team was over the whole ruddy house like ferrets.' Arnott's
barely concealed admiration flirted with Geoffrey's ego and
he rattled on, eager to display his cleverness.

'It was then I discovered the pornographic magazines
and gadgets in the dressing-up box.'

'The leather trunk in the study?'

'Precisely. You saw all that disgusting ordure?'

Arnott nodded.

'I need not elaborate. Until that moment it was for me a
calculated exercise to redress the balance. Swayne had
ripped up my career like yesterday's newspaper, without
a thought. Then he had jettisoned his own professional
standards, manipulating the law in order to release a murderer on a technicality. And despite this his own career was
unaffected. Not so much as a rebuke! No one accused
Swayne of unprofessional conduct, lack of integrity. It was
double-dealing of the worst kind, which as a former alien
did not surprise me in the least—don't tell me the old boy
network died with the Empire. It's one rule for them and
another for the rest of us.' Arnott hoped Geoffrey was not
going to slide off into political clichés and surreptitiously
checked his watch. But Geoffrey was now in full spate,
unstoppable.

'That was what drove Naomi to despair: she believed

in the establishment, tradition, ideals, chivalry, all that
rubbish. Whereas I never had. She would *not* accept the fact
that we had been flung into outer darkness while Swayne
got away with it. That fiasco in Dublin with terrorists wild
with delight outside the courthouse was the turning-point
for my poor Naomi. It was the last straw. She never was
the same after that, do you see. And this same clever lawyer
everyone thought so smart, this same manipulator of justice,
was a pervert!'

Colour suffused Geoffrey's neck and flushed darkly across
his brow, his emotional outburst vanquishing the pain in
his knee as no medication could. Arnott made soothing
gestures with his craggy hands, desperate that the ward
sister, hearing the man's frantic crescendo, might rush in
and break the spell.

But he was too angry to stop now and began again,
pressing his face close to Arnott's, whispering.

'When I saw all that filthy literature and women's clothing in the trunk I sank on to the floor in that horrible room,
appalled by the depravity of the man.'

Geoffrey shook his head as if to clear his thoughts and
after a moment's reflection, continued.

'Then I heard a car. I rushed through to the sitting-room
at the front and looked down into the mews. Swayne was
back! Why? He had already gone away for the weekend,
I assumed. He let himself in and came upstairs. There
was no escape. All I could do was hide in the sitting-room
and see what he did next. If he went to bed I could let
myself out later when it was quiet. If he was just passing
through I could keep hidden until he had gone. And all the
time the bomb was ticking away downstairs. I had to stay.
If Swayne didn't go away that night I must defuse the
explosive and try to escape unnoticed. If he left I could
stick to the plan. I had at least forty minutes to spare. I
sat tight.'

Geoffrey reached across the locker and poured a glass of
water, staring out at the rain as if Arnott's presence was

invisible, the narrative an internal catharsis purging himself of the emotional turmoil. To free himself to get back to his work. *That* was the important thing.

CHAPTER 20

Geoffrey picked up the story, speaking softly, forcing Arnott to crane forward to catch his words.

'Swayne was in a great hurry. I was sweating: the heat had built up in that converted stable of his, a rat-run of little rooms. Airless. He was whistling away to himself, running to the top of the house, banging drawers and suchlike and for a minute or two I thought he might be changing to drive down to the country straightaway. Then I heard water gushing in the bathroom. He was having a shower. I crept on to the landing and stood at the half-open door of the study, watching him when he came out, a fancy little fellow with a towel draped round his scraggy gut, slightly drunk and obviously pleased with himself over something or other.' Geoffrey's glance slid away from his rapt listener.

'The steam had penetrated the study, the whole place was like a Turkish bath. I waited, thinking he would either go to bed or keep to his usual routine and clear out for the weekend.'

'You took a chance there, standing within six feet of the man in his own house.'

'Swayne had more interesting things on his mind!' Geoffrey grimaced comically as if he were party to a secret joke. Then he shivered and seemed to pull himself together, brace himself to continue.

'It was then he must have decided to award himself a little luxury, a prize for something seemingly concluded to his entire satisfaction.

'You see,' Geoffrey confided, 'I had observed the man for weeks, years one might say. Could almost read his thoughts.

It was as if Fate had cast me as the unwilling witness to his success, perhaps a necessary audience for his odious gratification. In that appalling proximity I became Francis Swayne's alter ego, the human accolade.'

He took another sip from his glass, fastidiously dabbing his mouth with a tissue. It occurred to Arnott there was something pernickety about Tallent. A latent spinsterishness. As if the knee injury had become some sort of mental castration from which he could never recover.

'Swayne opened the trunk, selected some flimsy garments and made up his face. I was riveted, hypnotized by the ghastly spectacle of the man putting on a brassiere, french knickers, applying lipstick, prancing round. And then, when one could bear it no longer, suddenly released.'

He paused as if for dramatic effect, a trick Arnott suspected perfected to enliven lectures.

'Swayne unlocked a drawer in his desk and took out a wig, smoothing it in his hands as if it were a bird. It was just like Naomi's, not one of those brassy peroxide things transvestites wear in sex revues.' Geoffrey pursed his lips, his eyes behind the strong lenses magnified, unblinking as they gripped Arnott's attention. 'Utterly convincing,' he continued. 'Real hair, neatly set with a natural fall, obviously expensive. I know about such things, you see,' he added with asperity. Arnott nodded, urging him on, not daring to break the narrative.

'Seeing him in all that frou-frou nonsense was nauseating yet faintly comic. But when he produced the wig it was if the chicanery was exposed. He had gone too far. I pushed open the door and stood in the man's study, knowing I need never trouble myself with Swayne ever again.'

Arnott sat bolt upright.

'You killed him?'

Geoffrey glanced up with a look of hilarity. 'No need to, dear man. I laughed in his face.' Geoffrey's colour had returned and he relished his whimsical rapport with Arnott, inviting him to share the peepshow.

'Swayne sprang at me, thought I was a burglar. That man didn't even recognize me! He'd broken my career, killed my wife, destroyed my reputation and didn't even recognize me.' Geoffrey's laughter sounded harsh but his manner was relaxed, Arnott presumed, by the deadening effect of the painkillers. 'I did not enlighten him.'

'We grappled for a few minutes and eventually I got an armlock on him and forced him into the chair. The wig had flown into a corner of the room and his lipstick and eye stuff was all smudged. A disgusting wrestling match. But he was strong, much fitter than I had bargained for. At last I pinned him in the chair and managed to unwind the rope round my waist and tie him up. Poor devil was hampered by the black negligee, it was like shackles when it got twisted in the fight. But I held on and trussed him up after a fashion. You see, I'd had a much better idea. Better than the explosion. I was going to humiliate him, splash him all over the newspapers as he'd done to me. Not merely the educational press this time but the gutter brigade, a little postscript to his notoriety in Dublin, the so-called white knight of the freedom fighters now rescued by reporters from his embarrassing ordeal. I decided to tie him up in his ridiculous transvestite trappings and call the press from a safe distance, leave the door ajar for the photojournalist gang. There was no need to burn the house. I would make a laughing-stock of the man, not a martyr to Irish revenge-seekers, a respectable victim. I knew Francis Swayne, you understand. The sheer absurdity of his predicament would be tittle-tattled round the clubs and inns of court. He would never escape the ribald comment, the sniggers. I explained my intentions to him with precise detail, savouring every word. He imagined I was some sort of crackpot, an anonymous instrument of divine providence, he still didn't know me or even guess at my festering, longstanding grievance.'

Arnott grudgingly admitted some admiration for the plan, and made a determined effort to discipline his own flights

of fancy. LAWYER MUGGED IN MYSTERIOUS CIR-
CUMSTANCES. He could imagine the headlines.

'But first I had to defuse the bomb,' Geoffrey said. 'I
thought I had tied him up well enough but he was a wiry
little devil. Just as I was securing the knots he got one arm
free and snatched up the paperknife from the desk and gave
me one godalmighty slash to the groin. I really lost my
temper then and practically broke his arm before I got
him trussed up again. You won't believe this, but all this
wrestling and crashing about was fairly subdued, no shouting, all silent enmity. Neither of us wanted to bring the
neighbours knocking at the door to discover us dressed for
charades. The party at the back was noisy and right up to
the stabbing Swayne really thought he would win. He
didn't consider me any sort of adversary, contemptuous like
all those upper-crust yobs.'

Arnott searched Geoffrey's face for signs of madness but
he seemed sane enough. At worst, a man born in the wrong
century to whom vengeance seemed a valid reason for
action.

'I gagged him then. That did it. I wonder he didn't have
a heart attack, eyes bulging, his blood pumping through his
slimy body. It finally dawned on him that I might just get
away with it. I had to go down to the kitchen to stop the
timing device. To make sure he couldn't escape while I
was downstairs I gave the rope an extra twist or two and
tied the end to the base of the desk, all this time bleeding
like a pig from the gash in my thigh.'

He absent-mindedly stroked his leg under the mound of
bedcovers, pausing as if to present the sequence of events
in a scholarly order.

'In the kitchen I fiddled with the mechanism and defused
the bomb. It only took about ten minutes and I was just
about to pack it up in my satchel when I heard this frightful
crash from the room above. I dropped everything and ran
upstairs thinking he'd managed to get loose. But as soon as
I entered it was clear he'd knocked himself out, slewed the

chair sideways, still pinioned, his head all askew. I bawled at him then, dragging the chair upright and only then realized it was all up with him. He was dead. Because the chair was secured to the leg of the desk it had toppled and jerked the rope tight around his throat. He was dead. I couldn't believe it. But there was no doubt. Swayne had choked himself in his panic to get free. I panicked myself then. Believe me, Arnott, it took courage to pull myself together, not to run. Killing the man had never entered my head. Ironic, wasn't it, the coroner getting it right by default? Blind justice one might say. Swayne died accidentally, by his own hand. If he had sat tight he would still be poncing round the courts today, less bumptious maybe, but alive.'

Arnott whistled through his teeth. 'More like rough justice if you ask me.' He was genuinely shocked. It was as if he were watching a conjuror, astonished that the Chinese box was empty after all. The man had no reason to lie, his whole demeanour was, if anything, entirely without regret or remorse.

Geoffrey nodded. 'Quite so. Obviously the corpse had not tied himself to the chair. The only thing to abort a search for a murderer, and heaven knows what that would dredge up, was to concoct a suicide. I carefully untied him and after a lot of manœuvring in the bathroom hoisted the body up to the beam as if he'd hanged himself. Which in fact he had. For all his strength Swayne dead wasn't much of a weight. Putting back the wig was the worst part. By the time I had cleaned up the room I'd nearly passed out. There had been an initial loss of blood from my wound fortunately absorbed by a felt mat by the desk. I'd fixed myself up with a towel from the kitchen but it was impossible to stop the bleeding and in desperation I knew I would never make it back to Fulham on foot. Collapsing in the street with a stab wound would take a lot of explaining. So I took Swayne's keys and the felt mat and let myself out, relocked the door and threw the door keys back inside well away from the letter-box. Not perfect but it would have to do. Then I drove back to Fulham.'

'Using Swayne's car? Where was yours?'

'I had jogged to the mews from Tom's place in Fulham. People in tracksuits run round London streets at all hours. One is perfectly invisible. I knew Swayne would probably not be missed in town over the weekend. I intended to return his car next day, leave it nearby, no one would notice on a busy Saturday morning.'

'What made you change your mind?' Some mechanism in Arnott's rusty memory whirred into play and the reptilian eyes narrowed. 'Was it the stained seat?'

'Precisely so.' Geoffrey sighed, pursing his lips in incredulity that such an unforeseen and messy detail could flaw his calculations. 'By the time I had driven back to Fulham, blood had seeped right through the towel. There was no way I could clean it and for all I knew my blood and Swayne's were incompatible. Anyway he hadn't any fresh cuts. A bloodstained car seat would have set bells ringing even if the suicide seemed plausible.'

Arnott waved this aside, prompting Geoffrey to finish, dreading the reappearance of the ward sister. 'Go on, man.'

'I hid Swayne's car in Tom's garage, a ramshackle double-ended affair leading to a backyard, and crashed out for an hour. Then I assessed the situation. It couldn't have looked worse and my leg was in a very sorry state. I had to get it stitched up but first there was the problem of Swayne's car. I even contemplated driving it off a cliff somewhere but the whole episode had escalated badly. I had to regain control. The car was an albatross round my neck.'

His myopic eyes were heavy with the strain of marshalling the facts in the pedantic way his scientific training seemed to impose. A powerful lassitude was claiming Arnott's witness and the unanswered questions he was impatient to put were thrust back. Nagging queries about the black woman, the disposal of the stained rug from Swayne's study . . . Arnott mentally urged Geoffrey Tallent to rally and after a

seemingly final struggle the clipped accent of the professor
continued.

'It then struck me that—' he wiped a moist eyelid—
'there was one supreme coincidence I might turn to my
advantage. His car was practically identical to mine. Same
model, same year, same colour. Nothing for it. I had to
switch the cars. Tom's workshop was excellently fitted out
—rather odd that a rheumatologist had all that welding
equipment on hand. He messed about with sculpture in his
spare time, modern stuff, looked as if it had been salvaged
from skips, you know the sort of junky art the so-called
designers admire these days. In no time I unscrewed the
number plates and replaced everything, swapped the luggage, licences, the lot. Mine was in better shape mechani-
cally but I was gambling on no one being sufficiently familiar
with it to notice. Before dawn I shuffled the cars round and
drove mine back to Kensington. Then I went back and slept
all day. Finally, well after eleven the next night I presented
myself at the casualty department with all the drunks and
Saturday-night brawlers and got myself attended to.'

He coughed. His voice was beginning to go and Arnott
moved in, rubbing Geoffrey's cold hands in agitation.

Geoffrey focused on Arnott in a confused stare, frowning
at the rough touch of the old man's craggy fingers.

'It was while I was waiting at the hospital in Fulham
Road that it suddenly occurred to me I had left what would
be assumed to be Swayne's car parked near his house,
correctly locked up and not a whiff of suspicion there. But
I still had the car keys in my pocket. I went cold then.
Swayne would not have left the car in the street, his luggage
inside and the door unlocked. Neither would a careful man
like that abandon his car with the keys in the ignition. He
would have the keys at home and there was no way I could
replace them.'

'But mightn't he abandon an unlocked car if he was
contemplating suicide?' Arnott put in.

'I don't think so.' Geoffrey paused, considering this and

carefully elaborated. 'It wasn't in his nature to give anything away even on his deathbed. In the event the coroner's verdict was misadventure, accidental death in the course of a sexual game. Swayne had packed for his holidays, why should he invite car thieves to help themselves by leaving it open?'

Arnott shook his head, wondering if he would have been alerted if the car keys had not come to light. He sighed. It was impossible to comprehend his handling of the whole business. Especially now, when he knew so much. Geoffrey ploughed on, the words tumbling out. It seemed vital to him to explain the difficulties which had arisen, to justify the problems which had proliferated through no fault of his own.

'Details worry me,' he said. 'I knew I would never rest unless the question of the car keys was resolved. I couldn't go back to the mews again and let myself in to replace them on his desk. My injured leg precluded a second illegal entry over the wall and I had carefully thrown the house keys back inside, impossible to fish them out. Finally, the only way out was to post the keys through the letter-box the same as before. I caught sight of some handbills displayed in the hospital waiting-room with the dirty comics and old magazines.'

'Advertising the hospital fête,' Arnott crowed, slapping his knee in gleeful recognition.

'Quite. I waited until Sunday lunch-time when I knew the mews would be crowded: a warm day, the pub open, it was a foregone conclusion that all the usual noisy drinkers would be assembled, enjoying the sunshine. Slipping the keys back inside the house under cover of delivering handbills would go unnoticed.'

'Was that when Swayne's cleaning woman recognized you? She died. You knew that?'

'Did she? Overweight, of course. Heart attack, presumably.' Geoffrey was brutally indifferent. 'Nobody saw me return the keys with the handbill, of course. But you're right. The cleaner did speak to me. But earlier, several days before when I was sizing things up. She burst out into the mews as I was standing at the door. Asked me my business. These blacks are a belligerent lot. None of the fawning gratitude us refugees displayed when we arrived here. "I seen you hangin' about here,"' she said. Geoffrey's spirited recreation of Pamina's West Indian accent was comically accurate. His ear was unerring, the irony of the professor's own superior claim to his adopted mother tongue escaping him entirely.

'You didn't see her again?'

'Why should I?'

Arnott let it drop. Pamina must have orchestrated her own destruction after all. Funny, that. Arnott half smiled. If the black woman had kept her wits he might never have pursued Swayne's killer so relentlessly, a kinky barrister was hardly worth it . . .

Geoffrey was rambling on, his words fading, Arnott drifting in and out of focus, sounds ebbing, the familiar surroundings floating away. His lids fluttered, eyes widening, disorientated behind the mended spectacles.

Arnott leaned across and, dipping a tissue in the tumbler, trailed cold droplets across Geoffrey's face in a desperate effort to revive him.

It was at this moment the ward sister swept in. Arnott leapt back, foolishly aware of being caught in the act. Without a word she pointedly consulted the pendant watch pinned to her dress and raised an eyebrow.

Arnott sighed and, pocketing the cassette, stole a last glance at his man before following her out. He was snoring lightly like a man relaxing after a hard day. The professor had shot his bolt.

Arnott bitterly listed all the things he had not had a chance to ask. And Pamina? Was the man uninvolved in the death of Pamina? The lack of evidence on that score was like a black hole. If I was Sherlock bloody Holmes, he nagged himself, my Professor Moriarty would have coughed the lot. Fat chance of that crafty sod giving me a second crack of the whip . . . Especially when he knows I kept the tape.

CHAPTER 21

It was impossible for Sabina to get away. Aragon must be packed off to Glasgow without delay or Harry would instantly question the girl's state of shock. Doubtless discover the cause of it.

Also, there was Sybil to contend with. An unstated complicity was drawn up between Aragon and Sabina to keep the old lady out of it. It was with relief that Aragon found herself bundled on to the train, escaping back to reality after the nightmare ride. Even Rick's defection seemed inevitable and the girl curled up in a corner seat, white-faced, wondering what would happen if the professor died . . .

Sabina had risen to the crisis, successfully fending off Sybil's anxieties, pleading with her not to mention to Harry the bizarre joyride, assuring her that protecting Aragon from Harry's displeasure would save the situation. Nervously, Sybil agreed, unaware of the near-disaster from which Aragon had emerged, uninformed of the professor's accident.

Yet, lurking in the shadows of unasked questions, Sybil acknowledged a new cowardice. She felt diminished.

She seemed to have aged in the last few days, a persistent tremor in her veined hands exhibiting the fear within. Of what? Of getting old? Of being shielded from the by-blows of family life? Of death itself? She suddenly felt as if wrapped in tissue paper, put away like a Capodimonte porcelain figure, too fragile to be exposed to the rough and tumble of Sabina's secrets.

Harry was no fool. His shrewd eye detected the change immediately. In the few months since his last visit to Fernside his mother had imperceptibly slid into another decade. He blamed that tumble off the terrace. When she herself suggested he found her somewhere else to live, nearer the village, 'more convenient', his misgivings seemed to be confirmed. At least there was Mrs Carter, solid as ever, her bluff Yorkshire common sense a raft in the shifting sand. He was concerned about Sabina, too. She was looking thin and very pale. Nervy. The sooner he got her back home the better. Fernside must seem a dull hole after Hong Kong.

Sabina's efforts to slip away to see the inspector came to nothing; it was impossible to shake off Harry whose tender attentions were almost adhesive. Eventually, after two messages from the Feathers delivered by a deadpan Mrs Carter, Sabina managed to telephone from a call-box in the village.

'I'm so sorry, Mr Arnott. It's impossible to see you. How is Geoffrey?'

Arnott grimly gave a shortened version of Tallent's confession and a run-down on the professor's medical condition. Sabina, nervously glancing round at the empty street, interjected brief questions. Her shoulders sagged with the tragic waste of it all. So much destruction . . .

'I've got the tape,' Arnott said. 'It was a trade-off with Tallent for coming clean.'

'*I* don't want it,' she gasped.

'Useful if he plays up. A knife up your sleeve, lass.'

Sabina groaned. Would it never end? 'You keep it, Mr Arnott. I shall have to write to Geoffrey. I'll tell him you're keeping it. I've persuaded Harry to give him a chance.' She set out Harry Morland's terms, leaving unsaid the vital omission which would undoubtedly have voided any co-operation from her husband. 'Harry knew about the academic fraud, of course. But he wants me to go back with him straight away. He is being very kind, regards Geoffrey as a long-standing spectre which only he can exorcise. I ran away,' she faltered. 'Left Roger and the others to face it alone . . .' She pulled herself together and began again, trying to make it sound businesslike. 'Harry is willing to give him his chance. I shall be flying back to Hong Kong in two days' time. But I promise to send a letter explaining everything to Geoffrey myself.'

'Anything in writing would be most unwise, Mrs Morland.' He paused, letting this sink in and then set off on another tack. 'What about your own work? Thought twice about pitching in with the mad scientist?'

Sabina shivered. 'Too much has happened. I knew nothing about Naomi killing herself in that horrific way. He spoke as if she were alive. Believe me, Inspector, it came as a terrible shock. He kept up the pretence about his wife right until the night of the firework party. Can you credit it?'

'Perhaps I understand that poor bugger better'n most,' Arnott grunted.

Sabina steeled herself to pose the ultimate question.

'Now that you know the truth, Inspector, what are you going to do about Geoffrey? Must it all be dragged out all over again? He's guilty of causing Francis's death, I know that, but . . .' she stuttered.

Clearing his throat, Arnott spoke in his stilted official voice, the words exploding in her brain like children's sparklers.

'The coroner's verdict was correct, Mrs Morland. Misadventure. I've no reason to contest it. With your permission I'll finalize matters with the professor. The investigation is closed,' he said with finality. He replaced the receiver.

Sabina Morland gripped the phone, listening in wonder to the resumption of the dialling tone. It sounded more beautiful than a fanfare of trumpets at the gates of Paradise.

Arnott wore his bookmaker's suit to the hospital and presented himself at the official visiting hour. He passed by the ward sister, smiling broadly to himself, countering her silent disapproval with a wink. He followed the male nurse who offered to take him to Geoffrey whose bed had been pushed into the 'sun lounge' to escape the noisy influx of visitors to the ward.

Geoffrey was reading, a scientific journal propped in front of him, his spectacles still roughly taped at the bridge. He smiled as Arnott bundled in, seemed pleased to see him. Arnott, too, found it difficult to restrain an affection for this unlikely fellow conspirator: perpetrator of GBH, a confessed arsonist and that other thing everybody seemed to think so wicked—plagiarism, that was it!

He slid into the visitor's chair by the bed, assimilating the pale winter sunshine which glowed in the empty sun room, warming his cheek.

'How goes it, lad?'

Geoffrey grimaced, inclining his head to the shattered leg under the blanket.

'They've tacked it together. It should be all right apart from a bit of a limp.'

'Could've been worse. Put an end to that potholing lark. Never understood it meself, crawling about in the dark like some bloody beetle.'

Geoffrey smiled wanly and laid aside his magazine, giving all his attention to Arnott.

'You weren't quite straight with me, Arnott. The Sister says you're with Special Branch. She erroneously concluded I am some sort of top-flight boffin,' he snorted.

'Can I smoke in here?'

'If you must. It's allowed out here, unfortunately.'

Arnott was adept at turning a deaf ear and lit up, relishing the luxury of finding a chink in the ward sister's armour.

'I've got some bad news and some good,' he said. 'What'll you have first?'

'In my weak condition I had better stick with familiarities,' Geoffrey replied lightly. 'The bad, I think.'

Arnott leaned back, pausing to choose his words. Eventually he said, 'Sabina Morland's leaving. She's going back to the Far East. She won't see you.'

The light faded from Geoffrey's expression, his graceful

hands clutching the sheet and then falling open, a relin-
quishment of hope.

'She played the tape?'

'No. I've got the tape.' Arnott patted his pocket. 'We had
an arrangement, you and me. The tape in return for putting
her mind at rest about Swayne. I'm cheating. I need your
cooperation.'

Geoffrey pursed his lips. 'It's no use thinking I can buy
it back,' he snapped.

Arnott passed on, ignoring the spite. 'This isn't a touch!
I'm not short of a bob or two, lad.' He dragged on the
cigarette, watching the smoke curl up to the glazed panels
slimy with moss, spoiling the clarity of the sky. 'Mrs Morland's quitting. Best for all concerned if you ask me. But
she's fixed it with her old man. After your convalescence
you're to report to his head office in London. It's a job,
man,' he said. 'No need to look like that! Morland knows
nothing of your little fandango and I'm keeping the tape.
Insurance for your good behaviour. You get the facilities
you want, a living wage, a laboratory in Bracknell and an
assistant or two. And if you keep everything straight
up—no substituting evidence like I've heard about—you
might,' he slowly pronounced, 'you might just get off the
ground again.'

'And you keep the tape,' Geoffrey persisted.

'Bugger the tape! If it'll make you feel any better we'll
trade.'

He fished in his pockets and produced a dog-eared
envelope, passing it across the bed. Picking it up distaste-
fully, Geoffrey glanced at his craggy companion before
opening it. Between finger and thumb he held up a four-inch
square of printed paper, roughly smoothed out but still
badly crumpled, a sort of tax permit. He turned it over,
interested but nonplussed, eventually holding it against the
light as if it were a banknote. 'Well?'

'That's my little memento,' Arnott explained. He held
his cigarette butt under Geoffrey's nose, smiling wickedly.

Geoffrey recoiled, flicking at the ash which had dropped on to the bedsheet. Arnott swivelled on the plastic seat, looking round the room. And then with deliberation lazily stubbed out the inch of cigarette in a pot plant on Geoffrey's locker.

'You being so finicky made you forgetful,' he said. 'I knew something was wrong with that car when I saw it in the pound. Couldn't put my finger on it then but it wouldn't go away, niggling at the back of my 'ead like a ruddy flea.' Geoffrey stared at Arnott with distaste, suddenly exhausted.

'It's a parking permit,' Arnott said. 'Like a tax disc if you don't look careful but the car number's all filled in, dates and zone allocation for free parking, residents only. Not something you're familiar with up here, is it? From what I know about lawyers they're a nit-picking lot and Swayne sounded true to form by all accounts. Even drunk he'd never chance a fine, worse, leave it where it was likely to be clamped. But I didn't know then that the car'd been swapped. A conjuring trick. Now you see it, now you don't.'

Arnott lit another cigarette and Geoffrey realized their roles were interchangeable. Now it was Arnott's turn to confess and his to accept the burden.

Arnott said, 'It wasn't till I had a dekko at the car you left on the drive the night of the fireworks party that the penny dropped. I borrowed your keys overnight—excuse me, Swayne's keys!' he said, poking the bedclothes with a nicotine-stained finger. 'As soon as I was inside that little motor I knew it smelt wrong. Really smelt wrong,' he repeated. 'You can't abide it, even put a sticker on the dashboard reminding any poor misguided sod who might want a fag it's not on. But it lingers. And cigar smoke clings like nobody's business and your car still gave off a faint whiff. But a stink's not evidence. I searched that car with a dinky little torch that barely lit up an inch at a time but all I came up with was this fancy red dog lead which meant nothing at all till I showed it to Mrs Morland later. Even that was hardly going to tie you down. Bloody 'ell, who'd suss out cats have leads and harnesses like sodding lapdogs?

I buggered about in the dark for an hour and it was only when I opened the ashtray I found the permit. Swayne's own car number clear as daylight. In your car. That put the lid on it. That little bit of paper all screwed up into a pellet and shoved in there out of sight. Forgotten.'

Geoffrey sighed. 'I only saw it later after I'd driven back from London. It was stuck to the side window. I meant to dispose of it.'

Arnott grinned wolfishly, raising both hands like a performer inviting applause. 'That scrap of paper with the wrong car number on it linked you to Swayne as strongly as any fingerprint.'

'What are you going to do?'

'Me?'

Arnott lumbered to his feet, clapping Geoffrey on the shoulder before shambling to the door.

'I'm doing nothing at all, old son. From now on it's all pleasure. I forgot to tell you, Professor, I'm retired.'

He went out, closing the door behind him with infinite satisfaction.